Playing Along

Rory Samantha Green

Write To Be You Press

ISBN number: 978-0-9 884 948-1-7 (paperback)

Published by Write To Be You Press

Sweet Dreams (Are Made of This)

Visit Rory at her website **www.writetobeyou.com**
or her Facebook page
www.facebook.com/RorySamanthaGreen

To my mother, a true inspiration...

To my sisters for never-ending encouragement, love
and fellow fantasizing!

And to D, B and C for being my constant soundtrack

With Thanks

It has taken quite some time for this book to breathe the air it's been asking for!

The first person I'd like to thank is one of the top fiction editors at one of the top London publishing houses who gave me the gift of the most glorious rejection:

> "After much soul searching, and about a hundred conversations here, I have very reluctantly decided to pass on this wonderful novel. As you know I really did love the story, and fell head over heels for George. I will have to content myself with saying 'I told you so' when she goes on to sell a million copies. I hope you can tell this is a really reluctant turn down, and I have no doubt at all that I shall regret it."

I never met you, but thank you for motivating me to keep George and Lexi alive rather than suffocating them in the nether regions of my hard drive.

Now, I just need to sell those million copies...

Thank you to Sarah Lutyens and Kim Witherspoon for trying and trying!

To Tiff for going to 'that' concert, planting 'that' seed' and then watering it faithfully.

To Beth and Keith for late night tea and chats and for encouraging me to stop hiding.

To Jennifer for shining the light on the self-publishing path, and to Hitch at Booknook.biz for invaluable advice.

To my cheerleading reading squad: Mum, TT, TC, Chloe, David, Karen, Sarah, Beth H., Dawn, Brett, Lynne, Barry, Emma, Kay, Kris, India, Dilly and Eden. You helped me to believe!

And to the readers I have yet to meet—I hope you enjoy 'Playing Along'!

Life gets rough. We all need stories that make us smile...

RSG

"Fame is a bee
It has a song—
It has a sting—
Ah, too, it has a wing"

Emily Dickinson

"Sweet dreams are made of this
Who am I to disagree?
I travel the world and the seven seas
Everybody's looking for something"

Eurythmics

THEN

GEORGE
1st November, 1994
Stanford in the Vale, Oxfordshire

"Your brother's grown up a bit, hasn't he?"

George holds his breath when he hears these words swoop past his bedroom door. He's thirteen, but his sister is two years older and her friends are an enigma. They smell like grapefruit and cigarettes and layer mascara on their lashes until they look like pandas. Most of them have boobs. Big ones. He's fascinated by the divide. George's sister, Polly, has maybe said one word to him in the last two weeks and that was muttered in disdain when he had mistakenly knocked her make-up brush off the counter and into the toilet. It had floated forlornly in the bowl like a drowned rodent.

"Arsehole!"

But now there's a chance of redemption. Despite his skinny legs and spotty rounded face, it seems as if one of the awesome grapefruit girls has noticed something in him. Something unique. He reckons it will take a very special woman to appreciate his nuances. His love of Grover from Sesame Street (so underrated—why did Kermit get all the limelight?) and his adoration of the most amazing music the universe has to offer—Bowie, U2, Portishead, Dylan, New Order. The woman who takes his heart must take his record collection as well.

"My brother?" replies Polly in dramatic shock. "Yeah, you could say he's grown up—into a first rate troll."

The grapefruit girls giggle and their laughter snakes under his door and rings painfully in his ears. George bites his bottom lip, scraping his teeth against peeling skin. Another nervous habit.

"And listen to this... he claims one day he's going to be

3

in a famous band and be on the cover of *NME* and have groupies. What a joke!"

George, prepared for the inevitable cackle of mockery, grabs his headphones and his CD player and presses play with an urgency. "Fools Gold" by the Stone Roses floods his brain. He turns up the volume as loud as it will go and hurls his notebook across the room where it ricochets off the wall and slides under his bed. The notebook is filled with songs. George has been unpacking heartache from his sensitive soul since the age of ten.

His sister's harsh words are never as brutal as the words he calls himself.

He knows what he wants, but he's pretty damn certain that a boy like him is never going to get it.

LEXI
November 1st, 1994
Pacific Palisades, Los Angeles, California

"I'm psyched about the game tomorrow!" Andrew enthusiastically polishes off his second burrito, gazing longingly at Lexi across the table. She smiles at him mischievously knowing that she drives him crazy with her Juicy Fruit breath, her shiny brown hair, and her legs which have conveniently slimmed out and toned up since she started diligently attending an after school kickboxing class.

"I'm excited too," she replies, playfully nudging his size twelve basketball shoes under the table. "I hope you win, so we can celebrate."

Lexi and Andrew are *the* couple at Pali High. Just embarking on their senior year, they have been an item since the eleventh grade. Andrew first kissed Lexi on Zuma beach with the waves lapping at their bare feet two nights after passing his driving test. His parents had given him a convertible Mustang for his sixteenth birthday and when he drove her home, one hand on the wheel, the other holding hers, Lexi had a sweet taste lingering in her mouth and salty wind in her hair.

"So unfair," her best friend, Meg, had complained the following morning. "It's not supposed to happen like that. He's supposed to drool, or run out of gas, or step on your toe or something. Why is your life like an Audrey Hepburn movie and mine like a bad TV sitcom?"

And Lexi certainly didn't want to be smug, but there was some truth in Meg's observation. Things just seemed to go her way. Her parents had raised her to believe in herself and face life with a positive outlook. Not that she was syrupy or self-obsessed. She worked hard at her studies and had an excellent Grade Point Average. She volunteered at a local homeless shelter, fingerpainting with vulnerable kids after school. She'd started up a current events debate club in her junior year and persuaded many of her friends to join. They now competed nationally. Oh and of course, she kickboxed and played on the girls' volleyball team, and thankfully had the sort of hair that didn't frizz on damp mornings when the fog rolled in off the coast.

Lexi had lost her virginity to Andrew on the floor in his bedroom on a Sunday afternoon while his parents shopped at Target. He had lit a scented candle stolen from his mother's bathroom, and the smell of orange mimosa flooded the room. "Can't Help Falling in Love" by UB40 was playing on his CD player.

When it was over (slightly painful, but not nearly as uncomfortable as she had imagined), he leaned on his elbows beside her and whispered in her ear, "I can't help falling in love with *you*..."

One year later, sitting opposite him watching him wipe guacamole from the side of his lips, Lexi feels in her heart that she loves him too. In fact she is sure, along with almost everyone else at Pali High who either knows them or admires them from afar, that they will most likely end up getting married. Lexi's mother has saved her own wedding dress for the occasion, wrapped in delicate layers of archival tissue in an ivory box on the top shelf of her cupboard. "It's just waiting, my beauty," her mother has promised.

Lexi can picture their home now (a cozy New England style house, a few blocks from her parents, with whitewashed floors and shabby chic couches), two or maybe three kids (she really doesn't have a preference for boys or girls) and most definitely a dog, a black Labrador called George. She imagines a fulfilling and creative part time job as well, maybe a teacher or an art therapist, something that leaves her with the free-dom to be a hands-on mom. So what if she is only seventeen? It's just a dream, but life has already proven to Lexi that dreams do find a way of coming true.

NOW

GEORGE
1st November, 2009
Greenwich, England

"George... I love you!" On certain nights this professed love is yelled out a hundred times from men and women alike. Most nights it disappears into the roar of the crowd, but at some gigs a single voice will miraculously separate out and hover above the throng of faceless fans and George hears it and needs it to be true.

George is at the piano finishing the final chords of "Beyond Being," a poignant ballad based on his teenage existential musings and a lyric which popped into his head one day as he polished off a carton of mint chocolate chip ice cream. The audience sways in time and cell phones punctuate the blackness like rechargeable flames. George hangs his head as the song comes to a quiet end, his voice wavering with a sad clarity.

Thousands of fans cheer and whoop in adoration and George looks up shyly with his trademark grin. "Thank you very much for coming. We appreciate you might have better things to do with your Saturday nights, like watching *X Factor*, and the boys and I really enjoyed playing to you tonight..." This, as intended, whips up the crowd into an even louder frenzy as George and his band mates lope off the stage with a schoolboy charm that has captivated fans across the world from Denmark to Chile, and every destination in between.

George has come a long way from the corner of his brown bedroom. His band, Thesis, stormed onto the music scene with an unstoppable force after his best mate and guitarist, Simon Ogden-Smith, persuaded George to start up a Myspace page and stream some of their music. George, Simon,

Simon's cousin Mark, and Mark's sister's friend Duncan from Australia, had been playing local pubs in Islington and had been slowly building up a loyal fan base. But the Myspace page catapulted them into a whole new stratosphere, and with a swiftness which at times found George's throat closing with unprecedented anxiety, they burst onto the alternative music scene and made their mark. Three months after being signed by a record company they were flown to Los Angeles to record their first album, *Twelve Thousand Words*. George Bryce, still a sweaty lonely teenager at heart, found himself surrounded by attractive, fawning women called Claudia and Agnes and Nell. They willingly offered their breasts to him without any pleading involved and he indulged in a whole new adolescence at twenty-two.

The band's first big hit was a rocking anthem called "Grapefruit Girls," an opportunity for George to get his revenge on those elusive females who had inducted him into the hall of shame. George became an unlikely heartthrob, a self-deprecating lad who wore T-shirts with Grover on them and gave interviews about obscure comic books and rare vinyl. His boyish looks, lopsided smile and thick shaggy black hair, once his greatest insecurity, suddenly became irresistible. Even America, notoriously hard to break for an unheard-of alternative band, lapped up the accents and the awkwardness. Critics either loved or hated Thesis and George made a point of reading every review, because no matter how famous they became, he never stopped caring about what people thought of him.

Tonight they have sold out a third night at the 02 Arena in London. Three albums in six years and each one more successful than the last. George is obsessive about the set list. Simon is obsessive about sandwiches.

Off stage Simon squeezes George's shoulder. "What a night, huh? The best of the three, my boy. You were rather on form this evening." Simon is like the brother George never had. He loves him unconditionally, with an unspoken tenderness.

George, distracted, calls over to Duncan, their drummer, who is dripping like a tap. "What happened to you in 'Under the Radar'? You came in so late? It threw me." Duncan blows his nose on a manky Kleenex dug up from his jeans pocket.

"Chill out, George. I've got man flu—I told you that before. It was cool—no one noticed. They were crazy for us out there."

"Correction," chips in Mark, the bass player, who has worn the same pair of lucky orange socks during every performance for the last twelve months, "they were crazy for George, Dunc. We're just the wallpaper."

This is a running joke in the band, and while George secretly knows it might be accurate, he also realizes he would be nothing without his mates. The thought of being on stage without them makes him feel queasy, like approaching a bungee jump with no harness. Inevitable destruction. Confidence smashed to smithereens. He needs these three men to keep him in one piece. It is only here, in this group of four, that he has ever felt a sense of belonging.

They have two songs yet to perform in their encore and the audience is going wild chanting the chorus from "Grapefruit Girls." There is a fine line between being off stage for too long and reappearing too quickly.

"I'm wondering about that smoked turkey and cheese baguette I had before the show," says Simon thoughtfully. "I'm thinking some mustard next time, you know, to add a bit of zing."

"Did you just say zing?" asks Duncan.

"Try a sharper cheddar," offers Mark.

"That's an idea," says Simon, beckoning to Zac, his guitar tech who promptly appears with his trusty red Fender.

Thesis are both renowned and rebuked for their clean living. Of course the scathing half of the media revels in slamming them for their cautious approach to a rocker's lifestyle, accusing them of making music to knit to. George recoils from the criticism but is truly dedicated to his fans. He genuinely believes that in one way or another, the music they make impacts the lives of the people who listen to them. He knows only too well what it feels like to be a fan locked in relation-ship with one album or even one song. Playing it incessantly. Never enough. He only wishes that he had the same experi-ence with women.

George's endless conundrum—girls. The irony of being adored by thousands but never truly known by one. Some-times George feels that no amount of recognition will ever erase the sense of rejection indelibly tattooed on his ego, leaving him painfully thin-skinned. Even with the opposite sex flocking around him now. Even though he's had a string of short-lived "girlfriends." Even though Fanny Arundel, one of the most seductive and quirky singers of his generation, has recently been sending him suggestive texts on a weekly basis. He still feels faulty, and the women he meets just don't fill the gap. In fact they seem to dig the hole deeper and deep-er.

Back on stage for the final two songs, George faces the screaming crowd and murmurs affectionately into the micro-phone, "We missed you," before launching into the opening lines of "Grapefruit Girls." The band follows tightly behind: Simon, buoyantly one with his guitar; Mark lingering and soulful on bass, and Duncan brandishing his sticks with a momentous energy. The entire audience bounces in antici-pation of the addictive chorus.

I wanted you, wanted you, wanted you
I needed you,
You needled me,
Bleed bittersweet, I faced defeat
Soured Hours, love left scoured

Oh, oh, oh squeeze me tightly
Myyy Graaapefruit Giirls
Myyy Graaapfruit Giiirls...

George, soaked with perspiration, feels the adrenaline coursing through his veins like a frantic blue stream. The auditorium is a seething mass of love and adoration. He knows they feel connected. Understood. Couples will return home on the tube smiling and still be up at two a.m., entangled, ears ringing, recounting the events of the unforgettable concert. Misfit teenagers with acne and lank hair will reignite their ailing hopes, believing they too could be like George Bryce one day, a talented loner who has crossed over into cool without even trying. Forty-something women will imagine George either as their son or their lover and both fantasies will leave them warm. Hundreds of others will head straight to their laptops and download blurry pictures from their mobiles, blogging on fan forums or obsessively comparing notes in chatrooms. There is no question that George is at the top of his game. Everyone feels it. Everyone except George.

LEXI
November 1st, 2009
West Hollywood, Los Angeles

"Lexi, get over here! This one looks good..." Andrew's shriek reaches Lexi in her bathroom where she is dutifully applying concealer to the dark circles under her eyes. She pushes her nose close to the mirror scanning for wrinkles and instead notices a very fine, but decidedly black hair growing from the tip of her chin. She lunges for the tweezers.

"Lexi, get your butt out here!"

"It's official," she yells back, "I am morphing into a witch. Or a crone. Or possibly both?"

Andrew appears in the bathroom doorway, eyebrows

dramatically raised.

"Morphing into?"

Lexi pulls her thick brown hair into a low ponytail and squints at her reflection.

"Very funny. It's thirty-two. Thirty-two hates me."

"Welcome to my world. Heston just told me the other day that he thinks I'm getting a muffin top," he lifts his t-shirt to reveal a perfectly chiseled six-pack, which he lamely attempts to squeeze.

"Heston is weird, Andrew. Why don't you find yourself a nice older man to settle down with? You've got it all backwards. You should be the toy boy."

Andrew and Lexi are roommates. They share a duplex in West Hollywood just south of Melrose with lots of charm. In other words, the shower leaks incessantly and they have to plead with the oven to persuade it to work. They each have a small bedroom with a walk-in closet, of primary importance even in dumps. It was Andrew who walked out of the closet four years after they parted.

Weeks after graduation from high school, their relationship just seemed to fizzle. He was spending far too much time with his basketball friends (still now, she wonders about all the extra "practices" he needed to attend). Even at eighteen, their sex life had become predictable and sparse. It felt like they were brother and sister. Looking back, he spent more time advising her on what color lipstick to wear than he did kissing her.

The plan had been for Andrew and Lexi to attend Columbia University together, her parents' alma mater. The polo shirts were packed. Lexi was a girl who stuck to a plan, so when Andrew decided to stay on the west coast and accepted a place at UCLA instead, she was crushed, but determined to appear unruffled. She was Jeanette Jacobs's daughter after all, hardwired for optimism. Lexi bravely boarded that plane in September with a smile on her face and a firm belief that her four years at Columbia would set her on an even better track, revealing to her the life she was meant to lead, and perhaps the new man who was meant to lead it with her.

It took some time for her rose colored glasses to warp and crack, eventually becoming so loose at the screws that they fell apart completely. She tumbled in and out of bad relationships with boys who were too young, men who were too jaded, or tutors who were arrogant and balding. She failed her European History final. She broke her wrist kickboxing. And she was mugged on Amsterdam Avenue walking home one night from volunteering at the Braille Institute for the Blind. It was on that particular night that the thought occurred to her that she too had been blinded by the fuzzy glow of her adolescence. Could she really have peaked at seventeen?

Only this morning she had asked Andrew that question for the thousandth time as he scanned the job opportunity pages for her on the *LA Times* website.

"Lexi, you were hot at seventeen and you are even hotter now. You're just in a bit of a slump..."

"Yeah, so hot that I turned you gay."

"Don't start taking responsibility for that again. I've told you—it's genetic. I've traced back three generations of Mc-Clouds and I'm almost positive there was a flaming uncle on every branch of my family tree. You were put in my path as sweet temptation. And you were—so sweet—still are..."

"Andrew, this isn't a slump. This is more like a bottom-less pit."

"Enough! Today, we are finding you a job!"

Andrew pulls the tweezers out of Lexi's grasp and thrusts his iPhone under her chin instead. "Look at this!" he says triumphantly, pointing to an ad halfway down the screen. "I've found it—your ladder back into the land of the living. This looks perfect!"

Lexi remembers how that word *perfect* used to invite her in, offering her countless opportunities to prove it true. Now she wishes that it never existed. Surely such a word should be banned permanently from the dictionary?

GEORGE
4th November, 2009
Maida Vale, London

"Are you? You are, aren't you? OH MY GOD! OH MY GOD! Emma is going to *die*. It's you, George Bryce—can you... I mean, can I? I mean... oh my God, I can't breathe..."

George is standing in line at Tesco holding a four-pack of toilet paper, a box of PG Tips and three Crunchies. The teenage girl in front of him is beginning to hyperventilate. He's not certain how this has happened. After their second album, he was still able to go out relatively undisturbed, usually wearing a baseball cap or a beanie pulled down over his eyebrows. He could have been anyone. But since the release of their third album, *Corners and Tables,* his image seems to have seeped into the consciousness of far too many members of the general public.

He quickly puts down the toilet paper (thinking why now? Why this?) and rests a calming hand on the girl's shoulder, "It's okay, take a deep breath."

What he really wants to say is, "George who?" Unfortunately, his gesture appears to have the opposite of the desired effect and her breathing gets heavier and beads of sweat are starting to drip down her forehead.

"Oh sweet Jesus, are you touching me? Are your hands on my shoulder right now? I'm never, ever going to wash this sweater again for AS LONG AS I LIVE!" George is beginning to worry how long that might be if she continues to stay in close proximity to him. He wonders how Chris Martin deals with interactions like these. He most likely comes up with some amusing comment and defuses the situation with ease while making a quick escape. George, on the other hand, feels rooted to the spot.

The girl has managed to fumble in her oversized bag and pull out her mobile phone.

"My hands are shaking... look," she holds out a trembling limb as proof. "Can you just take my phone and call Emma, and tell her that it's you, and we're standing together in Tesco and that we... you and I... are talking? She's under F."

"F for Emma?" he can't help but wonder.

"Yeah, because she's Fucking Gorgeous Emma... she's my best fucking mate."

"Oh, right," George compliantly accepts the phone, hating himself for noticing that the histrionic teenager in front of him is really quite pretty. When he was fifteen he would have run a mile and wished the whole time that she was running after him. But now he wants to get back to his flat and have some tea and eat a Crunchie. He wants to watch two episodes of *Flight of the Conchords* and think about the lighting for the upcoming US tour. He has an idea.

"Look, Emma's not going to believe it's me if I call her. Why don't I just take a picture of the two of us and you can text it to her?"

The girl smiles and it dawns on him that she will live on this moment for months to come, possibly longer. He leans in next to her face and holds up the packet of toilet paper between them. With a big cheesy grin he presses capture, checks the shot, and hands her back the phone, pointing her towards the front of the line.

"It's your turn to pay."

"You are *amazing!*" she says, staring at him adoringly.

"I can but try..." the words sound right enough, but underneath them he feels a familiar tug. The longing to be accepted when he was growing up. The fruitless attempts to fit into his family when it was clear that he was never going to. The realization that the young stranger in front of him with the scraggly blond hair and the blue nail varnish probably thinks more of him than his parents ever did.

Even now they struggle to approve of his chosen profession, having hoped that their sullen little Georgie might have outgrown his youthful sensitivity and pursued computer programming or a management position like his father.

"How can you stand all that smoke?" his dad asked recently, as if he was still gigging in small pubs with flaky ceilings.

"Ah, Dad—they banned smoking in all public venues a while ago. You should get out sometime—come to one of our shows. I'll get you good seats—I've got connections."

At fifty-nine George's father is in a permanent sense of humour failure. "Too much noise, son. I don't know how you haven't lost your hearing yet."

"What?"

George has condensed his visits to Oxfordshire down to two a year, Christmas and his mum's birthday. They've refused his offer to buy them a new house, insisting instead on remaining in the cottage where he grew up and driving an old Ford Granada.

"We don't need much, Georgie," his mum has explained on numerous occasions. "We wouldn't want our friends to think we were showing off. It's hard enough having to hear all the envious comments about the triplets!"

The triplets. Archie, Padstow and Trevor—Polly's precocious four-year-olds. The rotten apples of his parents' eyes. George detests the matching outfits she forces them to wear like uniforms and the way they yell when they see him, "Uncle Georgie...*you're* FAMOUS!" stressing the word famous like it was a contagious disease. Which of course it sometimes felt like—but for God's sake, at least the little brats might look up to him, instead of following the rest of the family unwittingly into the lair of disdain.

He distractedly pays for his items, feeling a twinge of

guilt as he accepts a plastic bag. Just thinking about his family darkens his mood. Christmas isn't that far away. He has the trip to LA and the latest video to make before that, but even so, he can feel the dampness looming.

LEXI
November 4th, 2009
Venice, Los Angeles

Lexi has parked her car and is scanning the street for number fifty-five. Based on the ad Andrew had shown her, she was anticipating one of those funky, architect designed office buildings off Abbot Kinney.

> *Up and coming environmental awareness company, looking for enthusiastic, earth loving public relations specialist. Must have prior experience and plenty of ideas. Fantastic opportunity to be part of a grass roots business and work in a creative space. E-mail resume and references to Russell Hazleton. Only apply if you are willing to Let the Green Times Roll!*

Promising, right? So the last line might have been slightly suspect, but Andrew thought it was cute and Lexi was willing to overlook excessive perkiness if it meant a paycheck and a new beginning. But walking down Victoria Avenue, she is finding herself feeling slightly more dubious. There are no funky office buildings, just a row of run-down houses looking rather sorry for themselves. Lexi can empathize.

When she'd returned to California from Columbia in her early twenties, she had a degree in marketing and public relations and an addiction to cappuccinos. Though severely battered, her commitment to positive thinking was still limping along and she'd hoped that coming home would instigate a full recovery. She showed up just in time to be a bridesmaid at Meg's wedding, to discover that Andrew was gay, and to land a PR job for a small internet start-up company selling maternity wear called "Bumps Ahead." Really the name should have been a give-away.

Ten years on, she is godmother to both of Meg's children and unemployed after a string of PR jobs that always appeared to be 'perfect' but soon revealed themselves to be as shaky as the economy. Lexi's optimistic hardwiring is beginning to dangerously short circuit, after recently being let go from an interiors magazine because yet again, the company had lost their funding. She had dreamt once of opening her own PR company, but has convinced herself that clients would be impossible to hold onto. In fact these days, Lexi feels as if she can't hang onto much of anything.

She finally spots number fifty-five and attempts to summon her inner Maria, an old trick her mother had taught her as a girl when her self belief needed bolstering. She imagines Julie Andrews, suitcase in hand, striding away from the convent, arms swinging forcefully. *I have confidence in me! What is so fearsome about a captain and seven children?* But it seems that her once loyal Maria has long since gone into retirement, because the only thing Lexi can summon is a sinking feeling that this job, like all the others, is not going to be the one.

GEORGE
4th November, 2009
Maida Vale, London

George is crashed out on his sofa balancing his notebook on his knees and eating his third Crunchie. Just as he did at fifteen, he relies on good old-fashioned paper and pen, and has stacks of archived books piled in an empty kitchen cupboard. He promised Simon he'd work on the lyrics for "Over Time," a song they've been playing with for the last few weeks, but instead he's made some notes and sketches for a lighting idea he has for the North American tour. It's crucial to George that the shows do not become a circus act. He likes to keep things simple and let the music speak for itself.

The truth is, George can't come up with the line he needs to ground the song. He'll recognize it when it arrives. The lyric that embeds itself under the skin and finds a way to resonate with a million people he'll never meet. How to transform the intimate into the universal—a magical skill he knows he has, but can't always rely upon. He fishes around between the sofa cushions, stretching his long, lanky legs, and pulls out a yellow rubber ball with a worried grimace drawn on one side in thick black pen. George contorts the ball in his hand, causing the anxious expression to look even more pronounced.

It's his stress ball. A present from Simon three years ago when George's creative flow might have been better described as a creative concrete mixer. The inevitable pressures of producing a sophomore album that would favourably compare to their collectively adored first try, had seriously stalled him. The right side of his brain had gone on hunger strike, literally. He was starved of inspiration. Simon had panicked. It was he and George who grew the seed of the band into the massive, many-limbed tree it had become. It was they who had barricaded themselves in their student digs at university, writing songs until their fingers blistered. George will never forget the intensity of that time. They knew they were creating something special, but it was hard to imagine that releasing their music into the world would see that inkling confirmed.

So when George came to a standstill after *Twelve Thousand Words*, Simon kicked into motion. He overloaded his friend on a daily basis with new chords and riffs and rousing choruses. They ran laps around Regent's Park every afternoon. They ate Nando's extra hot chicken sandwiches and they kicked a football endlessly around the studio. His friend's tenacity drove George crazy, because really all he wanted to do was hide under his duvet and mope, but eventually George started writing again, and *Sounds As If*, their second album, was born.

The agony paid off: NME, May 2007 - *Sounds As If Thesis have avoided the sophomore slump. The follow-up to Twelve Thousand Words raises the listener high in all the right places.*

Simon knew how to resuscitate George, something George had never experienced before. When he was a child, it was always Polly who had some intense drama going on. It was Polly who garnered all of his parents' attention because she had grazed her knee, or lost her precious bookmark, or found a spider, or didn't like her haircut, or had argued with a friend. George had learned early on how not to ask for help, mostly because it never seemed to be available.

He gives his stress ball another tight squeeze and frowns back at the misshapen mouth, silently defying the creative concrete to build another wall.

LEXI
November 4th, 2009
Venice, Los Angeles

Number fifty-five is a ramshackle bungalow with a rickety front gate. A dilapidated lime-green Mini parked in the front yard has been converted into a makeshift garden, an explosion of vibrant wildflowers blossoming where the hood once was. A massive black and white cat is fast asleep on the warm roof. It's unexpected and Lexi is momentarily charmed, remembering the phrase *Creative space* from the ad. She takes a deep breath and knocks boldly on the front door.

Russell Hazleton opens the door with what can only be described as a flourish. He is a short man, probably somewhere in his late forties, with a long white blond ponytail hanging over his shoulder and a black fluffy goatee—a disarming combination.

"You've met Boris, I see..." he says, gesturing to the sleeping cat. "When he's not running the show around here you'll be dealing with me, second in command, Russell Hazleton, pleasure to meet you. You must be Lexi, because you don't look like the UPS driver." He greets her with a very weak handshake that slowly builds into a firm pumping action. She isn't certain if he has any plans to let go.

"That's right, Lexi Jacobs. It's very nice to meet you too, Russell," she says nervously, as he keeps a tight grip on her hand and continues to shake it vigorously.

"I can see you're wondering right about now, Lexi, what might be going on here. Well, I'll fill you in on my little secret and let you know that you've passed the first test."

"Test?" asks Lexi, confused, and suddenly feeling overdressed in her grey Theory suit and leather ballet pumps. Russell is wearing denim shorts and a Barack Obama tank top. He finally lets go of her hand.

"Yes, test. It's this nifty character study I've invented to assess suitable job candidates. I call it the shake and fake. You can tell a whole lot about somebody from how they shake your hand, you know. I operate on a spectrum from limp to powerful, all the while noting your response. You hung on in there. You didn't recoil. I felt you were willing to meet me in my energetic vibrations. You've got the job!"

Lexi is tempted to turn and run. She is, after all, still only at the front door.

"You look surprised," he adds.

"Well, um, yeah, you could say, surprised. That would be a good word. It's just I was expecting more of an interview and, maybe, you know, a chance for me to ask a few questions, so that I can decide if I actually *want* the job."

"Very sensible," he says, moving aside and allowing room for her to enter. "We can make that work. Come on in..."

Lexi steps tentatively over the threshold, trying not to hear her mother's voice warning ominously, "Stranger danger!" But once inside, it's impossible not to be overwhelmed by curiosity. Russell's house is an eccentric emporium of recycling. Every object imaginable appears to have been reincarnated and given a second chance in life. Toasters hold CDs. CDs are lampshades. Lampshades are fruit baskets. An upside-down oven is acting as a wine rack. Old t-shirts have been patchworked together and transformed into tablecloths and cushion covers. Bicycle wheels with painted tires hang on the walls like modern works of art. It really is quite captivating.

"This is extraordinary," she says.

"Perhaps," Russell replies modestly. "But my true aim is to take the ordinary items in life and save them from the well-worn fate of trash."

"Well, you've certainly achieved that," says Lexi.

"I love myself, Lexi, but I love the greatest mother of all above and beyond that. We are all children of the earth and we owe it to her to behave with respect and integrity. I don't know about you, but I for one have had it up to here with humans flipping the bird at our ailing matriarch. It is in our power to save her..."

His fervor is certainly compelling.

"Looking around here," says Lexi, "I can see you clearly intend to make a difference."

"I really do," says Russell.

"But, if you don't mind my asking," says Lexi cautiously, not wanting to offend him, "What is the business exactly? What do you do?"

Russell sucks in his breath, as if preparing to duck under water.

"Anything. Everything. I have a lot of excellent ideas on how to improve our commitment to the earth. I have volumes of valuable information stored in a paperless vault," he taps the side of his head pointedly. "I've already transformed a local retail outlet. They now run all their delivery vehicles on vegetable oil and they've cut down on trash output by eighty percent."

"That's very impressive," says Lexi.

"I just need a bit of assistance getting focused and getting out there. I find myself in somewhat of a jumble," Russell admits, glancing around his jam-packed living room. "I sure don't have a lot of money, Lexi, but I could pay you a small salary to begin with, and my bet is that Let The Green Times Roll will soon rocket. If things work out with you and me, I would gladly cut you in on a percentage."

Lexi is hesitant. She knows she really isn't in a position to be picky, and while Russell seems harmless, she is skeptical as to what kind of business could be fashioned from this museum of oddities.

"I think what you're doing here is admirable, Russell, and your passion is evident, but I'm just not certain what the future of all this could be."

Russell scoops up a dozy Boris, who has squeezed his way through a cat flap (previously a Supertramp album cover).

"That's just it, Lexi. No one is certain of the future. Our whole planet is in jeopardy unless people like you take a risk on people like me. I've read your resume. You have plenty of experience. I like your energy. Just say yes."

Lexi is caught off guard by Russell's directness. He might be making a more pertinent point than he realizes. She flashes back to all the jobs of the past few years that had initially appeared so suitable, only to unravel time and time again. Maybe for once she should stop trying to get it right and risk getting it wrong instead? She knows her mother wouldn't agree, but perhaps a little reverse psychology is exactly what she needs to turn things around.

"Okay, Russell. I accept the challenge," she says, deciding the only thing she has to lose is another job.

"You do?" he asks, looking shocked, leaving Lexi questioning how many applicants have declined the position before her.

"I do," she responds, feeling only half as confident as she sounds.

GEORGE
7th November, 2009
Camden, London

"It's a croissant, you see, but with two types of chutney, one sweet, one sour, and layers of thinly sliced roast beef." Simon licks his lips longingly, running his hand through his spiky red hair.

"Dude, you need to get laid," says Duncan, throwing a baseball cap across the room. Simon ducks as it skims over his head. "In fact, so do you, George—what is it with us? Am I the only one getting any action around here?"

"I am," offers Mark, the bass player and the only member of the band who is married.

"You don't count!" says Duncan. "What happened to Fanny, George? She's desperate to give you a guided tour."

"Yeah, maybe," says George, noncommittal. "She's just a bit weird."

Fanny Arundel—the UK's answer to Katy Perry. Irreverent, wry and super sexy, she provokes controversy wherever she goes, singing about puppies and nipples and the war in Afghanistan, sometimes covering all three subjects in one song. She used to be a nurse before being discovered by Sebastian Stonehill, a respected record executive, who happened to be her patient in Intensive Care. He signed her to his label two weeks before succumbing to an infection, post open heart surgery. Much to the public horror of his wife, Fanny sang at his funeral and now wears numerous variations of a nurse's uniform on stage in his memory. She drives young men to distraction.

"George, mate, weird is wonderful. Who knows what she might get up to—all sorts of kinky shit. Handcuffs, whips—you ever tried any of that?"

George should be accustomed to Duncan by now, so why does he still squirm when Duncan talks about sex? He's almost positive Duncan should have been diagnosed with ADHD when he was a child. He is in his element perched behind the drums, but even without his sticks in hand, he is in perpetual motion.

The band have gathered together at their recording studio in Camden to continue brainstorming ideas for the next album and to discuss the upcoming North American tour with their manager, Gabe. George likes to describe Gabe as half Prince Charles, half Bob Marley. He is the product of a very rebellious aristocratic mother from Hampshire and an equally rebellious music producer from Kingston, Jamaica. As a result of straddling the two worlds effortlessly, he has all the finesse of a diplomat and his strategic choices for Thesis have been crucial to their rise. He also buys lunch.

Gabe walks into the room with a tray piled high with sandwiches, conveniently allowing George to dodge answering Duncan's question.

"It's my boys!" he says with a big grin. "Names are on the wrappers, dig in, and Simon, keep your comments to a minimum." Simon lunges to grab his baguette and unwraps it carefully, holding it up to savour the moment before taking a bite.

"Now you've all got food in your faces, let's get down to business," says Gabe, pulling out his Blackberry. "We're scheduled to fly to Las Vegas on the twelfth of November where we have a three-day video shoot for 'I Knew It'. On the 16th we've got five radio drop ins and some print interviews. On the 17th we fly to LA. I'll give you the schedule of interviews and TV appearances closer to the time, but we're booked in for *The Tonight Show* for certain. Then there's breakfast with the competition winners—"

"Oh man, Gabe, give us a break! I hate those bloody breakfast things—do you remember the whack job last time with the rancid breath?" Duncan shakes his head disgustedly.

"Dunc, these things are important," says George, "I mean what's the point of all of this if we become too superior to meet with our fans?"

"Meet with them is one thing, having to smell them while we eat with them is another."

"Don't come, then," says Mark, renowned for being blunt.

"Well, of course I'll come, I was just—"

"Whingeing," interrupts Mark. "You were just whingeing as usual."

"Sorry we can't all be so bloody unflappable like you!" mimics Duncan in a forced English accent, his unpredictable temper rapidly heating up.

"Now, now, children," says Simon.

George starts to feel the familiar anxiety rising in his chest again. Sometimes he has a nightmare that this... all of this... could crumble and deteriorate as quickly as it appeared and then he would be... and then he would be who? The horrible question haunting him more and more frequently.

The room is suddenly silent.

"Okay, then," says Gabe, "can we get back to the schedule before we have to call in the group therapist and all do our Metallica impersonations? Duncan?"

"What, mate?" Duncan is up, pacing back and forth behind the sofas.

"You cool?"

"Yeah—Gabe—I'm cool. I'm fine."

George knows Duncan is the wild card in the foursome. He has the potential to detonate and it worries him. It's as if he's just on the brink of being completely out of control but somehow always manages to pull it back in.

"Good to hear," says Gabe, "so let's talk about the acoustic show."

The acoustic show is George's baby—an unexpected treat for the fans—an intricately paired back set, played to an audience of a few hundred. Tickets are only available by entering a lottery on their website. They've chosen LA because it's the city where they recorded their first album and holds a certain nostalgia. Plus they love the sunshine and the sushi bars.

"We've confirmed The Avid in Hollywood for the show. Built in the twenties—got a great vibe. We'll film the gig and I'm thinking let's leave it open to interpretation, give you guys a chance to improvise instead of micromanaging the entire evening. You up for that, George?"

George is not known for his risk taking, but he's really looking forward to the show and wants to explore what it might be like again without the buffer of a stadium crowd.

"I'm definitely up for it," says George, painfully aware that the smaller the gig the greater the chance of being exposed.

"Oh and I forgot to mention," adds Gabe, "I heard from Fanny Arundel's manager. It turns out that she's coincidentally shooting her video in Vegas at the same time as us. Thought you might be interested in that bit of info."

Fanny has had her sights set on George since meeting at last year's Brit awards, and his lack of interest up until now has only fueled her pursuit.

George cringes inside. Truthfully, Fanny scares the shit out of him. He's sure he could never live up to her raunchy expectations.

"You'll definitely be into that, won't you, mate?" teases Duncan, his juvenile tone reminding George of everything he would like to forget.

LEXI
November 7th, 2009
Pacific Palisades, Los Angeles

Lexi is sitting with Meg in her backyard watching Jack and Annabelle play Happy Hippos on the lawn. Meg has remained Lexi's best friend, except somewhere along the line, they seem to have swapped destinies. It is Meg who has the husband, house, children and dog, while Lexi is always the friend with a 'story' to tell. Usually the kind of story that leaves Meg asking, "Why do these insane things always happen to you?" But Lexi realizes that Meg finds her a welcome distraction. She often confides to Lexi that getting married too early has left her itchy. She's on the subject now.

"Sometimes I feel like I'm wearing long underwear and I want to rip it off and run through the streets naked."

"Really?" says Lexi. "I want to cuddle up on the couch with a man who isn't Andrew and watch *Before Sunrise* with no mascara on and baggy sweatpants."

"Ahh, I know, Lex," says Meg sympathetically. "You *will* meet somebody. I promise. A gorgeous specimen like you? There is no way you're going to grow old without baggy sweats and no mascara nights."

Lexi knows she's pretty and has always been complimented on her elegant profile and her green eyes swirled with amber and grey. There is something gentle and open in her expressions and she has an offbeat sex appeal that might well come with the territory of being a fallen prom queen. Her parents only introduced her when she was young as "our beautiful Lexi," and she came to rely on the label, like it was part of her name, printed neatly in typewriter ink on her birth certificate. But Lexi isn't so sure how helpful that is any longer. Over the last few years, it seems as if her love life and her career path have been in vicious competition, vying for which aspect of her world can fall apart quicker. Alongside her ill-fated job opportunities have been several unfit boy-friends. There was Michael, a dentist, the son of a dentist, who apparently hailed from a long line of dentists. He was obsess-ed with floss and told Lexi she had the sexiest molars he had ever laid eyes upon. Lexi had been in 'like' with him for a short while. He knew how to cook Moussaka and he didn't appear to be gay. But she left him after one year because she was bored.

"It's very normal to be bored by a man," explained her exasperated mother. "I've been bored by your father for decades!" But Lexi hadn't felt quite ready to be permanently bored, so she paused for a little while before dating the oppo-site extreme. She met Hank in the check-out line at Whole Foods. Hank had his pilot's license and was halfway through writing a seven hundred page novel. He flew her to Catalina and asked if he could paint her toenails on the beach. He had a mind like a marble maze and after a year, Lexi found it an effort to keep up with his wayward thoughts. Since Hank there had been numerous guys, some who had lasted for months at a time. She's never short of men being interested, it's her own lack of interest in return that concerns her.

"You just haven't met the right guy yet, Lex," says Meg encouragingly. "He'll come along."

"That's just it, Meg. He might not come along and I'm going to have to accept that. And so are you. And so is my mom."

"I don't know, Lex. Maybe it's like these guys are choos-ing you rather than you choosing them. You could be more proactive, go online, make a checklist, be assertive. I mean come on, you're not even on Facebook yet. Ryan Glazer might get back in contact with you! I was friended by that bitch, Penelope, from grammar school. She's a yoga teacher now."

The girls had shared a crush on Ryan Glazer in the third grade and he'd been the first boy to come between them. Meg cried for two straight days after he offered Lexi a bite of his peanut butter and banana sandwich.

Lexi groans, "No thank you, Meg! The computer is so unromantic," although Lexi has lost a true sense of what romance even is anymore. It used to be straightforward. The Prince *had* shown up. The glass slipper *had* fit. But now the Prince was out clubbing in boys town and the slipper had cracked into hundreds of pieces, leaving Lexi still picking up the tiny shards, all these years later.

"It might be unromantic but it *is* effective. Hey, Jack! Jack!" Meg suddenly yells at her four-year-old, "hippos DO NOT punch their sisters!"

"I wasn't punching her, Mommy. I was stroking her," says Jack innocently.

"With your fist?"

"But she likes it. Very, very much."

"She does, does she? Let's ask her. Annabelle, do you like it when Jack punches you?"

"Yes—me like it... punching is fun!" sings two-year-old Annabelle, jumping up and down.

Meg rolls her eyes. "She's got a great future ahead of her. I give up. If I get involved—I'm overprotective. If I don't—I'm neglecting their needs. Can you watch them while I get a drink? Is it too early for alcohol?"

"Yes!" says Lexi, as Meg disappears into the kitchen.

GEORGE
7th November, 2009
Maida Vale, London

It's three in the morning. George sits on the side of his bed wearing only boxers and plucking the strings of his oldest and most loved guitar. He saved up for it when he was a boy, washing his neighbors' cars and taking their dogs for walks. When he'd finally earned forty pounds, he'd cycled to the local charity shop and handed over the money. The guitar had been balanced in the window for months, next to a leery garden gnome and a pair of scuffed pink stilettos. He'd named it Stardust, in honor of Bowie, and had grown up talking to the instrument the way other kids conversed with imaginary friends. Stardust knew all of George's hopes and fears and translated them back to him in beautiful vibrating sound waves. All these years later, the scratched-up body still smells faintly of cedar wood and George always finds the weight of the instrument in his lap comforting. He presses his fingertips into the fret board and listens to the echo of 'A' minor reverberate. The window is wide open and his bedroom is bathed in a dense, cold darkness. George can't sleep, but even so, he feels like something deep inside of him still needs waking up.

LEXI
November 7th, 2009
Pacific Palisades, Los Angeles

Jack and Anabelle continue to wrestle merrily on the grass. For a brief second Lexi imagines this is her garden, her children, her life and she feels not the usual pang, but an unfamiliar ambivalence that catches her off guard. If she doesn't want this, what does she want? She used to think that this picture was all that mattered, or was it just that her mother had done the greatest PR job of all and marketed a potential package to Lexi that would never actually suit her? At least she has a new job to look forward to. Russell said she could start on Monday, and while the whole set-up is more than slightly odd, she had left Victoria Avenue feeling a trace of hopeful.

Meg interrupts her thoughts and hands her a tall glass of iced tea and her iPhone "Hey, can you give me your honest opinion of my profile picture? Is it trying too hard?" Lexi takes the phone and sees that Meg has chosen a shot pre-children, where she still looks fresh and quite sassy. She understands how Meg might be sensing some of her own dreams slipping through her fingers.

"Well, it could be more current—but you look great. Very flirty. I'm sure Penelope is seething."

"Mission accomplished. Ooh, look at this," says Meg, taking the phone back from Lexi and scrolling down the screen, "Thesis update. Did you ever buy their new album? The one I told you about last week—it's compulsive."

"No, I haven't bought any new music in ages. Oh God, I'm getting stale, aren't I? I'm supposed to be single and hip and you're meant to be wearing mom jeans. What's happening?"

"George Bryce is what's happening, Lex. Check this guy out—he's adorable."

Meg is legendary for her feverish crushes on numerous famous men and Lexi guesses this lead singer is the latest in line.

"Meggy—I love it when you turn fourteen on me again." Lexi remembers the days when they were both infatuated with Pearl Jam and would spend hours debating which of them would be better suited to marry Eddie Veder. She'd lie in bed at night fantasizing about touching her cheek to his sweaty chest moments after he ran off stage.

"Well, I need *some* outlet, don't I?" says Meg defensively. "They're coming to LA in concert soon—it's a special acoustic thing. I'd die to see them live."

"Would you just like totally die?" Lexi teases, grabbing the phone back from Meg to look at a grainy picture of George Bryce, posing with a delirious looking fan, a random pack of toilet paper lodged between them.

"Mock me if you will, but I'm entering the lottery to win tickets to their concert. I can take Tim for his birthday. Cross your fingers."

"Whatever you say," says Lexi, as it occurs to her that she too is due some luck, and good old fashioned finger crossing might definitely be worth a try.

GEORGE
12th November, 2009
Gatwick Airport, London

George and the boys are fielded through the busy airport by an ultra efficient woman called Candice, who works for Virgin Atlantic Special Services. Gone are the days of waiting to check in, or waiting in the tedious security line, or waiting at passport control, or waiting for luggage. George will never fully adjust to the VIP treatment. He feels guilty that they have become exempt from the mind-numbing activities that lend a familiar rhythm to the passage of life. He actually misses deciding where best to position himself at the luggage carousel and knocking into strangers while hauling his duffel bag off. He is, however, looking forward to the eleven-hour journey and is planning on revisiting the lyrics to "Over Time" again.

Candice is leading them briskly towards the first class lounge. As they pass through the throng of hassled travelers, George keeps his head down but can still hear people whispering "look!" and "isn't that..?" It's strange how he has come to feel the pointing fingers even when he can't directly see them—like sharp jabs in the ribs. In the past, Gabe has tried to advise him on the pitfalls of fame when he notices George is struggling. He once told him to imagine he is surrounded by an invisible force field—like a protective barrier designed to keep out the critic and let in the love. George managed this for about a week, until his fluorescent blue aura suffered a slow puncture and allowed all sorts of negativity in with absolutely no discretion. The best thing that came out of that failed attempt was the third single on their latest album,

"Punctured Aura." It went straight to number three on the UK charts.

Duncan is keeping step with Candice while George, Simon, Mark, and Mark's wife Anna trail slightly behind. Gabe follows.

Duncan leans in to Candice, "So, Candy, have you ever performed any 'special services' for Mick Jagger?" He is clearly amused by his own joke.

"Oh, Mr. Cross, you *are* naughty," says Candice, obviously not unused to men coming on to her somewhere between security clearance and the first class lounge.

"So I've been told. Call me Duncan."

"Well, Duncan, Mr. Jagger is in fact one of our clients, but I shall say no more. One day when I'm old and grey I might write a book."

"I'll buy it, but I need to know how to get *in it* first."

Simon mutters to George, "Jesus, Dunc's out of control, are you listening to this? I think she's old enough to be his mother."

George chuckles, "Duncan gets away with it. I'd sound like a right twat if I said any of that."

"It's because he's Australian. They can say anything and women fall all over them."

"You reckon? Whatever became of Angela?" George can't forget the six foot model from Melbourne who was permanently draped around Duncan's neck when the band had first formed. "I thought she was the love of his life."

"Come on, mate... you're still a hopeless romantic. Angela was just another girl. Duncan's not husband material. Do you honestly think that there is one woman out there meant especially for you?"

George lets the question hang in the air. He wants to believe it. He used to believe it. Mark seems content, but then again Anna is forever moaning at him about this thing he never does right or that thing he could have done better.

Maybe he should just forget about finding the 'right' woman and be a bit more reckless instead. There's a zillion opportunities. He's a rock star, for God's sake. Shouldn't he start behaving like one? Does he want to end up like his parents, numb and shriveled, barely speaking to one another except to say pass the remote control? But then again, it's not as if Simon's a rock 'n roll model himself. He's usually too busy eating.

"I don't know, Sim, I thought I did, but recently I'm not so sure. Why don't you and I make a pact, right here, right now. This trip we're about to take—let's throw caution to the wind and—you know—explore some options..."

"I'm liking this, George, it's sounding good. Are you talking female options?"

"Yeah, among other things. I'm not talking about you trying a new gluten free pumpernickel bread." Simon shakes his friend's hand.

"I'm in."

As they arrive in the first class lounge, a pretty receptionist greets the band with a big smile and shiny pink lip gloss.

"What a pleasure to meet you all. Mr. Bryce, I'm going to embarrass myself now, but I can't tell you how much I adore your voice."

George returns the smile. "Oh, I'm sure with a bit of encouragement you could." The receptionist blushes and giggles nervously, lowering her eyes. *See* thinks George, *easy*.

LEXI
November 12th, 2009
Venice, Los Angeles

Lexi is driving to her fourth day of work with Russell. The first three days on the job have been peculiar. Daunted by the task at hand, Lexi wonders how she is ever going to make sense of the minefield of messiness in Russell's home and in his mind. For all his talk of getting focused, the reality is that Russell simply doesn't know how. Every time she shows up for work, he spends at least ten minutes giving her a play by play of Boris's activities in her absence.

"After you left, he appeared a little forlorn. He chased his tail for some time before settling. He slept fitfully last night. I think he was having a nightmare about the neighbor's canary. He only ate half of his bowl of food. He might be constipated." Lexi nods dutifully, desperately wanting to yell, "TOO MUCH INFORMATION!" but incapable of being that impolite. Eventually Russell moves onto a jumbled outpouring about CO2 emissions, greenhouse gases, plastic recycling technology and grains and pulses. At that point, he usually squeezes them both a large glass of orange and beet juice and Lexi sips it slowly, imagining her tongue turning red.

Today she has decided enough is enough. Whatever it takes, she is determined to figure out how to harness the unruly child that is Let The Green Times Roll and tame it to be a well-behaved business. And if that doesn't work—she's out.

GEORGE
12th November, 2009
Virgin Atlantic flight VS043 to Las Vegas

George stares out of the window of the 747 as it begins crossing the Atlantic. Simon is fast asleep with his headphones on and his mouth wide open. Mark and Anna are watching a film, Gabe is playing on his iPad and Duncan has lowered the divider between the business class seats and is shamelessly chatting up the French woman sitting beside him. George has already signed ten air sickness bags for the flight attendant's friends and family. He reckons they might show up on eBay next week. The thought of someone paying silly money for his signature still floors him. There isn't a morning that goes by when he doesn't ask himself, how did this happen?

The captain has had the seat belt sign on for the last ten minutes and things are currently smooth, but George is expectant, waiting for the next jolt. Being a nervous flyer and being in a successful band are not a good combination. Half your life you're in the air. He's often imagined the headlines should Thesis perish in a plane crash—after all, hasn't that been the fate of many a famous musician? He wonders if his family would feel guilty? More likely they would feign a few weeks of grief and then gleefully become the recipient of his royalties. Polly and the triplets would be set for life, and his parents might finally buy a new house without feeling forced to show any gratitude. He pictures it now, a ten-page spread in *OK magazine*—**Living without George. How the family of George Bryce are coping in the aftermath of his tragic early death.** He can just make out the triplets' sickly expressions, as they pose in identical black shirts, next to a framed picture of the band.

George attempts to shake off the image and concentrate instead on the view outside. The sky is a twisted ribbon of white and grey clouds, and he finds the thought of the churning water below oddly soothing. Better to plummet into the ocean than crash into a row of houses on hard ground. *Hard Ground. Hard Ground. I Found. I found. And we sing the lonely sound. The only sound. This desire's not a crime. See my need build over time.* The words start a ritual dance in his head, as the melody creeps up from behind, and the song finally begins to form. George feels his body relax. Before he knows it they will land.

LEXI
November 12th, 2009
Venice, Los Angeles

Russell is slicing the beet into rough chunks and still talking about Boris. "It's rather remarkable how quickly he has attached to you. Cats, as you know, are renowned for being antisocial, and Boris is very particular, but ever since you arrived—"

"Russell!" Lexi's tone is firm. Russell looks surprised, as if unexpectedly woken up from a nap.

"Russell," Lexi continues, now she has his attention, "we have got to concentrate here. Boris is the least of our concerns. You have hired me to get this business into shape, so let's do it!" She is unaccustomed to sounding so assertive but it actually feels pretty good. She wonders if she should stand up and bang her fist on the table, or would that be a bit over the top?

Russell looks wounded. "I thought we were doing that, Lexi. We designed that new filing system from the old cereal boxes. I've never been so organized in all my life."

"Yes, that's a start, but we need a game plan. A target. A vision. Mother Earth is waiting for us to do the right thing— remember?" She is quickly learning to speak Russell's language.

"You're right, I know you're right. I just get..." Russell trails off.

"Scared, you get scared, Russell. We all do. Now let's tackle some of that fear and turn it into biofuel!"

Lexi is on fire! Maybe she should become a life coach instead? Russell has a sparkle back in his eye. "Speaking of bio fuel, Lexi, I had this idea for a consultancy service..."

GEORGE
12th November, 2009
Virgin Atlantic flight VS043 to Las Vegas

George has fallen asleep with his notebook splayed open on his lap. All the lyrics for "Over Time" had arrived in his head and landed on the page while the plane was still flying. The flight attendant with the signed air sickness bags comes by with a tray of orange juice and water. She stands for a moment and stares at him. His lips are slightly parted and his black hair is flopping over one eye and she imagines running her fingers over the contours of his face. She knows she's about to do something she shouldn't. She goes back to the galley and puts the tray down. She finds her handbag and takes out her phone. She walks casually back to George and surreptitiously snaps a picture. Her heart is racing.

LEXI
November 12th, 2009
Venice, Los Angeles

By the end of the day, Lexi has drunk four glasses of orange and beet juice, eaten a very unwieldy raw salad and paced a thousand circles around the house with Boris and Russell at her heels. Having spent hours bouncing around ideas, mind mapping the results, scrapping everything and starting over again, they have finally thrashed out a potential format for the venture. She is giddy with relief and Russell has quite literally let his hair down, shaking out his limp ponytail.

"I say we celebrate!" he announces, picking up a disgruntled Boris and twirling him around the room.

"All hail to the spider!" adds Lexi, glancing at her watch remembering she is due to meet Andrew tonight for dinner and a movie and is already running late.

The spider was her idea. It refers to the different 'legs' of the business plan, with Russell operating as the center hub and heart. This particular spider will have four legs with room to grow—a consultancy service for businesses looking to improve their commitment to the environment; a website where Russell can sell the recycled products he designs; a series of lectures and creative workshops to be run in schools on how to re-use and re-cycle, and last but not least, a book. Of course a percentage of all profits will go to charities saving the rainforest, the polar bears, the ozone layer and the pine nut. Lexi has no clue if she really can get the Green Times to Roll, but there's a better chance of it now than there was four days ago.

Russell is hyper. "Light bulb! Why don't I pull out some Diamante vinyl and I can whiz up a couple of my world famous lychee margaritas and you and I can smoke a little grass? I've got a special blend which I've been saving for just the right occasion."

Lexi tries not to laugh, "Diamante?"

"Neil Diamond, my dear girl, Neil Diamond. He's a god."

"Oh, of course. I think my mom likes him."

"She must have excellent taste, then. What do ya' say?"

Lexi doesn't want to hurt Russell's feelings, but she knows this is not an invitation to be contemplated. She stands up and looks around for her bag.

"It's tempting, Russell, but I promised to meet up with a friend tonight."

Russell looks deflated. "No worries—Boris and I will share a straw—it's not like it hasn't happened before."

"But listen, today was great. I really think we can do something with this now. Start narrowing in on ideas for the book and lectures and write them down. You could even do a blog. I know you want to save trees, but it's time to see something on paper."

"You're right again. I'll get going on it. And Lexi—" She pauses at the front door. The sun is setting on Venice beach and there is a soft orange glow filtering in through the front window.

"Yes, Russell?"

"Boris wants to say... thank you."

Boris has passed out on the couch having been danced around the room and is purring contentedly.

Lexi waves in his direction, "You're welcome, Boris." She leaves the house and walks past the Mini and back towards her car. It will be a miracle if she can actually make this happen, but she is already feeling a small sense of achievement and winks at her inner Maria, who has come out of retirement and is busy making play clothes from retro print curtains.

GEORGE
November 12th, 2009
Las Vegas, Nevada

George thinks Las Vegas is like chewing gum—after fifteen minutes the flavour has been sucked away and he's looking to spit it out. Oh, but that first fifteen minutes! That first burst of neon and colour and perennial buzz and tasteless monstrosity and rush of desert heat—that first fifteen minutes is sublime. They're here to shoot the third video for this album and George is frustrated by his lack of creative input. They'll be working with a director called Pedro Myerson, who is known to be a temperamental genius. He has his own 'concept' for the shoot and Gabe has encouraged George to step back.

The band is grabbing dinner at the Venetian Hotel—an eerie impostor of the Italian city, except with a Delmonico Steakhouse and Abercrombie and Fitch. They are basically sitting in a giant indoor shopping mall built alongside the Grand Canal, complete with floating gondolas and a fake starry sky. Gabe is trying to convince George that Myerson is the right choice.

"Trust me, man, this guy is like Scorsese. The song is big —it needs a cinematic eye." George actually prefers not to be featured too heavily in the videos at all. Most of the last few shoots have involved actors or been obscured and shadowy concert footage. He would like it to stay that way, but Gabe sometimes has different ideas.

"But we've barely seen a proposal, Gabe. What if he wants us all dressed in drag playing cricket in the desert?"

Gabe guffaws, "I think you're onto something, George. Listen—I know you like to keep the videos simple, but it's time for a change. Let's give them something to talk about."

George is distracted by Duncan. He's wound up like a spring and is rubbing his hands together. When they first formed the band, the four of them had vowed not to succumb to the temptation of drugs. "It's such a bloody cliché," George had insisted. He had experimented when he was younger, but found most drugs either made him feel seriously depressed or numb. He was naturally prone to melancholy and didn't need a substance to enhance that, and when he was numb he couldn't write. He needed to write. He knows that the others have most likely strayed over the years. George has told himself it isn't a problem until it's a problem.

Duncan's pupils look like pinpricks and George is beginning to wonder if now it's a problem. He's bouncing in his seat, "Vegas, baby, Vegas! I'm talking Tom Jones, Frank Sinatra, Engelbert Humperdinck—all the greats! This place is a riot. Who's going to hit the tables with me?"

Anna looks protectively at Mark. "I'm really tired. I think you and I should go back to the room and get some sleep."

Mark nods obediently, "Yeah, not tonight, Dunc, Anna and I are going to hit the sack." Duncan's mouth hangs open, "But it's only eight o'clock, mate—live a little."

"It's not eight o'clock in London, Duncan," says Anna frostily, "it's four o'clock in the morning. We aren't on Las Vegas time yet."

"Give me a fuckin' break! Vegas doesn't keep time, Anna, haven't you noticed there's no clocks anywhere?" Anna stands up and takes Mark's hand, virtually dragging him away from the table. Mark shrugs at the boys and dutifully follows. Duncan shakes his head in disgust, "Man, he's whipped."

Mark had confided to George on the plane earlier that Anna has been uneasy recently, complaining that they don't have enough quality time together. "She wants to take baths in candlelight—and give each other massages. I've got to make more of an effort." George had listened sympathetically, secretly wishing he had the same sort of issues to contend with. He steps in now remembering his pact with Simon earlier. "Relax, Dunc. Simon and I are up for it—aren't we, Simon?"

"Yes Sir!" says Simon, saluting. "And by the way—this club sandwich isn't bad. I wasn't sure what to make of the four layers but when I—" Simon is cut off abruptly by a peroxide blonde with an extremely oversized bottom barreling towards their table. She is squeezed into tight white jeans and a T-shirt with the words *Beauty is in the eye of the beer holder* emblazoned across her ample chest.

Zeroing in on George, she turns to her friend and screeches in a loud southern accent, "I know who this is! You're that Irish singer, the one with the funny name. I've seen you on MTV winning all those awards. You're Bow Wow, aren't you?"

"Well, uh... I could be," George says, desperately attempting to remain composed, while Duncan, Gabe and Simon are all stifling the giggles.

The woman is oblivious. "Didn't I tell you, Lorraine? Didn't I say we'd see someone famous in Vegas? Can you sign this?" she says, lifting up her t-shirt to reveal rolls of dimpled fat and a bra with generous square footage.

"You got a pen, sweetie?" she asks Duncan, who is reveling in the sideshow.

"Sorry, love, I don't. But Bow Wow might."

George holds up empty hands. "I can't currently oblige, but it was nice of you to stop by," he says, inching himself away from the woman's formidable bust, as Simon kicks him under the table like a twelve-year-old.

Unperturbed, she pulls her t-shirt down and walks away declaring to her friend, "Did you hear those European accents? Those Irish boys are sure polite."

Gabe opens his arms wide, "Welcome back to Vegas, lads!"

LEXI
November 12th, 2009
The Grove, Los Angeles

Lexi was indeed late to meet Andrew and they missed the beginning of the movie. He got very huffy and insisted they wait for the next showing, and after sharing a pizza, they are now wandering around the huge Barnes and Noble bookstore in The Grove shopping mall.

"Are you sure nothing's going on with you and your new boss? You seem to be working very late."

"No way! He listens to Neil Diamond and drinks wheatgrass."

"The maiden doth protest! Isn't that a sign that you're lying?" Lexi clenches her jaw. She feels like screaming. Andrew has been especially annoying recently. His latest lover, Heston, has recently dumped him and he's acting like a clingy child. In high school she had mistaken his possessiveness for true love.

"Andrew. Back off please. I've had a long day. You found me this job for goodness sake, and suddenly it's like you're trying to make me feel guilty for working at it."

"Cool your jets, Lexi, I'm just joking."

"Cool my what?"

"Your jets. It's a saying. It means calm down."

"Cool your jets? It's not something I've heard you say before."

"I'm a man of mystery. You don't know everything about me, do you?"

"I didn't used to, but I do now. Most things."

"Really. Most things?"

"Cool your jets?!" She finds it hard to stay icy with Andrew and can feel herself thawing. He puts his arm around her shoulder and pulls her in for a hug. She sinks into him, feeling very tired and sadly aware that it has been a long while since she's been held by a man. Touched by a man. Kissed by a man. Too long.

Just as she's burying her forehead into the soft nook of his leather jacket, she hears a familiar voice behind her, "Well hello there, Lovebirds!"

Lexi turns around to find her mother looking extremely self-satisfied, clutching two books to her chest.

"Mom, what are you doing here?"

"Picking up books, honey. What does it look like?"

"But this is so far away for you. Where's Dad?"

"He's at home. Watching *The Bachelorette* or something." She rolls her eyes in an exaggerated arc. Lexi's mother, Jeanette, is in her late fifties and looking good on it. She gets Botox twice a year and highlights four times a year. This is low maintenance for LA. For the most part she is content to age naturally. Her father is ten years older and ten years grumpier and has recently become fixated by reality T.V. shows. He shouts insults at the screen and then talks about the participants as if they were close family friends. "Can you believe that Jessica chose Ethan? What the hell was she thinking?" Lexi is their only child and they have both doted on her excessively since the day she was born. She will always be a dazzling prom queen in their eyes.

"You don't usually come out on your own?" says Lexi, beginning to feel concerned.

"I was bored. I felt like driving."

"Hello, Jeanette," Andrew steps forward to greet her.

"How are you, Andrew, honey, you look thin."

"I'm fine. It's probably the break-up. Heston left me, you know."

Jeanette seems confused. "Oh please, Andrew, you're not still pretending to be gay, are you? I thought that was just a phase. Lexi and you were so happy together. You were such a lovely couple. I hoped maybe you two were getting back together? Why else would you be standing embracing each other in public?"

Lexi is mortified, "Mom, come on! How can you say that? People don't pretend to be gay."

"Well actually honey, they do. Your father and I once—"

Andrew takes his cue, "Jeanette, it's always a pleasure but I'm going to browse over there now... in the homosexual section." He kisses Lexi's mother on the cheek and wanders off. Lexi sighs.

"I'm sorry, honey, I didn't mean to upset you both. You can't blame me for wanting you to be happy."

"I *am* happy, Mom."

"No, you're not."

"Okay, maybe not happy, happy. But I'm not unhappy. I've got a new job. I've got a..."

"A what?"

"A... a... I don't know... a hunch that this could be my year." Lexi has a memory of having said that to her mother many times.

"You're such a special girl, Lexi. You always have been a light... a light in our lives. Do you remember when your debating team won the nationals? You wore your hair in that gorgeous long braid and Andrew was so handsome. I still have the picture in my wallet. See," Jeanette reaches into her purse.

Lexi puts her hand on top of her mother's to stop her. "I know you do, Mom. I don't have to see. I get it. You and Dad just want me to keep winning, but my idea of winning and your idea of winning might not be the same anymore."

"We still think you're a winner, honey, we always will."

Lexi feels the tears pooling in the corner of her eyes. She wipes them away quickly and links arms with her mother. "Looks like you've got some steamy reads for tonight," she says, glancing down at her mother's book choices, the latest Jackie Collins novel and a paperback titled *Forget Your Husband! Train Your Dog Instead!* "Why don't you go home and give Dad a hug and get into bed with some tea?"

"Good idea, honey. What will you do?"

"Oh, let's see, Mom. Make out with Andrew in the back of the movie theatre?!" Both women laugh, and Lexi wills herself to keep smiling. The tears that she was about to cry are not far behind, but she is stubbornly resolved to keep them at bay.

GEORGE
13th November, 2009
Las Vegas, Nevada

It's three a.m. again and this time George is lucky to have finally stumbled upon his room, having wandered the gaudy air-conditioned hallways for twenty minutes. He is a little worse for wear, after commandeering a roulette table with Duncan, Simon and Gabe, betting on all his lucky numbers (album release dates), winning 400 dollars, losing 500, and downing countless tequila shots at Duncan's insistence. In fact his head is starting to spin and Italian frescoes are somersaulting in his brain. He fumbles with the key, attempting to shove it into the slot the right way up. He needs, very definitely needs, to lie down. Now.

"Can I give you a hand with that?" He recognizes the

woman's voice. Is it his mother? Polly? His fifth year art teacher with the large hoop earrings? His mind is not prepared to currently decipher anything. Perhaps the person behind him is all three women morphed together. Perhaps she is a guardian angel come to swoop him away to Las Vegas heaven? He turns around and comes face, to very close face, with Fanny Arundel. Her black hair is razor straight with a thick Cleopatra fringe.

"Hello, George, I guess I finally found you." For a brief moment, he feels sober again. How has she miraculously appeared in this hallway? Has she been following him?

"Fanny! Fanny, Fanny, Fanny!"

"That's a good sign, darlin', at least you remember my name. For a while I was beginning to think you might have forgotten."

"Forgotten? Me? Never. Such an interesting name—how could I possibly forget?" George is too drunk to consider an escape. The only door he can go through now is his.

"George Bryce—are you plastered?" says Fanny, teasingly.

"What? No. NO. Just wiped out after a long, long plane journey. I'm going to bed... to my bed...okay?"

George has managed to get his door open and is now trying to put it between him and her. She is clearly not going to give in and pushes past him into the room flopping directly onto the bed.

"You can't fool me, George Bryce, clean living patron saint of pop and rock. You're shit faced and I'm just a tiny bit high. Good combination." Fanny looks at him with a mischievous smile and kicks off her four-inch heels, the same shade of deep crimson as her lipstick. George is suddenly mesmerized by her mouth. When was the last time he kissed a woman? Four months ago? Five months ago? She was a DJ on Radio One, very enthusiastic with yellow skinny jeans and an impressive knowledge of eighties music. It hadn't lasted. He felt suffocated when they kissed—she never came up for air. But at this moment, in Las Vegas, reserves of self control plummeting, the thought of kissing Fanny's red lips is like a million slot machines winning the jackpot. He drops down on the bed next to her, the sound of an avalanche of coins ringing in his ears.

"So, maybe. Maybe you *are* sort of right about the drunk thing. But, you know, Fanny... as they say, when in Vegas..."

She clicks her tongue and begins to wriggle out of her Little Miss Chatterbox tight pink t-shirt.

"Is that what they say?" asks Fanny, unveiling a skimpy red lacy bra.

"They do say that. I believe they do. Whoever they are. Do you know who *they* are, Fanny?" George tries to move but his limbs are not cooperating. Fanny rolls over on top of him and deftly gets up onto all fours.

"No I don't, George, but I do know that you are *so so* cute..." Something in the tone of her voice reminds George of Polly cooing at the triplets, but in his drunken haze, nothing can deter him now. "And I've waited patiently for *too too* long..."

She lowers her breasts dangerously close to his mouth where they float like two summer cherries. The first time George had met Fanny, she'd brushed her hand against the front of his jeans and whispered, "Stand to attention, officer." Embarrassingly, he had, and needed to make a hasty retreat to conceal the evidence.

"Don't you just hate waiting?" says George, wearily, feeling like he has made the most profound statement of his entire life.

Fanny unhooks her bra, releasing two pert dark nipples and a breathy sigh. "Time's up, Georgie, welcome to Fanny land..."

LEXI
November 13th, 2009
West Hollywood, Los Angeles

Lexi can't get back to sleep. She thinks maybe she was woken by a small earthquake. Or maybe not. Whatever it was, she feels rattled. She looks over at her clock. Three thirty in the morning. An insomniac's netherworld. When she moved back to LA she had spent months not being able to sleep. But then her doctor prescribed a mild sleeping pill and she found herself dreaming again—disappearing into hours of uninterrupted slumber. She had never even taken the pill. Just the thought that she could if she wanted, appeared to have resolved the issue. The moon is full tonight and pressed cleanly onto the city-lit sky, like it's been stamped there with silver ink. Lexi sleeps with her shutters open because she likes to be woken up by the light. It helps her to gauge how the day might go. Bright. Misty. She can recognize now the sort of clouds that will burn off by lunchtime, bringing the possibility of a sunny afternoon. Those are her favorite kind of clouds.

But the sky tonight is thick and cloudless, bare except for the luminous moon. She attempts rolling over, but something tells her that she's not falling back to sleep any time soon. She decides instead to get up and get a glass of milk and a sneaky vanilla wafer. Maybe she'll just turn on the TV and check to see if there was an earthquake. There usually is a local channel with a 24/7 seismic cam. Maybe she'll find an infomercial and buy a Thighmaster or an automatic card shuffler. Andrew and she could start a poker group and invite her parents. Should she be worried that her parents are having marital problems? Her mom did seem a bit odd tonight at the bookshop. Being an only child, Lexi was the intimate observer of her parents' marriage and mentally documented how her mother repaired all breaks, even the hairline fractures which might have gone unnoticed. "I've left that teabag in for too long, honey. Here, let me make you a new one."

Her mother was intent on preserving appearances and would do almost anything to sustain that. In comparison, Lexi loses tempo quickly in relationships—perhaps the legacy of Andrew—she wonders if she'll ever find a middle ground. Lexi holds that thought as she rifles through the kitchen cupboards. Well stocked with vanilla wafers and a tall glass of milk, she settles down on the couch and flicks on the television. She presses the mute button so as not to disturb Andrew. He'd been very disgruntled by her mother's comments that night.

"What if I am just pretending to be gay, Lexi? Maybe that's why I can't seem to stay in a relationship with a man. Do you think your mom is right? Should we have sex one more time, just to check?"

"You're insane!" Lexi had screamed, outraged, slamming her bedroom door.

"I was just kidding!" he had yelled. "Very sensitive tonight."

"You or me?" she had shouted back, pressing her forehead to her bedroom door.

"Both of us!" he had replied.

They just couldn't seem to manage a civil conversation for long recently.

Lexi starts surfing through the channels searching for news. Home shopping. Cheap jewelry. Cher in Las Vegas. *Friends* re-runs. Music videos. Beyoncé shaking her bootie. Maroon Five looking very sleazy and then... who is this? Lexi turns up the volume slowly. She knows this song. She's heard it before but she's never seen the video. She loves this song. Who is it? The video is filmed in moody black and white. The band are standing in the woods, sheltered under trees, the camera jumping about. The lead singer is so attractive. He has these incredibly intense eyes and Lexi feels completely drawn in by them. And the lyrics. She's never really listened to the lyrics before.

> *It was a suitable dawn*
> *A beautiful dawn*
> *Your fragile heart*
> *So torn apart and I'm*
> *Here now, here now*
> *And I hear you, hear you*
> *As my love rises like*
> *a suitable dawn*

The singer's voice is so damn sexy and his eyes, she can't get over those eyes. And then she realizes. The band is Thesis. Meg's latest obsession. Of course. This time she might have to agree with Meg—the lead singer is seriously cute. As the video fades away, she feels a bit like a teenager again, hungrily daydreaming about making out with Eddie Veder. The pit of her stomach is heavy and fluttery both at the same time. *Oh I'm so stupid* she thinks *he's gotta be at least ten years younger than me. He looks like a baby.* She turns off the TV and eats another vanilla wafer. Distracted, she turns the TV on again and continues to channel hop. Maybe she'll find another Thesis video. Nothing. She clicks the off button and tosses the remote onto the couch. Earthquake or no earthquake, she really should go back to bed. She's got work in the morning. Russell to wrangle. The ozone layer to save. Who knows, maybe the work she ends up doing with Russell really will make a difference? Even in the last week, she's stopped taking paper bags at the market and replaced all the lights in the apartment with energy saving bulbs.

Lexi walks quietly back to her room thinking there must be thousands of other people awake right now, so why does she feel like the only one in the world? It's four in the morning and the moon is full but her milk glass is empty. She crawls into bed and pulls her cozy comforter up around her chin. She can't seem to get the Thesis song out of her head. *Your fragile heart, so torn apart, and I'm here now, here now...* Hmmm. She wonders who the lucky girl is who had that song written just for her?

GEORGE
13th November, 2009
The Venetian Hotel, Las Vegas, Nevada

George is dreaming. He's dreaming there's a massive snoring elephant asleep on his head. The snores are deafening. His skull feels ready to crack. He opens his eyes and for a split second thinks he is at home. Then he remembers he isn't and thinks he must be on tour. Which city? Which hotel? On an average touring year they might visit a hundred. He can't remember, and the snoring is getting louder and louder and the elephant is clearly still in the room. It is then he rolls over and sees the culprit. Fanny Arundel. Fast asleep, mouth wide open, emitting a noise unacceptable even for a sumo wrestler.

"Shit," says George and climbs out of bed. His head no longer feels like it belongs on his body. He marvels at how he is managing to keep it on straight. He looks at the clock, 5:47 a.m. Fanny is sprawled on top of the sheets wearing a red lacy bra and a minuscule thong. George still has on his boxer shorts and socks—very rock and roll. He has absolutely no recollection of what happened. Did they or didn't they? The last thing he remembers is Duncan ordering another round of tequila shots, while Gabe and Simon took bets on who could store the most olive pits in their cheeks. The roulette ball landed on 7. The rest is anyone's guess. How did Fanny Arundel get in his bed? He hopes they didn't have sex. Firstly, because what a bloody waste if he doesn't even remember it, and secondly, because she's a certified crackpot. Even with that body, which is currently very hard to ignore, George knows she's trouble. Plus the snoring is nothing less than awful.

He goes over to the window, thirty-five floors up, and stares across the plugged-in landscape. It looks like a world of electric Legos just waiting to be dismantled and put back together in another configuration. A full pale moon is hanging over the horizon, preparing to switch places with the hot desert sun. What to do? George rubs his tender head considering his options. He could try and find Simon's room or Gabe's. He could just take his suitcase and sneak away and pretend he was never here with her. If he doesn't remember a bloody thing, surely she won't? She does have a reputation for being a cokehead.

For a second he stays with his nose pressed to the window, bewitched by the half light between night and morning. He's always loved this time of day. "A Suitable Dawn" was the first song he'd written for this third album and it had been one of their biggest hits to date. He had written it while walking through the flower gardens in Kyoto on a sleepless, jet-lagged night. He'd wandered around until morning, and then the lyrics had come to him complete, like delicate petals landing in a perfect symmetry. He wrote it for the woman he had yet to meet. The woman he still hasn't met.

"Good morning, lover boy..."

George pushes his forehead harder against the glass. "Morning, Fanny."

His reverie is over.

LEXI
November 13th, 2009
Venice Blvd, Los Angeles

Lexi never did fall back to sleep after returning to bed, and finally got up at six and downloaded the most recent Thesis album. She's only listening to one song on the car journey to Venice though, "A Suitable Dawn." Over and over again.

GEORGE
13th November, 2009
The Venetian Hotel, Las Vegas, Nevada

"You and I, George, I knew we'd be hot." Fanny meows and beckons George back towards the bed.

"Did you?" says George, grabbing his jeans and t-shirt and dressing hurriedly.

"Yes. You're such a tease. All this time, you've been holding out. Holding back all that passion. Christ, my mouth feels like sandpaper—have we got any wine?"

George takes a bottle of water from the fridge and puts it on the bedside table.

"It's a little early for wine, don't you think?"

"Oh George, you sound like my mother. But not last night. Last night you didn't sound like my mother at all. Especially when you told me..." her voice trails off.

"What? What did I tell you?" he's starting to think she might be bluffing.

"I'll remind you later when we have a re-match. What's the hurry anyway, come back to bed."

George looks around for her clothes, if in fact she has any. He spots a polka-dotted miniskirt and a pink t-shirt on the floor, next to a pair of red shoes. He picks up the bundle and slides the shoes in her direction.

"Look, Fanny, last night was... was last night. And you... you are a really talented... talented singer. And me... I'm hopeless at... well hopeless in the mornings really, just a grouch. Not a morning person. Not at all. And today we've got this video shoot and—"

Fanny stands up and stretches her arms high above her head, her breasts barely restrained by the bra. When she turns around, George gets a prime view of her famous tattoo, *high blood pressure,* brazen in bright red cursive script an inch above her bottom. She whistles as she exhales.

"Say no more, George Bryce. I get it. We speak the same language. I'm an artist too, and I know how important it is to get into that Zen space before a performance. I totally respect that. I sometimes channel Sebastian when I'm in that zone. He was my mentor, you know. He gave me my big break. When he died, my world shattered around me." Fanny slips into her shoes and stumbles towards George. "He speaks to me now, George. When I'm meditating. Sebastian told me that you and I were going to be hot together. He told me it would all work out in the end. He was here last night watching us..."

George is utterly creeped out and wishes she would leave.

"Great!" he says a little too enthusiastically, steering Fanny towards the door. "Well then, Sebastian must be about as tired as I am, and probably has a hangover equally as gruesome. He's going to want to rest. In your room. Do you know where it is?" Before he can dodge her, Fanny leans in and kisses George full on the lips, trying to push her tongue insistently into his mouth. He pulls away, aware that there are scores of men who would cut off any number of limbs to find themselves in this position, but ironically, George just isn't feeling it. He hands Fanny her clothes.

"You should get dressed."

Fanny takes the rolled up ball of fabric but doesn't bother to put anything on. She opens the door and swaying down the hallway, *high blood pressure* on full display, calls behind her, "Reach out, George, reach out."

"Most definitely," says George, closing the door as she vanishes around the corner. He briefly questions if he should worry about Fanny roaming the halls half naked, but reminds himself that surely in Vegas that's hardly out of the ordinary.

I'm such an arse he thinks. He can't even manage to

throw caution to the wind without throwing God knows what else into the gale. The day looms ahead of him. A video shoot with a control freak director. Another forty-eight hours in this surreal city. Fanny, the ghost channelling stalker. At least he has the acoustic show to look forward to. He leans his back against the door and surveys the hotel room, a space so thoroughly devoid of soul. George has to be one of thousands of people staying in this beast of a hotel, so why, right at this moment, does he feel like the only one?

LEXI
November 13th, 2009
Venice, Los Angeles

Russell greets Lexi with a freshly prepared glass of green juice. "New recipe!" he declares proudly.

"Thanks," says Lexi who is still feeling the effects of her sleepless night.

What she wants to do now is get to work, rein Russell in, and start making some progress. She's decided that designing a website is the first point of call.

"So," says Lexi, enjoying her new professional vigor, "I was thinking website. Our priority now is to generate interest from organizations who might consider using your consultation services. We need to get businesses on board and then we can get testimonials. It's all about word of mouth." Lexi produces her iPhone from her bag.

"I'm going to start calling contacts today. I know a brilliant website designer who I'm certain would give us a break on the price, considering the current climate."

"Okey dokey," says Russell, "Boris and I will just take out the compost then. Boris has been a tad anxious ever since—"

"No!" says Lexi, with more force than intended. "No Boris talk right now, Russell. The compost will have to wait." She takes a sip of the green juice (a foul tasting concoction) and begins pacing back and forth, something that appears to have become a habit in this job.

"I've been asking myself—what's the most unique selling point of this business? And I realized the answer is—you. It's your passion and expertise. It's your stunning devotion. We have to get you out there as the face of Let The Green Times Roll. We need to make a video to play on the home page. You... talking to the masses... pleading with the consumers and the capitalists... inspiring millions... like a leader. Make the world stop and listen, Russell—I know you have it in you!"

Russell looks deeply moved. Boris sits next to him on the kitchen counter staring uneasily at the juice. "You really believe in me, don't you, Lexi? I don't think anyone has ever said those things to me before, ever. If I were to be entirely honest it would seem the majority of people I meet regard me as a bit," he pauses, obviously trying to come up with the most suitable word, "freakish."

Lexi stops pacing, feeling terrible for having thought exactly that about Russell less than two weeks ago. But since getting to know him a bit, she *has* changed her mind. If she's been practicing leaps of faith, then believing in Russell might well be the biggest leap yet. She looks Russell square in the eye.

"Aren't we all, Russell? A bit freakish? This planet would be very tedious without people like you to add a bit of... of..." it's her turn now to find the perfect word. But she quickly remembers that perfect is banned. "Pizazz."

"Pizazz?" he says, letting the word buzz on his tongue. "Pizazz, I like that."

"I thought you might."

"I guess it's down to work then! Boris and I will begin typing my inaugural speech and you can make your calls and drink your juice. But one last question."

"Yes?" says Lexi, hoping he's not going to suggest they smoke weed again.

"Can Boris be in the video?"

"Of course Boris can be in the video, Russell," says Lexi, relieved. "It wouldn't be the same without him, would it?"

"No," says Russell, thoughtfully, "I guess it wouldn't."

GEORGE
13th November, 2009
Las Vegas, Nevada

Pedro Myerson is followed around by three PAs at all times. One holds an arsenal of medicines in a Perspex container (George thought they were an assorted array of Tic Tacs before Simon set him straight). One holds his paper-thin laptop. And the third one doesn't hold anything, but apparently is necessary in case the other two unexpectedly drop dead. They have obviously been programmed to keep an appropriate distance from their revered boss, and yet appear to anticipate his every need, stepping forward at intervals, as if summoned by a silent dog whistle. Initially amused by the spectacle, the band are rapidly losing patience with the eccentric genius.

"This guy's got his head up his butthole," declares Duncan, as the four band mates lie in the hot sand shoulder to shoulder, while Myerson and his DP prepare lighting for the next take.

"Talking of, George, how was your midnight feast? Fanny was salivating looking for you. I was tempted to give her my room number instead."

George might have guessed it was Duncan who put Fanny back on his trail. He is certainly not in the mood to indulge in his banter now. The video shoot is even worse than he might have imagined. Myerson is incredibly patronizing and earlier in the day communicated painstakingly slowly his thoughts about the shoot.

"I see you all in white. Bright white. Asleep in the sand—

okay? The hot desert sand. Do you understand? It's like it's searing through your skin. Skin. Okay?"

"It *was* searing through my skin, just now," Simon had said glibly. "It's bloody hot out here, mate." Pedro had ignored the comment and continued, directing the remaining portion of his vision to George.

"This song, 'I Knew It'. This song you wrote is powerful. It juxtaposes elements of light and dark. The pure and evil forces residing within us all. The images need to reflect these themes. Suffocation. Purification. Do you understand me? Mortification. I knew it, right? I knew it. Okay?" George had hesitated, somewhat at a loss for words. Was Myerson hoping to enlighten him about the meaning of his own lyrics? He had in fact written the song about something far less lofty, but far more familiar to him. The certainty of uncertainty. How the only thing you could ever rely on in life is just how unpredictable things are.

Case in hand. He now finds himself and the boys half buried in scorching sand, decked out in hideous white suits, with a scattering of decapitated palm trees hovering above them. George is wishing he had indeed spoken up. He could have said, "No, Pedro, not okay. Let's film casinos full of middle America and us on a stage in the background; like the bad band at a bar mitzvah. Bad band. Okay?" That would have been poetic irony. Oh, and as an afterthought, he could have suggested a set-up with Fanny, because all arrows were pointing towards them being a match made in heaven, where surely they could persuade old, dead Sebastian to complete the threesome?

But he had been too hung-over to be assertive. Plus he wants to trust Gabe. He needs to trust Gabe, who now sprints over to the boys and says excitedly, "I've just seen this shot on the monitor. It's the ticket, boys. It looks magnificent. Really."

George is unconvinced. The set is swarming with a

multitude of people, doing a multitude of seemingly extremely important jobs.

"Have they finished lighting this shot—can we move now?" asks George, who is having a spontaneous memory of being five years old on holiday in Cornwall, while Polly buried his entire body beneath the sand, forcing him to swallow a massive mouthful until he nearly choked to death. He vividly recalls hearing his mother say, "Look how sweet, Lawrence, the children are playing."

"I'll check," says Gabe and runs off again.

"There's something wrong with this picture," says Mark. "That Myerson chap has three assistants and there's only one of him. There's four of us and we have—Gabe."

"I'll gladly take one of his, mate," says Duncan, "I've had my eye on the short one with the big—"

"Box of pills?" interrupts George.

"Is it lunch yet?" adds Simon.

"Anyway, I thought Anna was your assistant, or is it the other way around?" says Duncan sarcastically.

"Give it a rest, Dunc," says Mark.

"We said, didn't we—when we first started out—we said we'd keep it real." George stands up, feeling aggravated. "There's enough people who are essential when we tour without having to hire an entourage just for the hell of it."

"Well, this is real enough for me," says Simon. "I have sand in every crevice imaginable and no sandwich on the horizon. I'm ready to be a diva. People!" he yells, shaking the dust from his mop of red hair, as make-up and wardrobe rush to his side.

George declines help from an eager wardrobe assistant trying to brush off his suit and does so himself. He heads straight for the craft service table sheltered under a canopy, offering a selection of cut up vegetables, cheese and oversized biscuits. A young guy, no more than eighteen years old, is manning the table. He looks slightly flustered as George approaches.

"Uh, hi. George, um, wow. I think, you know, in your trailer, they've got special food for you."

"No, this is great. Carrots, I love carrots." George grabs a handful. "So *you* know *my* name, what's yours?"

"Eliot, my name's Eliot and damn, you know, I am such a big fan," Eliot fumbles awkwardly with a stack of plastic cups, almost knocking them all over. "Not cool," he mutters under his breath.

"No, honestly, that's really nice to hear, Eliot. You play anything yourself?"

"Yeah, I do. I, you know, write some lyrics and play guitar and my friends and I we've started a band."

"Excellent. Called?"

"Extra Utensils."

"I like it. Who are your influences?"

Eliot looks embarrassed, "Besides you? Wow, like, Bon Iver, The Shins, Bright Eyes."

"Impressive selection. You have anything recorded?"

"Yeah, we have some stuff, like on my computer."

"Eliot, listen to me. How old are you?"

"Eighteen."

"I thought so. You've got a lot more misery to suffer through. It carves an edge—you'll need it. See that guy with the afro and the glasses over there," George points to Gabe, who is circling a palm tree on his phone. "I want you to take him some celery and some cheese sticks or something, and tell him I told you to ask for his card. Don't do anything with it now. Put it away. In four years' time, call him up and send him a demo. Tell him to pass it on to me. I'll remember you. Vegas Eliot with the carrots."

Eliot looks bewildered. "Are you totally serious?"

"Totally serious," says George.

"Wow, like really serious? That's sick. You must have people like asking you for stuff all the time. Why me?"

George shrugs.

"Because, Eliot, you didn't ask."

He grabs another handful of carrots. "Hey good luck. I'll see you later, mate." George wanders back towards the mayhem, feeling invigorated, having bypassed the celebrity trappings to make contact with a real human instead. A klutzy boy with sweaty palms whom he knows only too well. A boy whose life he could possibly inextricably alter. The power of this influence at times feels extraordinary. It goes beyond the music. Beyond the record sales. He feels the weight of the responsibility and with that a craving to get it right. To do something better.

"George. Mr. Myerson would like to see you in his trailer immediately," instructs assistant number one, striding towards him with the box full of pills.

"I see," says George, eyeing the portable pharmacy. "What is all that stuff anyway? What's wrong with him?" He reckons this is quite a loaded question. Duncan has now sidled over to George with a large bucket of popcorn.

"Mr. Myerson suffers from BPV among other thyroid-related conditions," the assistant replies robotically.

"What does that stand for?" asks Duncan, "Bloody poncy video?"

She is clearly unamused. "Benign Positional Vertigo. He gets dizzy."

"Well, that explains it," says George, helping himself to the warm popcorn and aiming a kernel in Duncan's ready and waiting open mouth.

LEXI
November 17th, 2009
Venice, Los Angeles

Russell has tried on about six different outfits, each worse than the one before. Lexi's phone marathon paid off and she managed to reach an old contact, Billy, who agreed to design a website at a reasonable cost. He liked the idea of a video introduction but suggested Lexi film it herself, if budget was an issue. So she has borrowed Meg's Flip video camera and positioned it carefully on a tripod in the front yard, with the blossoming Mini strategically placed in the background. What she hadn't factored for are the Santa Ana winds, blowing a hot, dry, billowy breath across the entire city all the way to the shore, where Lexi is struggling to keep the camera standing. She knows the Santa Anas can drive ordinarily sane people berserk. She can't exactly categorize Russell as sane to begin with. He appears now in the doorway, wearing linen trousers and an embroidered Mexican poncho, longing for Lexi's approval. She shakes her head for the seventh time.

"Sorry, Russell, it's just not right. You look like you're going to a wedding in Cancun." He looks thoroughly fed up.

"Am I that obvious? June 2000, The Ritz Carlton. Boris's vet, Arnold, married Lucinda. It was a splendid event. Everyone told me I looked very festive."

"You do. Look festive but... it's not the look we're going for in the video. We need casual but concerned. Serious yet comfortable. Trustworthy. Natural but not too crunchy granola... do you get the picture?"

Russell's ponytail, whipped up by the wind, snaps against his cheek.

"I'm trying my darnedest, Lexi, but nothing seems good enough for you. You might have noticed that fashion is not a priority for me. I have far more pressing matters to think about. I'm not going to parade around out here anymore humiliating myself. I'm changing into my organic, hemp, long sleeved T-shirt... and that will just have to do."

Lexi grips the tripod to stop it from toppling. She can't believe that now she's on Russell's hit list, when just a few days ago she could do no wrong. She's only trying to help.

"Okay," she says, tired of constantly being conciliatory. "Why didn't you just put that on in the first place?" She feels like sticking out her tongue. Clearly the winds are working their voodoo on her as well. This video is set to be a disaster. That's if they even get around to filming it. Russell walks back into the house in a huff, followed by Boris with his tail hanging between his legs.

Lexi's phone rings and Meg's grinning face beams out from the screen. She picks it up, ready to vent.

"Shoot me now—I'm having the day from hell, and it's not even lunch yet."

"I don't want details," says Meg. "You're coming for dinner with Tim and me tonight."

"I am? I *do* want details."

"Forget it. We'll pick you up at 7:30. Look ravishing—like you always do."

"I'm really not sure, Meg, I mean I haven't even begun filming Russell yet. It might go late tonight."

"Well, make sure it doesn't. Okay? Look, Annabelle's fallen in the toilet again! Gotta go, hon. I'll see you at 7:30. Byyyeee!" Meg hangs up.

"Byyeee!" Lexi repeats sarcastically, this time pointedly sticking her tongue out at her phone, while her hair blows in a wild halo above her head.

GEORGE
17th November, 2009
United Flight to Los Angeles

Goodbye Vegas, hello LA. George is relieved to put sin city

behind him and move on with the itinerary. There should already be a loud buzz building around the upcoming acoustic gig—intentionally masterminded by Gabe. All the radio stations will be talking about it. Other than record execs and some industry faces, the tickets for the show are being given to fans registered on the website. They won't find out until the night before if they have been allocated seats or where the venue is, and every ticket holder will receive a free limited edition t-shirt. The t-shirt has a picture of a dog on it, sitting at a corner table with a pint of lager, and a single yellow rose in a vase. *Thesis, LA 2009* is inscribed in small font on the back centre of the shirt. George designed the t-shirt. He is a stickler for details.

The band are also appearing on the cover of this week's *SPIN* magazine and have a double page spread and the cover of the *LA Times* calendar on the weekend. George will religiously scour them all. So far most of the American reviews of the latest album have been favourable.

"Thesis rocks another well honed dissertation."

"Bryce and the boys have lost their milk teeth—*Corners and Tables* has some serious bite."

Of course there's also, "Back me in a corner and let me hide under the table—another dull, Coldplayesque album from Britain's most overrated soft rockers." A lot of bands don't bother reading reviews at all, but George does. He sometimes imagines Polly and his parents sitting and gloating over the bad ones, nodding conspiratorially. He really wishes that one day they would just come to one of his shows. His parents haven't seen him perform since the band was just starting out. There's always an excuse. Too noisy. Too far. Maybe next time. Polly came once to the Hammersmith Apollo with her husband, Martyn, but they left before the end of the show so they could get back to the triplets.

The plane is descending bumpily. George keeps his eye on the mountaintops and remembers he needs to show Simon the lyrics to "Over Time," the ones he worked on last time he was in turbulence. The captain's voice booms out loudly over the PA, "Captain Hank Adams here. Sorry for the rollercoaster ride, folks. We'll get you safely on the ground in just a few minutes, but for now, enjoy the Santa Anas. Apparently they make all sorts of weird and wonderful things happen in LA."

LEXI
November 17th, 2009
Venice, Los Angeles

By some miracle, Lexi had managed to get a decent amount of footage of Russell in his suitably neutral, chemical-free garment, coupled with the wedding trousers. Eventually they had to tie his ponytail into a tight knot at the nape of his neck to stop the wind from blowing it into his mouth. Russell complained that he looked bald, but Lexi convinced him that it was the only option. His speech was nothing short of stellar —stirring yet informational, with just the right hint of eccentricity. Boris took pride of place on the roof of the Mini, providing a creative backdrop. He did fall off at one point, rolling over while in a deep sleep and plummeting onto the grass, but Lexi had suggested they include it in a bloopers link, and before long, Russell was smiling again.

Now she is sitting in the back of Meg's and Tim's SUV surrounded by mangled Barbies, lethally sharp pieces of Transformers and a plentiful scattering of cookie crumbs. She feels something moist soaking into the back of her jeans.

"Uh, guys, did one of the kids pee back here or something?"

"Oh, shit!" says Meg. "Jack's Gogurt exploded yesterday. I must have missed some."

"Great," replies Lexi, anticipating a massive wet patch in the middle of her butt. "Well, at least it's just the three of us tonight. You won't mind me smelling like curdled yogurt."

"No worries, Lex, we're used to it, but you might just want to spray a bit of this." Meg rummages in her purse and passes back a miniature bottle of perfume. "It's yummy. Smells like grapefruit."

Lexi takes the bottle and spritzes her wrists.

"So what's the occasion anyway? Did I forget our anniversary, Meg? Where are you taking me?"

"Oh, nothing special. Tim was just saying today that he hadn't seen you in such a long time and so—"

"Meg—will you just tell her already?" Tim, who is driving, glares pointedly at his wife. Lexi has always considered Tim to be the quintessential all-American man. He's solid as they come. Great dad on the weekends. Plays golf. Works in investment banking. Favorite film is *Anchor Man*. Drinks lots of beer but knows when to stop. Worships his wife. These are all the reasons why Lexi knows Meg loves him, as well as being most of the things that drive her to distraction. He's clearly fond of Lexi, but were she to give it some thought, she would find herself hard pressed to recall a time when he actually had a conversation with her, short of, "Hey Lex, what's up?"

But tonight he seems to have her best interests in mind.

"Tell me what, Meg?"

Meg throws Tim a livid stare in return, "What are you doing?! I told you not to say anything. You're such a dick sometimes."

"Me? A dick?" says Tim, gripping the steering wheel tightly. "You're the one that came up with this dumb idea. I don't feel right lying to her."

"We weren't lying. We were just not saying everything. There's a difference, you know. Now you've ruined it!"

"Not saying everything? Are these the sort of morals you're teaching our kids?"

"Hello? Remember me?" Lexi begins waving from the back seat, unsettled by how much Meg and Tim are reminding her of her parents' recent spats. Is this inane bickering the destiny of all married couples? If so, she might begin to truly appreciate being single. "Will you two just shut up and tell me what's happening?"

Meg turns around and the guilty upturned corners of her mouth are unmistakable. "You look like you did in the tenth grade when I asked you not to tell Cameron Branch that I liked his calf muscles, but you told him anyway."

"It was a compliment. He was flattered!" says Meg, still adeptly avoiding the subject.

"Just spill it," says Lexi, her tolerance level waning.

"All right, but promise not to be mad?"

"I'm not promising anything right now," says Lexi.

"Okay—it's just that when I mentioned being proactive the other day, you didn't sound hugely into it, and I know things have been difficult recently and you've been looking for a job and after that guy with the thumb ring, you haven't been on a date for a really long time, which I get, because the thumb ring was gross, but I thought just maybe, *I* could be proactive for you, so there's this new guy at Tim's office, Bradley, and I figured if I suggested it, you would be like 'no, I'm busy, I've got work, I'm tired, blah, blah, blah,' but honestly I think you're scared now of ever finding anyone who can live up to your expectations, or your Mom's expectations, but six or seven years can just fly by and you look back and go 'shit! how did that happen?' and when it comes to men —you just have to make compromises—take it from me!" Meg finally draws a breath.

"Nice job, babe," says Tim, keeping his eyes on the road.

Lexi leans back in her seat and picks up one of the stranded Barbies. "So, you're setting me up with Bradley?"

"Yes," they both say in unison.

"Are we having sushi?"

"Noori Noori in Beverly Hills."

"Sounds good. Tim, would you mind turning some music on?"

"Sounds good? That's it?" asks Meg.

"That's it," says Lexi, refusing to fall prey to any of the labels Meg wants to stamp upon her, most notably Stubborn Single Friend. She might well have said no had Meg suggested it, but that's only because she wants to concentrate on her career at the moment. Dating has become so tedious.

"No prob," says Tim, clicking on the stereo and mumbling under his breath to Meg, "I told you so!"

The song "I Knew It" and George Bryce's enticingly tender voice floods the car.

Lexi coils the Barbie's synthetic blond hair around her middle finger, trying not to imagine anything about Bradley—she's learning from Russell that first impressions are often nothing to go on. She notices Annabelle has chopped into one side of the doll's hair leaving her with half a mohawk, streaked green with a marker. She's also scrawled tiny black hearts up and down each arm and hacked her pink dress into a micro-mini. She looks like Punk Barbie. Barbie after a binge. An apt nemesis to her Malibu counterpart. Lexi holds punk Barbie up to the window, and as the song picks up tempo, she dances her from side to side. A little girl with glasses in a neighboring car smiles at the impromptu sideshow. Lexi returns the grin.

GEORGE
17th November, 2009
Los Angeles

"I love LA," announces George, as the boys are shuttled from the airport to their hotel in West Hollywood in a black van with mirrored windows and built-in screens on the back of each seat.

"Not as much as I love Vegas," says Simon, who has had

a permanent smirk on his face, since spending a very long evening with one of the make-up girls from the video shoot.

"Better than a sandwich, huh, mate?" says Duncan with an exaggerated wink.

"Very amusing," says Simon embarrassedly, as he checks his phone for the hundredth time in the last hour. "Stacey says she might drive down to LA this week to see the acoustic."

"Don't reply." says Duncan, "Leave her hanging for a day or two and she'll be begging for more..."

"Oh puh-leaze, Dunc," says Anna from the backseat, "that's rubbish advice. You think all women have brains the size of a pea."

"Not all women, Anna."

"I would say Stacey's was more in the range of an artichoke," adds Simon.

"And he brings it back to food," says Gabe.

"Text her now, Simon. Tell her you'd love to see her again." Anna pats him reassuringly on the shoulder. Simon glances over at George to get his reading.

George is perplexed by the conversation. It's not that he's not pleased for Simon. Good on him for following the pact and putting himself out there. But he was convinced that Stacey the make-up girl was coming onto him yesterday in the trailer. What had he done to put her off? Or maybe she wasn't interested in him at all. Surely he can't be as clueless as all that? He should be able to distinguish between a friendly chat and a full fledged flirt fest. Maybe not. George finds American women have a knack of being boldly enthusiastic, making even Fanny look demure. According to their website and sales, South American women go insane over Thesis and doubly insane over George. When they toured Brazil he felt like McCartney. He could say with confidence that he saw women swoon. Maybe he should be trying to meet a Brazilian woman. Damn. Here he was again overthinking everything. It was like repeatedly burning the toast, no matter how hard he tried to rescue it before the surface charred to black.

"Earth to George," says Simon. "What would you do?"

"I'm an unreliable source, Sim. I'd...I'd write her a song."

"Ahh, you're so sweet," says Anna.

"Start by texting her," says Mark.

"A song?" asks Simon

"A *yes*," says Mark.

"You're all a bunch of girls," says Duncan. "I'm in the wrong band. I should be on the party bus with the Kings of Leon."

"That's an idea," says Gabe, "except they already have a drummer. Although... has there ever been a band with two drummers?" He turns to George, their in-house music trivia archive.

"Genesis, Adam and the Ants, The Grateful Dead..." rattles off George without faltering, while making a mental note to get some Cuban bongos for the acoustic show. He really needs to stop thinking about women, or the lack of them more accurately, and start thinking about arrangements, and musical saws and harpists. He wants the show to be raw and magical. An eclectic arc of instruments with his voice, simple and true, spanning the curve. So he can't seem to seduce one woman, but he will seduce a whole audience. Mesmerize a room full of fans. *That should be enough for anyone*, George tells himself, *enough for me*.

"All in favour of a sushi stop raise your right hand!" George admires the way Gabe can call the court to order. For a change, everyone agrees and Mark even playfully tickles Anna under her arm and she manages a very genuine giggle. Morale is up. George feels brighter. He does love LA. City of Angels. Land of possibility. Although you couldn't guess it from the car window. One bland mini-mall after another linked by wide, faceless streets. But George knows this is a town full of surprises and ultimately best explored through a zoom lens.

LEXI
November 17th, 2009
Beverly Hills

Ten minutes into the dinner and Lexi has decided this feels less like a double date and more like an unexpected ambush. Noori Noori Sushi is a trendy hotspot where the fresh sushi, displayed in plastic pods, circles the interior of the restaurant on a conveyor belt, running a loop inside the tables. Whoever is closest to the conveyor grabs the dishes, as well as fielding requests from the rest of the table. Technique is everything.

"I know it's tempting, guys!" says Jason, their excessively friendly waiter. "But take it from me, two hands are crucial. It's not as easy as it looks and picking up the plates requires both of these little buddies!" He waves his hands playfully in the air for a moment too long. "Okkaaaaay! Drinks? Sake? Sapporo?"

"Let's go crazy and have both!" says Bradley, Tim's work colleague from the bank and Lexi's date for the night.

"You're on!" says Jason, before Lexi can order an iced tea.

Bradley has recently moved from Chicago. He's wearing beige loafers, a gold watch and he uses the word "hilarious." A lot. Before Jason had arrived on the scene, he was proudly showing the table his right ear, which he claims used to be pierced.

He continues where he left off, "Check this out. I'm not yanking your chain. I'm telling you—I was wild in my college days—it was hilarious! Look." He leans in far too closely to Lexi, forcing her to examine his fleshy earlobe. She can just about detect a small ridge where the skin has healed. And now she's expected to eat?

"Yes, that's very, very funny. An earring—wow." Lexi nudges Meg's foot under the table, but Meg is undeterred.

"Lexi wears earrings—don't you, Lex?"

"Yes, yes—I do. Wear earrings. I do."

"Man that mutherfucker hurt when it went in. I mean—for sure I was hammered at the time, but let me tell you, the pain stays with me."

"You must be very sensitive," says Lexi, amazing even herself with the comic irony.

"You could say that," says Bradley, "I mean it's not like I listen to Barbara Streisand or anything. I mean that would be hilarious, right? I bet when you first saw me you didn't think 'now there's a guy who listens to Streisand,' because if you did —you'd be way off base." Bradley runs his hand nervously over the top of his hair, cemented skywards with heavy duty mousse.

He looks over expectantly at Lexi, "No, I didn't think that, Bradley. That wasn't the first thought in my mind at all. You, Meg? That's assuming that tonight *is* the first time you've met Bradley?"

"Oh, yes," says Meg, apologizing with her eyes. "Tonight is the very first time we've met, but Tim has told me so much about you, Bradley, none of which involved Streisand."

"Good man, Tim!" says Bradley, reaching over the table to shake Tim's hand. "He's a great guy, your husband, Meggy. Life of the party at the office. Hilarious. Absolutely hilarious!"

"You said it," says Meg, now returning the toe nudge under the table but with slightly more force.

This is going to be the longest dinner in history, thinks Lexi despairingly. Should she go to the restroom and pretend to be ill? Should she go to the restroom and sneak out the back door? She'd love to, but she knows unfortunately she's not that cruel. Lexi prays for the drinks to arrive quickly, resigned that she is in it for the long haul and her only hope might be to get embarrassingly drunk.

"So Bradley," says Tim, obviously eager to change the subject, "Why don't you do the honors and grab some of those eats. That yellowtail sashimi looks the business."

"At your service," says Bradley, "I'll deliver the goods."

Lexi feels momentarily sorry for him, as he leans towards the circling sushi. Who is she to be so superior? He's not her type, but without the hair mousse and the beige loafers he could be decent looking. So far he's apparently only interested in himself and is severely lacking in subtlety, but the night is early, he might have a question or two in him yet. He's nervous. He's harmless. He's... but before she can complete the last guilt-induced platitude, she turns to see a plate of immaculately arranged sashimi fly through the air, as if in slow motion. It glides over the table and lands with a monumental crash on the floor, splattering Lexi's metallic flip flops and Bradley's beige suede loafers with a spray of brown soy sauce. Paper thin slices of yellowtail and pale pink ginger lie strewn around them like road kill. Five sushi chefs cheer something Japanese in boisterous approval. Neighboring regulars snicker.

Lexi's not sure whether to laugh or cry. Jason rushes over wagging a disciplinary finger.

"Easy, fella. Let me guess, you only used one hand?"

"Busted!" says Bradley, holding up both. "I thought I could—"

"I've heard it all before," says Jason. "You thought you could impress your girlfriend and prove the neurotic waiter wrong. Why don't you try again, following my directions. I'll get this cleared up."

"That's hilarious!" says Bradley, reaching for his Blackberry. "I've gotta Tweet this—what a complete crack up. Get it? Crack up?"

Lexi grabs hold of Jason's arm before he can leave, pulling him towards her. Tim and Bradley have moved on, consulting with each other on exactly how to best remove the sushi plates inflicting the least amount of damage.

"Jason... the drinks..." says Lexi in a pleading whisper. "Bring the drinks—I beg you!"

"Right away," says Jason, giving her the thumbs up.

"And just so you know," says Lexi in a confiding tone, "He's *not* my boyfriend."

GEORGE
17th November, 2009
Beverly Hills

The band's van pulls up outside Noori Noori, a sushi restaurant Gabe has heard is excellent. As the valet parker opens the door, George catches the bizarre sight in the front window of a plate cartwheeling through the air, sending food flying. He pauses.

"Did you see that?" asks George, looking back at Simon quizzically.

"Food fight!" yells Duncan, "I'm in!"

"I might have steered us wrong," says Gabe. "Looks like it's a Yo Sushi production line."

"Spare me the gimmicks," says Simon, who considers authentic Japanese food to be a close second to a vintage sandwich.

"Let's go to that one on Melrose," says Mark. "You can't beat an old trusty."

"I'll call over there," says Gabe, apologizing to the valet parker as he reaches over to close the door again.

George has a sudden urge to get out of the car and walk. People in LA appear to have an aversion to walking which makes it even more appealing. *I'll be a rebel* thinks George. *I'll walk to Melrose.* He has this idea that he is less conspicuous in LA because the town is teeming with famous people—most of them gagging for recognition just to confirm they exist. In comparison, George just ends up looking vaguely familiar, like the boy you once went to school with or the guy who works in the supermarket. The more famous George becomes, the more he fantasizes about being innocuous. The paradox confounds him—how his lifelong ache to be special has led him to a place of yearning to be ordinary.

Before the door closes, he impulsively hops out.

"George, I thought it was unanimous?" says Gabe, looking confused.

"It is. It was—it's only that I've decided to walk."

"Are you off your rocker?" says Duncan. "We're in LA. You don't do that here."

"You might get shot," says Anna in all seriousness.

"Or abducted," adds Mark, forever dry. "And we're not paying ransom."

"Come on, George, I'm hungry. Get back in," says Simon.

"Look fellas—honestly—it's no big deal. It will take twenty minutes. I'll see you there."

Gabe looks especially concerned. "George, it's not a good idea, really. I just don't feel right about it. Why walk now?"

"I want to," replies George, wondering if this will be enough.

"It's because I let a juicy one rip, Gabe," calls Duncan from the back seat. "Release him!"

George feels determined now to follow through, even though he could just as easily climb back into the car. He knows this is beginning to border on the ridiculous. The most mundane thing has become an oddly meaningful act of defiance.

"I don't need a secret service detail—yet. I've got my phone on me. I just need to stretch my legs. I'll see you there, Gabe, I promise."

Gabe looks bewildered and reluctantly closes the door. As the van drives away, he rolls down the window, "Are you sure you know where it is?"

"I know!" says George, feeling a surge of liberation. He could get lost. Disappear. Resurface. Re-invent himself in another guise. He thinks of all his fans, all the people he's never even met who feel a claim over him. He could transform himself into one of them. Spend his days monitoring his own website contributing to conspiracy theories about his own disappearance. Trippy.

He glances one more time in the window of the Sushi restaurant. Happy couples on double dates. Laughing. Drinking. Fitting closely together as if carved from the same stone. He needs to walk.

LEXI
November 17th, 2009
Beverly Hills

After an excruciating two hours, a hundred more declarations of 'hilarious', and Jason the waiter slipping her his phone number when she went to the restroom, Lexi is now waiting to bid a jubilant farewell to Bradley. Meg hustles her into the back of the car as soon as the valet drives up, while Tim gives his friend a hug.

"This was a blast, Lex. I'll get your number from Tim," says Bradley, leaning awkwardly forward to kiss her on the cheek. "We'll hook up."

More likely I'll hang up, thinks Lexi. "You do that!" she says with a nervous smile, shutting the door a little too quickly, leaving Bradley on the curb, tipped forward, looking for love in all the wrong places.

"Drive," she orders Tim through gritted teeth.

"Well that was—"

"Dreadful," says Meg before Tim can finish. "That was dreadful. What were you thinking?"

"You told me to find someone to—"

"You're blaming me now? Blaming me for setting my

best friend up with Mr. Neanderthal Frat Guy, who scarily seems to believe you two were separated at birth!"

"Come on, Meg. He's not that bad."

"Not that bad, Tim? He threw the food. He showed Lexi his—" Lexi's head is beginning to pound. She wishes she could get out and walk the rest of the way. She feels like the sides of the car are closing in on her.

"STOP!" she yells from the back seat. "Don't say another word until you drop me home. Not a word."

GEORGE
17th November, 2009
Melrose Ave, Los Angeles

Even on Melrose, home of the trendiest shops and restaurants, the streets are relatively quiet. George is accustomed to bustling cities that gain a vibrant momentum after dark. In contrast, LA appears to empty out, allowing only for movement between cars and doorways, dutiful valet parkers clocking up miles in strangers' cars. George imagines what it might feel like for those guys, settling into the indent of the driver's seat, still faintly warm from the owner's body. Maybe he'll write a song about it.

He's been walking for twenty minutes and has only seen three other pedestrians. He remembers as a child making up stories about people he saw on the streets when he walked to church with his parents on a Sunday. He abhorred the constricting tie his mother insisted he wore and the way his father snapped at him for lagging behind.

"Hurry up, George, or you'll make us late. Are you daydreaming again?" And he usually was. Dreaming about what life was like in another family. Dreaming about the girl across the road with the brown riding boots and if she liked chocolate sprinkles on her ice cream or preferred it plain. His imagination was always roaming some unexamined landscape. Somehow, despite Polly's incessant histrionics, George constantly felt like everything that went wrong in their family was attributed solely to him.

LEXI
November 18th, 2009
West Hollywood

"I have your approval to divorce him, right?" Meg is clearly trying to blame Tim for the whole date debacle. It's the morning after and she has rung first thing while Lexi is making tea and an English muffin before work.

Lexi is well aware of Meg's propensity to dodge accountability. She simply hates owning up to a mistake and would choose to hop around on hot sand for an hour, rather than shelter in the shade of a tree and admit defeat.

"You can't get away with blaming it all on Tim," says Lexi, contemplating the sorry sight of her soggy teabag and wondering if Meg will concede anything.

"Yes, I can. He told me the new guy at his office was perfect for you."

"How would he know?"

"Well—he said he was tall and funny and—"

"Did he really say funny? Are you sure he didn't say 'hilarious'? And did he happen to mention that he was horny, because he's just moved here and gagging to get some action? And so *you* think to yourself—I know—Lexi, my best friend the charity case, who cares if I've never met the guy. He'll do. She's desperate too."

"Please, Lex. It wasn't like that—I promise. Tim just led me astray. He knows I worry about you. He thought you guys would hit it off. I trusted him. It was his fault—not mine."

"Not yours? Not even a tiny bit yours, Meg? Look, I know you mean well but just at this moment I need you to stop worrying about me. You and my mother. I'm fine. There is absolutely nothing at all wrong. I am totally and completely fine," and as Lexi reaches the end of her sentence, she feels the tears that have been slowly building over the last few weeks. They are unreservedly cascading down her cheeks, refusing any longer to be held prisoner. It's a deluge. She can't speak for crying.

"Oh, God—I'm coming over!" says Meg in a panic.

"You don't need to come," says Lexi between hiccupy sobs. "I really am fine. I just have a hangover, that's all. Hangovers make me sad. I have to go to work now."

"Lex, I'll make it up to you, I promise."

"You'll make it up to me? Does that mean you agree you were wrong?"

"Not exactly. I had good intentions." Aghhhh! Why was Meg so infuriatingly intransigent? Lexi wills the outburst to subside as she attempts to regulate her breathing.

"No more blind dates, okay?" she pleads, sniffing sporadically. "I'll accept jewelry." She has managed to calm her tears, the remaining few dripping pitifully into her tea.

"I'll think of something even better," says Meg in her reassuring voice, the one she uses with the kids when they have fallen over. "Now get to work, Lex. Take your mind off Bradley's earlobes."

Lexi shudders at the memory. "Thanks for the visual."

"You're welcome," says Meg. "What does it say on that mug your mom gave you for your b-day, *Yesterday's history, tomorrow's a mystery but today is a gift?*"

Lexi looks down at her tea realizing she is holding onto the very same mug. She thinks back to high school, how she was always the one consoling Meg, telling her to get back in the saddle, brush herself off, confront the next hurdle. God, she must have been irritating.

"That's the corniest thing ever, Meg."

"Better than the horniest thing ever, right?"

"Ha ha. Can we just talk later?" says Lexi, pressing *end*

on her phone before Meg has a chance to object. But as soon as she puts it down, it rings again, this time flashing Boris's picture on the screen. Why on earth is Russell calling so early? She reaches for a Kleenex, wipes her nose and takes a shaky breath before answering.

"Russell?"

"Lexi, I'm so sorry, I know I'll be seeing you in less than an hour but I just can't keep it in any longer. I've just got to tell you—"

"Tell me what?" asks Lexi, needing to get off the phone so she can continue to cry.

"Tell you about my chance encounter yesterday evening with Mildred Cotton."

"Mildred Cotton? Do I know her?"

"Not yet," says Russell cryptically, "but you will."

"Please don't make me crack a code, Russell, I don't have the energy for it this morning."

"I was taking Boris for a stroll on the boardwalk last night, after you left. The wind had died down—it was a lovely evening. Anyway, he was in quite a chipper mood and before I know it he's making advances towards this rather stunning Siamese, drinking in the view on someone's veranda. I've never seen Boris quite so forward, curling his tail and purring up a storm."

Lexi is bemused. Has Russell really called her at this time of the morning to recount some lengthy story about Boris and a girl cat?

"Russell, can this wait till I arrive?" asks Lexi, blowing her nose loudly into the telephone.

"I'll hurry," says Russell, clearly oblivious to her fragile state. "You see, while Boris is charming the feline, her owner comes out onto the veranda. She's just delightful. As coincidence would have it, we share the same vet. Her cat's called Cherub—isn't that unusual?"

Lexi hopes her uncontrollable sobbing will kick in again.

Anything to drown this out. She silently begs Russell to get to the point.

"Anyway, Mildred, that was her name, asks me about myself and I tell her about Let The Green Times Roll. She's noticeably impressed. It turns out that Mildred is the executive producer of *Wake Up LA*—you know, on channel 9 in the mornings?"

"Doesn't that start at 5:00 a.m?"

"Yes, yes that's the one. Maybe it should be called *Wake Up Early LA*. All the same, she is well connected, Lexi, and she wants to showcase us on her *New in Town* segment."

"At 5:00 a.m?"

"Well, maybe at 5:30."

"Sounds good. When things are up and running. No publicity is bad publicity."

"There's just one little glitch."

"What's that?" asks Lexi, finding herself increasingly annoyed and maybe even envious. Could it be that while she was out on a blind date with Bradley the bonehead, not only Russell, but Boris as well, seem to have stumbled across love matches? Surely that was a cruel injustice?

"Well, she wants me on the show next Tuesday. As luck would have it, something's fallen through and there's an available slot."

"Next Tuesday? Russell, that's less than a week. It's impossible. We won't even have the website up and running by then—it's far too soon to start publicity."

"I know, I know. I thought you'd say that, but it's only that I got carried away. I think I made the business sound a bit bigger than it actually is. I was feeling amped from shooting the video. You know—conquer the capitalists. Recruit the masses!"

"So just call up Mildred Cotton and tell her to book you in for next month. We'll be in a much stronger position by then to promote things."

"Yes, but there's a slight problem there too. I arranged to take her out to brunch after the show, to talk about the cats really. Cherub's been having some issues."

Lexi sighs, "What can I say, Russell? It's five-thirty in the morning, hopefully no one will be watching."

"I knew you'd be cross. My enthusiasm got the better of me." *Among other things*, thinks Lexi.

"I'm not cross, I'm just... ready to go back to bed."

"Are you unwell? Now that you mention it, you do sound a bit peaky."

"It depends how you define that. I think I'll be in a bit late today if that's okay? I'll see you around eleven."

As Lexi hangs up she hears Andrew's key in the door. She had assumed he was home and still sleeping.

"Andrew! In here," calls Lexi, plotting a plan for them to both skip school and hike up Franklin Canyon instead. Some fresh air and exercise will clear her head.

"Oh, boy," he calls back, appearing dramatically in the kitchen alcove, hair uncharacteristically ruffled. "Ask me if I've just had the best night of my entire life."

Lexi takes one look at his ridiculously smug grin and flops her head onto the table, almost tipping over her stupid mug. *Today is a gift, today is a gift, today is a gift*—the words loop around her brain, taunting her with their precooked wisdom. If only something would happen to convince her they were actually true.

GEORGE
18TH November, 2009
West Hollywood, Los Angeles

George wakes up to the sound of a room service tray rattling down the hallway outside his room. For a few years after uni, he and Simon had shared a small flat near Queensway in

London surrounded by cheap, musty hotels. The dawn chorus had been the jangle and scrape of suitcase wheels dragged along the pavement outside their window. Ever since then he has come to find the sound rather comforting, and the room service trays always call it to mind.

George knows the day ahead is going to be manic. He wonders if he and Simon have time for a quick half hour in the hotel gym before the madness descends. Since the days of running around Regents Park, many a solution has been reached or song idea premeditated while the two of them run side by side on neighbouring hotel treadmills. Sometimes George finds it easier to talk things through when he's moving. He picks up his phone, cringing at a text message from Fanny, *Greetings from my Pussy,* accompanied by a picture of a rather demented looking black cat. Simon answers immediately in a low whisper.

"You ready to run off your egg and bacon bap?" asks George, hopefully.

"Guess what, mate? You know how I texted Stacey back last night? Well, she hopped on a late flight and surprised me. Let's put it this way—I haven't had much sleep."

"Right. Excellent. Good on you, Sim. Um, well, I might just go on my own then, unless you change your mind. I don't suppose Duncan will be up yet and Mark's probably—"

"Hey, George—look, gotta go mate. We'll talk later, okay?" Simon hangs up before George can respond.

A profound sense of loneliness rises in his chest, and he knows he will continue to feel it, even as his day becomes populated with more and more people. The only time George doesn't sense that loneliness lurking is when he's on stage. On stage he feels large inside. Alive. In contact. So why is it that just last night he was fantasizing about walking away from it all? He wants to turn down the bloody volume inside his own head. He gets out of bed quickly and rifles through his bag, pulling out an old pair of shorts, a Sesame Street t-shirt and a black beanie. It's 8:30 and he doesn't have to be in the lobby to meet Gabe and the rest of the band until 9:30. George decides he will take a jog around the neighbourhood instead. He enjoyed his walk last night. He grabs his iTouch, selects his *run away* playlist and sprints out the door.

Later on that day, some die-hards might get word of where they are staying and start loitering outside, waiting to get a photo or an autograph. But now all is clear. The sky is a cloudless flat palette of blue, the mountaintops so sharply outlined, George can see snow. The very first time George visited LA, the plane flew through a thick layer of yellowing smog and he could virtually taste the pollution festering in his mouth. He didn't know then that the light played tricks on you here, and on magic days it shone so brightly that even the pavements seemed to dazzle.

This morning the smog has vanished, and George feels as if he is running through a film set, the fastidiously mani-cured front lawns glistening around him. He starts slowly, but picks up speed, trying to forget Simon and Stacey, Mark and Anna, Duncan and his many conquests, and Fanny and her pussy. He propels himself forward, keeping up pace with a Calvin Harris song, his feet almost weightless. He used to run like this when he was a teenager in the woods near to his house. Anything to get away. He would write lyrics in his head as he ran, always knowing what he was running away from, but never sure of what he was running to. George decides to forget about his pact with Simon. Simon's got it covered. He needs to keep his mind on the music. Nothing else. Just the music. Just the music.

A woman runs towards him halfway down a residential street. His heart is beating in time to the song. As they pass each other, they both look up, and even though her face is in his eye line for the briefest second, he could swear he sees tears in her eyes. His mind swerves away from thoughts of himself and for a flickering moment, he can't help but wonder why she is crying.

LEXI
November 18th, 2009
West Hollywood

Lexi manages to tolerate five minutes of Andrew waxing eloquent about his night's escapades until she stands up and announces, "I'm so happy for you. Carl sounds great. I'm going to—" Her thoughts begin tripping over each other. She is determined not to cry again, but has no clue what she is going to do instead.

"Are you okay, Lex? You look a bit pale?" Andrew is so loved up, Lexi's surprised that he can even focus his attention on another person's well being. She is beginning to feel consumed by jealousy and has visions of it devouring her like a ravenous beast, permanently furrowing her eyebrows and etching deep hateful crevices in her skin.

"It's nothing, I'm just a bit tired. I also went on a date last night."

"Oh, typical, here I am talking about me, me, me. How was it?" She contemplates telling the truth, but decides against it. Lying suddenly seems very appealing.

"Incredible."

"Really? Did you?"

"No, Andrew—never on a first date! Don't tell me you've forgotten how long you had to campaign for."

"Well, yes—but we were sixteen. Times might have changed—considering."

"Considering what?"

"Nothing—just considering—you know—that it's been a while."

"Just say it, okay? In fact... why don't you just join the club with the rest of them?"

"What Club?"

"The *Lexi is Desperate and Pathetic club*. I'll give you a friends and family discount on your membership."

"I only meant it had been a while since you were sixteen —so you might not have such rigid standards anymore."

"A while since I was sixteen? So what are you saying, that I'm old and washed up?"

"No, Lex. Geez, are you PMS or what? I'm in a great mood and I'm not going to let you ruin it."

"I don't want to ruin it, Andrew. I just want everyone to leave me alone." Lexi can sense the anger pulsing through her and she feels shockingly alert. She mainly tries to avoid it for fear of what she might become, but anger actually feels pretty damn good. Far preferable to sadness, and miles more empowering than jealousy.

"Fine!" says Andrew and storms out of the room.

"Fine!" Lexi shouts back.

She's left standing in the kitchen bristling. She picks up the mug and tosses it into the sink where it lands with a resounding clatter. Lexi decides to go for a run around the neighborhood—on her own. She doesn't need any of her friends right now. They're smothering her—all of them. She needs to be independent and self reliant and free. Pulling on shorts and a tank she imagines getting Russell's business off the ground and then leaving LA. Buying a ticket to Thailand or New Zealand or even Africa. She can picture it now—meditating by a Buddhist shrine in Phuket; building an orphanage in a run-down village in Uganda. Maybe she'll forget about men entirely and become a lesbian. If Andrew could switch sides, why couldn't she?

She's full of plans as she searches in her purse for her iPod and headphones. Pressing them into her ears, she enters the world of Thesis—a world where a complete stranger seems to understand her more than her closest friends. Lexi slams the front door behind her and starts running down the sidewalk, no idea where she is heading, only certain that she needs to keep moving. When the tears arrive again, she lets them flow. This time they feel cleansing. The music wraps itself around her.

> *you ask, can I fly like an elegant bird? will I sew you new*
> *   wings?*
> *this life is absurd, when corners and tables keep calling our*
> *   names,*
> *with no reservations and no one to blame, blame, blame, no*
> *   one to blame*
> *find your own reasons, sculpt your own dreams,*
> *I'm at a table for one, you're not what you seem...*

The piano mounts to a rousing crescendo and urges Lexi on. She's annoyed by the appearance of another runner approaching her in the opposite direction. It's as if he's interrupted something intimate, a private space she doesn't want trespassed. As he passes her by, their eyes meet for barely a second and she thinks two things: *God—he must be hot in that wool hat*, and *I wonder if he saw me crying?*

GEORGE
20th November, 2009
Hollywood, Los Angeles

As predicted, the last few days have disappeared in a flurry of arrangements, musical and otherwise. With the show on the horizon, the Thesis machine has kicked into seriously high gear and George has watched Gabe skippering a team of many, including instrument techs, roadies, publicists, and lighting engineers.

In rehearsals George has been feeling completely in sync with the rest of the boys. There are times when he sits down at the piano, fingers poised, when he wishes he could stop time and preserve the moment, so exquisitely full of antici-pation. But then he starts playing, and he opens his mouth to sing, and it's as if his ability to control anything evaporates, and he is overcome with the inevitable. Overcome with the music surging through him and out of him. Overcome with the invisible threads of sound linking him to each band member, each instrument, each note. George has heard it said before, but he's felt it himself, in those moments he is merely a vessel, and the feeling is all at once humbling and exhila-rating.

It's the day before the show and they have just com-pleted a final sound check. George sits on the edge of the stage dangling his legs over the side like a boy balanced on a bridge about to skim stones in a river. He looks out at the room full of empty seats and feels surprisingly peaceful. He remembers the first time they played Glastonbury, how his gut twisted before they went on stage at the prospect of being faced with a sea of writhing bodies and faces. He wondered in that moment how he could please a field of thousands if he couldn't meet the expectations of two? But it was only after they made it on the stage and began their set, that he allowed himself to be elevated by the massive crowd who, unlike his parents, would love him because of his music. It was that simple. The crowd wanted him to succeed. He sang from his core that night and experimented with being completely unin-hibited on stage, bounding around and letting his voice lead his body wherever it chose to go. Their debut at Glastonbury was legendary. Fans still reminisced about it today.

Gabe appears and sits down next to George. "Sounding superb."

"You're biased."

"Well, what else do you pay me for?"

"Got me there."

"We've just released the tickets on the website—your adoring fans will be going ape shit."

"Excellent. I should take a look online."

"So, my friend, we're almost there. One more run through tomorrow."

"Nope. I've talked about it with the lads. We don't want to over rehearse. It might take something away from it."

"Expect the unexpected and go with it then."

"Something like that." George fishes a pen out of his back pocket and writes **go with it** on the palm of his hand. "So what do you think, Gabe—you think we can keep this up until we're old men?"

"Well, there are many who have paved the way."

"Yeah, but what if I—"

"You won't."

George understands that neither of them knows exactly what he was going to say, but the specifics are irrelevant. What *does* matter to George is that Gabe is his anchor. The dependable voice of reassurance that went missing inside his own head a long time ago.

LEXI
November 20th, 2009
The 10 Freeway East, Los Angeles

Lexi is driving home exhausted. Looking back she considers the night of the blind date and the morning after to have been a blessing, disguised in beige loafers and a loud shirt, but a blessing nonetheless. Running around the neighborhood the next morning, Thesis resonating around her head, she'd had somewhat of an epiphany. It was as if George Bryce was speaking directly to her, telling her to find her own reasons and sculpt her own dreams. It all made sense now—she had spent most of her life relying on other people to determine her happiness—her parents, Meg, Andrew. She had absorbed their perceptions of her like invisible fumes seeping into her pores, becoming the person they thought she should be—

popular, positive, pretty. But even that hadn't worked and she had lost Lexi along the way—lost the woman she wanted to become. She had also lost her edge, which she is determined to regain at this juncture in her life.

Lexi had called Russell after the run and said she wasn't feeling well enough to work. She had spent most of the day crying, something she hadn't allowed herself to do since she was a very little girl. Somewhere along the line she had taken her mother's mantra, "Tears won't help, my beauty, let's look on the bright side" to be an indisputable truth, embedded into their family constitution. But tears *had* helped. They had flushed out something toxic swirling under the surface of her skin, and Lexi had woken up the next day with a renewed outlook. It was time to shed everyone else's wishes for her and discover her own.

Quite how she was going to do this was still a bit fuzzy, but she knew Russell and the development of the business played a crucial role. She had to channel all of her energy into expanding Let The Green Times Roll. She wanted to make an impact in the world—to hear the bouncing echo of her shout rather than the hushed breath left behind by a whisper. Now was not the time for a relationship. No way. This was Lexi time. Even thinking about finding a man would derail her. *I'm at a table for one.* And she was going to choose whatever she wanted from life's menu, instead of relying on someone else to do the ordering.

She'd spent the last two days in overdrive. Russell didn't know what had hit him when she got back to work.

"I was convinced you'd be livid about the television interview," he had said while brewing her an echinacea tea, "I told Boris to be on his best behavior." But Lexi had returned with a flame at her heels and assured Russell they could make it happen by next Tuesday. *He* will be ready to go in front of the cameras, and behind the scenes, *she* will be ready for business.

"And I'm very much looking forward to meeting Mildred Cotton," she had declared magnanimously, hoping to eclipse some of the bitterness she had initially felt.

"Yes, yes!" Russell had replied, blushing nervously, "Me too. I'm sure you'll find her as engaging as I did."

Now, two days later, stuck in Friday night traffic on the 10 freeway, Lexi is feeling entirely spent. She wasn't actually sick before, but today she can feel a sharp scratch at the base of her throat and when her phone rings and she sees it's Meg, she decides not to answer. They usually speak at least once a day, but she has avoided talking to her since Wednesday morning, purposefully trying to put some needed distance between them.

When Meg has texted, Lexi has replied only to say, "all's well just super busy at work." But two minutes later it rings again. Lexi feels a swift rush of guilt, what if something has happened to one of the children? She reaches for the phone.

GEORGE
20th November, 2009
West Hollywood, Los Angeles

"How the fuck did this happen?" The band are all together in Gabe's room and George is staring at the laptop screen completely dumfounded.

"I don't know, George, you must have lost your notebook." Gabe has had the unfortunate job of delivering the news that the lyrics for "Over Time" have been leaked on the Internet.

"I didn't lose my notebook. I've got my notebook. It's not even a song yet. The only person who's seen the lyrics is Simon."

"What are you implying?" says Simon indignantly. "You think I took our lyrics and sold them to a friggin blogger? Why would I do that?"

93

"Of course, you wouldn't—I don't know, but how the hell did they get *here*," says George, pointing angrily at the computer screen. "Did you show them to Stacey?"

"No! I didn't show them to Stacey. I didn't even have them. They're in your bloody book."

"Lighten up, guys," says Duncan, putting his feet up on the desk. "It's not like some kind of mainland security has been breached. So what if the lyrics are out. You can still write the fucking song..."

"Dunc is actually talking sense for once, George," says Mark. "Let it go—" George can't understand why they don't get it. He feels violated. Those are his words, his thoughts. Fresh. Barely born. The formation of songs for a new album is a painstaking process and it can take months, even years for the vision to articulate. He knew this song was integral but it's been hijacked now—thrown into the glare of scrutiny way too early. He *will* have to let it go—all of it.

"Anyway," says Mark, fiddling with his wedding ring, "I *do* mean to change the subject here, because I'd like to know why Duncan and I hadn't even seen the song yet."

"It was too early," defends George, "you know we don't show you things until they're in better shape."

"Why?" asks Mark.

"Yeah, why?" adds Duncan. "What's up with that? I thought we'd talked about bringing us in on the process sooner?" There had been some conversation about this after *Sounds As if* was released, but nothing had really come of it. George and Simon had always drawn the outline and then Mark and Duncan helped colour it in. The terms of their union were entirely equitable, all song royalties split four ways. If it wasn't broken—why fix it?

"I don't know why—it's just what's worked in the past. Hasn't it, Sim?" George looks to Simon to back him up. Gabe is staying conspicuously quiet.

"Yeah mate, but it's like it all rests upon you," says

Simon, finding it difficult to look George in the eye. "Maybe Mark and Dunc need to get more of a look in. You know, show up from the start instead of being brought in somewhere in the middle."

"I've got some lyrics, George," says Mark, quietly. "I mean, not up to your standard, but Simon's seen them and he thinks they're pretty good. I was going to wait to mention it, but now that it's come up, I was thinking I could contribute to a song on this next album." George slowly closes the lid of the laptop and stands up. He feels shaky. Not only because of the stolen lyrics but this completely unexpected mutiny on top of it. Was this the beginning of the chasm he had always dreaded?

"You should have said something," says George to Mark, unsure of what else to say. He doesn't have a history of knowing how to repair ruptures in relationships. He would never have guessed that the rest of them felt so undermined or considered him to be so domineering.

"I just did," says Mark.

"Come on, boys," says Gabe, the absent anchor, suddenly speaking up. "It's the big night tomorrow. We've all been looking forward to this and you've worked bloody hard. It's crap timing that the lyrics were let loose today, but the show must go on, right? I'm sure you all just need a bit of space to think about what's been said. We can pick the conversation back up in London."

"Gabe's right," says Duncan, "I vote we all go grab a brew and get pissed."

"Sorry, lads. Stacey's waiting for me," says Simon, looking eager to leave. George can sense him pulling away and the sensation is visceral, like a muscle weakening, withering from lack of use. How long have they all felt like this and why is he the last to hear about it?

"I'll come," says Mark, "Anna's shopping anyway." He turns to George. "You joining?"

George wants to try to sound normal. Wants to act as if nothing has changed, but his fear is that everything has. "Not right now," he says, hoping that he's the only one who can hear the tremor in his voice.

LEXI
November 20th, 2009
West Hollywood, Los Angeles

Lexi had attempted to answer Meg's call, but just as she was reaching for her phone she had noticed a police car a few lanes to the left. Using a hand-held in the car incurred a hefty fine and she wasn't going to risk it. She'd switched her phone off and turned up the stereo, reassuring herself that there was probably nothing wrong and she'd check her messages later.

She's barely walked through the front door when her home phone rings. Andrew is with Carl, the apartment is peaceful, and Lexi is preparing to go to bed for the entire weekend with 1000 mgs of vitamin C, a stack of trashy magazines and a packet of Red Vines.

"Hi there," says Lexi, hoping to sound as normal as possible. "Everything okay?"

"OH MY GOD!" says Meg in her most dramatic voice, "More than okay. I've been trying to reach you for an hour—can you talk?"

"I'm not feeling a hundred percent," says Lexi, "but I guess I can, for a minute or two."

"Okay, okay. Soooo—remember when I entered that lottery to win the Thesis tickets for Tim's birthday?"

"I remember," says Lexi.

"Well, they've sent me an e-mail and I won! These tickets are like gold dust, I mean all the Facebook fans were desperate to get their hands on them and I can't even believe it, but I actually got them!" Her voice is getting higher by the second.

Lexi wishes she'd never answered the phone. The last

things she needs to hear right now is Meg gushing about Thesis. Lexi's finally working on being a grown-up—following her eco learnings—finding her own passions. She doesn't need to get sucked into Meg's delirium. Although... she must admit that she has felt an uncanny connection between herself and George Bryce since seeing the video and listening continually to his music. She knows it's so silly, but it's as if the lyrics are speaking to her—guiding her in her new direction. Anyway. Whatever. Let Meg have the girlish crush on the twenty-something Brit boy. Lexi has more important things to concentrate on.

"Hello?!! Are you there?" says Meg.

"Yes, yes, I'm here," says Lexi, "I'm just feeling shitty today. That's awesome about the tickets though. I'm sure you and Tim will love it."

"Are you losing brain cells, Lex? I'm not taking Tim! After that fiasco on Tuesday—he's in the dog house—no booty for two weeks and no concert. Girl's night out. Tomorrow night—Sexy Lexi and Meg the legs!"

Sexy Lexi—she hasn't heard that one in a while—her nickname in the eighth grade when she had been the first of the two best friends to kiss a boy. His name was Lucas. His lips had tasted of chalk.

"Tomorrow?" repeats Lexi, feeling a swell of delight, "I'm not sure, Meg—I *do* have a sore throat." She has this odd sensation that she needs to protect her excitement and not let on how much she would really love to go. Meg is already infatuated with George. In high school, they had always lusted after the same boy.

"Forget your sore throat. I told you I'd make it up to you. You have to come. I'm not giving you a choice. Do you still have your white mini dress—the one you wore to The Spin Doctors at The Greek?"

It's just a concert, right? She's permitted to have some fun. She can't hold a grudge with Meg forever.

"I'm not so sure, but sounds like I better go look for it now."

"Yay!" says Meg squealing loudly, "it's going to be just like old times." And that's the part that worries Lexi the most.

GEORGE
21st November, 2009
The Avid Theatre, Hollywood

Customarily, an hour before performing, George and the boys shrink their world, close the door of their dressing room and won't permit anyone in—even Gabe. This hour is sacrosanct. They don't request gallons of Smirnoff, vats of caviar and cocaine, or pink toilet seats. They normally ask for a small table, three packs of cards, twelve bags of Walkers salt and vinegar crisps, a case of Orangina and two sixpacks of Corona beer. The band then embarks on rounds of Switch, a card game taught to Simon and Mark by their grandfather when they were eight. It's a ritual that George can't do without. They think Simon is reigning champion, but they have lost count along the way, relying on the hour instead to shut out nerves and bind them together. By the time they get on stage, they are like four teenage boys who have been shut in their parents' basement all afternoon, full of mischief and spark, prepared to make an impact.

Tonight should be no different, even though they will be playing to an audience of two hundred and fifty instead of twenty thousand. But after yesterday's revelations, George knows that something has been lost. Maybe even irretrievably. Earlier that day, George had asked one of the band's PAs to run to the English Shop in Santa Monica to buy a large party sized tin of Quality Street—top chocolates. He'd shared them generously as a feeble peace offering. The boys had all laughed and helped themselves, but still, George can't seem to shake yesterday's criticisms, roughly unpicking the stitches from an old, neglected wound.

LEXI
November 21st, 2009
The Avid Theatre, Hollywood

Lexi and Meg have third row seats. Center. When they arrived at The Avid theatre and were directed to the front, Lexi thought Meg was going to have a coronary right there and then.

"This is beyond! Just beyond, Lex. Do you realize we'll be able to smell him from here!"

"Lucky us," said Lexi sarcastically, but inside she was secretly thrilled. The last concert she went to see was Michael Bolton with her parents. She had sat between them and when he sang "How Am I Supposed to Live Without You?" her mother had squeezed her knee.

GEORGE
21st November, 2009
The Avid Theatre, Hollywood

There isn't a support act tonight. The doors open at 7:00 p.m. and the boys will come on at 8:00. There's a baby grand piano on stage, and a variety of unusual instruments will make appearances infusing the sound with something special. Andrea Evans, a harpist for the Los Angeles Philharmonic, will join them for "A Suitable Dawn." In rehearsals she'd sounded hypnotic.

At 7:45 Gabe knocks three times on the door, his signature warning. Mark has just won the final game with an eight of diamonds and Duncan is cursing him.

"Fucker—that was my victory!"

George stands up and stretches as Gabe opens the door,

holding a mug of hot water with honey and lemon. He hands it to George. Voice maintenance. George savours the hot, sweet liquid as it runs down the back of his throat. He catches sight of his reflection in the mirror and turns away. He doesn't like to look too much. He thinks maybe he needs a haircut. Or perhaps he should grow a beard? George is wearing black jeans and a checked shirt with a white t-shirt underneath. He's got his Tiger trainers on with the red laces— the ones he bought on Melrose Avenue last time they were in town.

He isn't vain about what he wears on stage and refuses to accept a stylist, wary of the four of them looking like a bunch of wankers trying to emulate another band. Come to think of it, this hasn't been discussed in a while. Maybe the rest of them have long hankered after themed outfits, but just can't bring themselves to tell him.

"Okay, lads—ready?" asks Gabe.

"Steady, go!" says Duncan.

"Yes, sir," says Mark.

"Couldn't be readier," adds Simon, licking the salt from his fingers and popping the final crisp into his mouth.

"Definitely maybe," says George (classic Oasis) as the four of them follow Gabe out of the room.

Tonight the show will open with George and his guitar entering from the back of the theatre, a spotlight tracking him down the centre aisle. He'll sing an acoustic version of "Grapefruit Girls"—an entirely fresh take on their biggest hit. The rest of the band will be waiting on stage.

The boys momentarily huddle, heads bent forward, arms resting on each other's backs.

"May the force be with you," says Simon.

"And also with you," say George, Duncan and Mark in unison. Another ritual.

As they part ways, George's guitar tech, Freddie, hands him his Martin and he's ushered away by Gabe and a bouncer down a dim narrow hallway towards the front of the building. He predicted earlier that his nerves might spike before this show but now the hour has arrived, he feels weirdly calm, like he's about to be tossed into the surf, but doesn't yet realize the power of the current.

LEXI
November 21st, 2009
The Avid Theatre, Hollywood

Lexi scans the room attempting to get a profile of your average Thesis fan. It's impossible. They seem to range from young guys in their twenties with low slung jeans and messy hair to fifty-year-old women accompanying their teenage daughters. Everyone is typing away madly on Blackberrys or iPhones—including Meg.

"What are you doing?" asks Lexi, tapping her shoulder.

"Updating my status on Facebook. I mean this is too good to pass up. Will you take a picture of me during the concert so I can post it?"

That afternoon Lexi had been enjoying feeling like a teenager again. Meg had called her a thousand times to consult on the appropriate outfit. Meg had finally decided to wear her new purple leather jacket bought on sale at Bloomingdales.

"You'll have to get tickets to see Prince next," teased Lexi.

Lexi had chosen her favorite night-time jeans, gladiator sandals and a loose orange shirt with three long, gold beaded necklaces. When she was putting on her lip gloss, she stepped back for a final appraisal, tilting her head to the left and smiling at her reflection, as if greeting an unexpected friend. When she was thirteen she would spend ages talking to imaginary boyfriends in her bathroom mirror, trying on outfits for varying events. Baseball games were popular. White shorts, colored tank top and her thick brown hair tied back in a bouncy high ponytail. Her imaginary boyfriend was always the star pitcher and winked at her when he arrived on the mound.

Tonight she feels pretty, but attempts to remind herself that it really doesn't matter how lovely she looks. Even if the hottest guy sat down next to her, right now, she's resolved to not give into temptation and allow herself to be swept away by him. Even if he tells her he used to play baseball. It's bound to end in tears, with her becoming so wrapped up in him that she loses her mind, or her job, or both. He's surely got a string of ex-girlfriends in his past who have fallen in the wake of his charms and never recovered. In fact, she's starting to really dislike this potential hot guy who is nowhere to be seen and is certainly not sitting next to her. And she's even considering swapping seats with Meg if he shows up now.

Lexi's internal diatribe against the nonexistent stranger is rudely interrupted by a young grungy-looking girl who has miraculously appeared in the neighboring seat. "Are these not like OMG tickets?" she says to both Lexi and Meg, who has finished with Facebook and is reapplying her lipstick.

"I know!" says Meg. "I love Thesis! They're the best ever and George is going to be—"

"Spitting distance," says the girl, completing Meg's sentence for her. "Sp—itt—ing distance," she drags out the word for emphasis. Lexi reckons she's about twenty-two. Pierced nose and bed hair. No make-up except for thick black eyeliner.

"You think?" says Meg excitedly. "Do you think we'll feel the saliva?"

"I hope so," says the girl, turning to the guy she's with and kissing him voraciously on the lips.

"Well, *he's* surely feeling the saliva," Lexi whispers to Meg, glancing around and noticing the theatre is now full to capacity.

GEORGE
21st November, 2009
The Avid Theatre, Hollywood

They emerge into the glare of the front foyer where the red floral carpet reminds George of London's West End theatres and smells like an odd combination of his granny's settee and spilt Guinness. This is mental. It's as if instead of the main attraction he could transform into one of the punters, clutching a ticket, wondering where his seats are. He pictures himself at seventeen fumbling in his pocket after a show, searching for ten quid to buy a t-shirt, averting his eyes down. He used to be very familiar with carpet.

Gabe looks to George and nods. George returns the gesture. The bouncer mutters into his walkie-talkie and the carved wooden double doors in front of them are suddenly thrown open. The blast of excitement is palpable and warm. The audience are all seated and George can almost see the energy rising from the tops of their heads like a blurred frenzy of fireflies. The lights go down and the noise dips with them, turning instead into an anticipatory hum.

George takes one deep breath, strokes the smooth torso of his guitar, and steps fearlessly into the waves.

LEXI
November 21st, 2009
The Avid Theatre, Hollywood

There is a buzz in the room escalating by the second and then, suddenly—darkness. A hush settles, but not a silent one—a hush filled with murmurs and possibility. Lexi feels a shivery tingle down her spine, as somewhere behind her she hears the opening chords of an acoustic guitar.

GEORGE
21st November, 2009
The Avid Theatre, Hollywood

The first song is flawless. George strolls down the aisle serenading the audience with a wonderfully slow rendition of "Grapefruit Girls" almost unrecognizable from the original. He makes it to the stage without tripping (tripping is always one of his greatest fears) and when the rest of the band appear, the room erupts with rapturous applause. Just as the song is about to end, Duncan comes in on drums with Simon and Mark close behind. George lays his guitar down, sits at the piano and plays with a rhythmic passion as the song transforms back to its previous incarnation and the whole room explodes with approval.

LEXI
November 21st, 2009
The Avid Theatre, Hollywood

When George Bryce walks down the aisle with his guitar, there is a raw vulnerability in his voice that makes Lexi want to weep. The song is divine. She has heard it on the radio many times, but this is the one time that will forever stand out. Stripped back to the bone, she hears all the lyrics tonight and the catchy chorus becomes poignant. When the rest of the band join in, louder, faster, the song takes on a whirling force, coaxing Lexi and the entire crowd to stand up and dance. She finds herself singing along like everyone else, bouncing up and down with Meg, feeling deliciously unself-conscious. Mr. and Mrs. Saliva next to her are screaming their heads off.

GEORGE
21st November, 2009
The Avid Theatre, Hollywood

George is already sweating profusely by the end of the song—hazard of the job. He senses a raw energy in the room and (this will forever be the hardest part to explain) he feels elated by the love of their fans—like he's receiving some kind of intravenous joy juice. When the clapping dies down, he whistles into the microphone.

"Forgive me for sounding so cheesy but you lot are really talented—you took that song and made it your own." *American Idol, X Factor*, any of the reality talent show references reliably get a laugh. George likes to get a laugh. "In fact—I may just have to step aside and let each of you, one by one, come up here and do the singing."

"I'll come up there anytime, George!" a woman's voice yells from the darkness.

"Well, thank you," says George politely, "that's an extremely generous offer. The boys and I love coming to this wonderful city of yours—you always make us feel very welcome indeed."

LEXI
November 21st, 2009
The Avid Theatre, Hollywood

When the first song ends, George starts to talk in his delicious English accent. "I'd like to invite each one of you to come up here and sing," he says with a cheeky grin that Lexi finds disturbingly attractive. He is irresistible.

"I'll come up there anytime, George!" hollers Meg. Lexi violently elbows her best friend, not certain if she should be mortified or proud, but the crowd are all laughing and Meg is clearly thrilled by her own bravado. Mrs. Saliva leans over Lexi to give Meg a high five.

GEORGE
21st November, 2009
The Avid Theatre, Hollywood

"We love you, George!" booms another voice from the crowd.

"No doubt if I knew you—I would love you back," replies George, without skipping a beat. Everyone laughs again. The banter with the crowd wasn't always easy like this. In the early days of performing, he used to be paralyzed with fright and could barely manage a hello, but in time and with prac- tice, he has acquired immaculate comic timing. More recently though, with mostly stadiums to perform, the audience feel miles away.

"Shall we get on with it then?" George asks, and the crowd respond with more cheers and whistles, as he plays the opening bars of "Under The Radar," pressing his lips close to the microphone.

> *how could I have missed you*
> *left someone else to kiss you*
> *you slipped under the radar*
> *I was looking away*

LEXI
November 21st, 2009
The Avid Theatre, Hollywood

The night unfolds with a seamless magic and Lexi is captivated by every song. "Does he write all the lyrics?" she asks Meg at one point, after he has sung "I Knew It" accom- panied by bongo drums.

"I think so," says Meg. "Or maybe with Simon, the redhead on the guitar. They're friends from school—I've done all my research on Wikipedia."

Lexi wonders about the process of writing a song. She then begins to wonder about his relationships with the other band members. Are they all friends from school? The other three are cute as well, the drummer especially has enormous charisma, and George somehow manages to convey a cama- raderie with all of them. He's the leader though. There is no doubt about that.

She marvels at the massive reserves of self-confidence he must have to do what he does, and to do it apparently so effortlessly. She then begins to imagine how many women he must have available to him. How old is he? Does he have a girlfriend? And before she can stop herself, she's picturing pressing her cheek to his sweaty chest minutes after he comes off the stage. *In fact,* she thinks, *why bother with the chest? Let's go straight to the lips.*

GEORGE
21st November, 2009
The Avid Theatre, Hollywood

Despite yesterday's friction, the show is going better than George had ever expected. The four of them are soaring and George wishes he could stop everything, just for a moment, and turn to his band mates, his three best friends and say, "See. This is why it works. *This* is why." But he can't, so he navigates the stage instead, going up to each of the boys at varying intervals and sharing a joke, or playfully leaning into them, or introducing a solo. When he sits back down at the piano to sing "Corners and Tables" he flubs a line, and smiles at Simon, who says to the audience, "Please accept our apolo- gies—he doesn't get out much." The whole room cracks up and they start the song again from the beginning.

LEXI
November 21st, 2009
The Avid Theatre, Hollywood

George continues to sing and the audience, Lexi included, continue to adore him.

He stops every two or three songs and makes a funny comment or tells a story with a relaxed casualness. He even forgets some of the lyrics and laughing, starts the song from the beginning. His fallible side makes him all the more endearing.

"I hope you're enjoying yourselves?" he asks, an hour into the show. The crowd shout and clap in appreciation.

"That's good to know, because we certainly are. In fact, Gabe," he calls to someone off stage, "Why don't we bring up the house lights for this next song. It's a special one and I want to see your reaction to the extra special visitor who's going to help us out."

The house lights come up and an ethereal looking blonde woman wafts onto the stage; a golden harp wheeled in behind her. She has long, thin, blond hair almost reaching her butt and is wearing a white cotton floaty dress.

"Please say hello to Andrea Evans, who is kindly on loan to us for the evening from none other than the Los Angeles Philharmonic." More clapping and whistling as George greets her and takes her hand.

"Is that his girlfriend?" Lexi asks Meg, indignant at the nerve of this woman inconsiderately intruding on her fantasy.

"Not sure," says Meg, "but she's gorgeous, isn't she?"

George and Andrea are positioned now together at the front of the stage. She is perched next to her harp looking like a mermaid, and he's on a stool with his guitar. They begin to play "A Suitable Dawn." Lexi wants to drift away on the crest of her favorite song. She loves this track so much. And of course he wrote it for Andrea—she can feel the chemistry between them on stage. It's so obvious. *She* was the lucky girl.

GEORGE
21st November, 2009
The Avid Theatre, Hollywood

When it comes time for "A Suitable Dawn," George sponta-neously decides to ask for the house lights on. He wants to look at the audience and doesn't feel too daunted at the prospect of seeing faces. He's unusually resilient tonight. He welcomes Andrea Evans onto the stage, whose work he really admires. As recently revealed in *NME*'s Top Ten Tastes column, George listens to a huge spectrum of music and classical is an important influence. When Andrea comes on stage, he takes her hand, thinking how lovely she looks. He met her six years ago when they first recorded in LA. Her husband is a successful conductor, twenty years older than her, and George usually ends up having dinner with them when he's in town. Andrea's looking exceptionally well to-night, considering she's just had a baby three months ago.

LEXI
November 21st, 2009
The Avid Theatre, Hollywood

Lexi is reeled in by George's mesmerizing voice and the heavenly harp, and something deep inside of her is shim-mering. She's singing along to the words and imagining he is singing just for her. And then the strangest thing happens. She could swear he makes eye contact with her. He's singing "A Suitable Dawn" and he's looking directly at her. Or at least she feels like he's looking directly at her. She holds his gaze for a number of seconds, feeling, bizarrely, like she is the only person in the room. *He can't possibly have noticed me*, Lexi scolds herself, cursing her mother for raising her with such an overinflated ego. Especially when he's up there with his super model harpist who probably isn't wearing any underwear.

As quickly as it arrived, the moment disappears. The house lights go down, sinking the audience back into darkness. Lexi feels intoxicated by it all. By how very real the connection felt—as if she's been harboring a secret for the longest time, only to discover that it's his secret too.

GEORGE
21st November, 2009
The Avid Theatre, Hollywood

Halfway through "A Suitable Dawn," something happens. George catches the eye of a woman in the crowd. She's almost dead centre in the third row. There are other women around her, but she's wearing orange and it's as if she's three dimensional, a technicolour figure on a flat grey backdrop. He recognizes her, maybe. From where? He meets so many new faces every day. Record company? Radio station? He's actually locked eyes with her and realizes it might be for too long and looks away to the women beside her, and around the rest of the room. But he doesn't lose sight of her. She's shining. She's beautiful. And she's singing his words back to him.

So many people singing his song. So many people who don't really know him. The words are flowing out of his mouth without thought, just feeling. He must have sung this song of longing a thousand times. Andrea is elegantly strumming the harp. And then it comes to him, like a flash from a dream you don't remember having. Running. She was the woman who ran by him three days ago. He's sure of it. She was the woman who was crying.

As he sings the final note, the audience are plunged back

into darkness but not before his eyes rest on her for one last moment.

He's intrigued. She's still beautiful.

He wasn't imagining it. But there's more.

George unexplainably feels like he knows something of this woman.

Something that nobody else does.

LEXI
November 21st, 2009
The Avid Theatre, Hollywood

The house lights don't come on again until the end of the show, and by then the band have left the stage. They've already played three encores and the audience have screamed and clapped until their throats are hoarse and their palms slapped pink.

Meg hugs Lexi and squeals, "That was out of this world good. Best, best night."

"I've seen them in concert six times," announces Mrs. Saliva, "but tonight was the bomb. They were amaaa—zzing! By the way, babe," she says turning to her boyfriend, "Did you see George checking me out?"

"No way, I'll kill the dude," says Mr. Saliva, pulling her towards him, his hands wrapping around her waist.

"That's so funny," says Meg to Lexi, "I thought he was checking me out too. I'm positive he was staring right at me when the lights came up."

"Oh Meggy—he probably was," says Lexi, trying hard to hide her disappointment. "You look so rock chick in your leather jacket."

"Wait till I tell Tim!" says Meg excitedly.

Idiot, idiot, idiot, repeats Lexi to herself, as she is pulled along with the throng of fans, all gushing about Thesis, all reluctantly making their way to the exit.

GEORGE
21st November, 2009
The Avid Theatre, Hollywood

The remainder of the concert goes perfectly. He doesn't ask for the house lights on again. What's he going to do? Say, *excuse me, I hope you don't mind, but can I just stop and get the phone number of the woman wearing orange in the third row? I think I've had a glimpse into her soul.* She's better off left in the dark anyway. After the final encore. After the precision bow, linking arms with the boys. After the applause has long died down. After the record execs have obediently licked their arses. Before all the schmoozing at the post party begins, George slips back onto the stage and looks out over the red velour seats. He's not entirely sure what he's hoping to find. Everyone's gone home. The third row is empty.

LEXI
November 21st, 2009
West Hollywood, Los Angeles

Lexi arrives back to find Andrew and his new flame, Carl, flopped on the couch both fast asleep in front of the TV. So much for whirlwind romance; they're already behaving like an old married couple after three dates. Having been in both camps, Andrew has explained to her that in gay dating there is no tedious game playing—it's like Twister without spinning the dial—you can just go directly to all the most compromising positions. *Maybe they experimented with compromising positions earlier,* thinks Lexi, as she sneaks past them to her bedroom.

It's midnight. Her ears are ringing. She lies down on her bed replaying the night's events in her head. But every time she tries to remember exactly what happened, she returns to the most far-fetched plotline conceivable. George Bryce, charming English boy, super successful rock star, poet, singing her favorite song and staring into her eyes. *I'm delusional*, thinks Lexi, reaching for her laptop and flipping it open. *He was checking everyone out. He must do that at all the concerts. That's what musicians his age do, right? He was probably high on ecstasy or something and preparing to indulge in a threesome backstage with Madame Harpist and her twin sister.* But even as she's trying to convince herself of his debauched lifestyle, that other Lexi inside of her, that alter ego who is either full of insight or totally vain, is murmuring, *you are special, Lexi. Your mother was right. He _was_ looking at you and he's different, he might even be the—*"SHUT UP!" says Lexi out loud. She will not be swayed. She decides the best thing to do is some research into George to confirm her suspicions.

She googles Thesis. A trillion pages pop up. She googles George Bryce and chooses images, scrolling through them intently, looking for the harpist or other girlfriends. Lots of him with the band. Some of him with famous singers; Annie Lennox at a charity performance, Tom Chaplin from Keane, Kanye West and some girl called Fanny Arundel, a slutty looking singer she doesn't recognize. She attempts to convince herself that she doesn't actually find him that attractive, but with each picture her interest is only further piqued. Lexi looks at her clock—it's 1:00 a.m.. *I'll just quickly check out their website* she decides *and then I'll go to sleep.*

GEORGE
21st November, 2009
Hollywood, Los Angeles

The post party is at an ultra trendy club in Hollywood, which George doesn't even know the name of. He's surrounded by faces wanting to talk to him. Hands on his arms, on his shoulders, in the middle of his back. Women he's never met kiss him on the lips and pose for photographs with him like he's a new attraction at London zoo. "You're so cute!" Who would have believed that 'cute' would be the adjective most used to describe him these days? He couldn't feel any less cute if he tried. He knows the gig went brilliantly but the satisfaction has worn off and he's beginning to worry about something else, but he can't put his finger on what. He's holding a beer in his hand and contemplates if it's the same beer he was holding before? He looks around the room hoping to spot Simon or Duncan or Mark or Gabe. There's an extremely thin woman with a nose ring hanging onto him, explaining in great detail a concept album she's working on.

"The concept is totally conceptual. It's an esoteric take on the rise of the birth control pill pushing the boundaries for women—freedom or poison? I'm totally into harmonica. I was thinking you and I could collaborate?"

"Collaborate?" repeats George, wondering if he's drunk again. Contemplating saying, *apparently I don't even do that with my own band. Why would I want to with you?*

"Take a ticket, darling," a voice from behind intervenes, as a forceful arm links up with his, pulling him away from the nose ring.

"Fanny," says George, actually feeling relieved that she's managed to extricate him, but simultaneously wondering how he'll now extricate himself.

"I'm next in line, right?" she says, possessively, manoeuvring him quickly across the room.

"You do pop up when I least expect it," says George, scanning the room again to see if he can spot an exit strategy.

"I like to shock people. Now—talking of popping up when you least expect it..." she brushes the tips of her fingers against the front of his jeans. George can't believe that her repertoire is that limited. He needs to move away from her. Why does she always have to find him when he's feeling defenceless? And drunk. *I'm not as drunk as I was in Vegas* he reminds himself. *I am in complete control of my faculties. She's bonkers. Bonkers is bad, George. Very, very bad.*

"I thought you were in Vegas," he says, at a loss.

"I was," she replies, "and now I'm here. And you were in Vegas. And now *you're* here. So what do you say, G, your place or mine?"

LEXI
November 22ⁿᵈ, 2009
West Hollywood, Los Angeles

One hour later, Lexi is still hunched over her computer, trawling through mindless comments on the Thesis fan boards. She's had to register on the website and couldn't decide upon a username, finally settling on Dawn77. She wants to go to sleep. She really truly wants to snap the computer shut and close her eyes so she can return to her private space with George, which has now been invaded by thousands of incredibly annoying fans who appear to be horrifyingly obsessed by him. But somehow she just can't bring herself to log out and turn away. She's finding Radar3Girl particularly irritating at the moment. Who does she think she is? The world's greatest expert on George Bryce's wardrobe? And she was clearly at tonight's concert. Her last post reads:

> Anyone notice George was wearing the same
> blue and black shirt he wore at Coachella
> last year? I think he's only worn it at
> three gigs in the last eighteen months but
> I think he looks SEXY in it. Were his
> jeans Levis?? Hees soooooo funny. This gig
> was off the hook!!!!!!!!!!!!!!!!!! And I'm
> loving the red laces. GO GEORGE!!!!!!!!!!!!
> I'm yours. I'm buying red laces tomorrow. I
> LOOOOVE YOU!!!!!!!!!!!!!!!!

Doesn't she know that people are dying in Afghanistan? Doesn't she know that an exclamation point loses meaning if overused? Lexi is tempted to post in response: `Fuck off Radar3Girl—you sound like you're 14 and if you must know, George was looking at me tonight!!!!!!` Luckily she restrains herself and finally shuts down her computer. She switches off the light and sinks into her pillow, her head spinning her a decade and a half back in a tornado of longing. But for what exactly—she can't say.

GEORGE
22nd November, 2009
Chateau Marmont Hotel, Los Angeles

This time there's no mistaking what has happened. George is in Fanny's en suite bathroom at the Chateau Marmont, muttering to himself, as he splashes cold water onto his face, "Fucking wanker."

He hasn't shaved in days and looks wasted. *Living the life* muses George.

His reflection peers back at him pathetically, like a little boy in need of a hug.

Fanny's impressive snores are reverberating right through the locked door. She'd fallen asleep minutes after a second very high-pitched, dramatic orgasm, orchestrated by her own skilled methods.

"No sweat, cupcake. I just need an extra top up," she'd explained, wriggling into position.

George wonders if at that point her dead boyfriend, Sebastian, had shown up to lend a helping hand. Fuck. He just wants to get away. What is he doing here? It's like she repels him and attracts him at the same time.

The woman in the orange shirt appears in his mind. The beautiful runner with the tears and the singing lips. It was her fault. She flicked his switch back on again. She made him want something he couldn't have, so he took something he could have instead.

LEXI
November 23rd, 2009
Venice, CA

Lexi has fully recovered from Saturday night and is back at work. She's returned to being a grown-up and hasn't looked at the Thesis website once this morning. Yesterday had been different. She'd only wanted to see if Radar3Girl had posted any more inane comments. She hadn't intended on staying on for another hour—watching videos of the band and perusing the merchandise in the shop. Anyhow, she's rationalized that it's far better to be fantasizing about some unattainable rock star than a real man, who could distract her from her work and make footprints on her heart.

It was all good research for Russell's website. She's picked up lots of excellent design ideas. In fact, Billy said he should have the initial site map up and running today—just in time for the onslaught of publicity they'll get after *Wake up LA*. Not. Thank God it's on at 5:00 a.m.

Russell is full of beans. Literally. He's making a mung bean stew to support his digestion before tomorrow's appear-ance.

"Are you sure that's the best idea?" asks Lexi. "You might fart your way through the whole segment."

"Quite the opposite, my dear. I need to flush out tonight so I can feel cleansed and focused in the morning."

"If you say so," says Lexi, making a note to leave early this afternoon before the flushing out process begins.

"Have you heard from Billy yet?" asks Russell, feeding Boris a spoonful of stew.

"Next on my list to call," says Lexi, "and then we'll do a

run through again for the morning. Do you know the inter-viewer's name?"

"Sophie Samuels. I've been tuning in over the last week. She has lots of hair."

Lexi considers how this might affect Russell's per-formance. Perhaps he's a bit envious.

Her phone vibrates alerting her to check her e-mail. Just in time—it's Billy with the link to www.letthegreentimes-roll.com. He's written, "Pretty darn impressive—if I do say so myself :)"

"Russell—go to your computer and type in your new website address."

"Really?" says Russell, full of pride.

"Really," says Lexi, moving in to lean over his shoulder.

The site appears in a flash of recycling symbols spinning in a kaleidoscopic formation with various objects colliding inside the image. The words—**Round and Round it goes, Let The Green Times Roll!**—circle the screen and a menu jumps out from the middle. The backdrop looks like recycled paper and the fonts are all in varying shades of green.

"It's fantastic!" says Lexi, feeling as if she's watching her toddler take his first steps.

"I'm just... just... flabbergasted, Lexi. It's so professional. So right."

"So *you*!" says Lexi. "I told you Billy would pull through. Go on—click on mission statement—it should be your video."

Russell clicks and the screen fills up with his face, in front of his house, Boris asleep in the background.

"Let me introduce myself, I'm Russell Hazelton and I'm going to show you how to let the green times roll... not only into next week... but far into our future. My future, your future, the future all humankind depends upon..."

Lexi laughs remembering how stressful that day was. It feels like forever ago, but it was all worth it. And as for Russell—she can see he's a natural. His quirkiness works wonders for him on camera. He'll nail it tomorrow. She has no doubt about that.

GEORGE
23rd November, 2009
Hollywood, Los Angeles

The band are in the waiting area at KROQ, one of LA's long running radio stations, about to be interviewed by Kevin and Bean. George had managed to slip out of Fanny's hotel room in the early hours of Sunday morning, while she was still sleeping. Now he really *was* behaving like a rock star. He had five text messages from Gabe on his phone, each one increasingly frantic, *where the hell are you, George? ARE YOU OKAY????*

Was he okay? It was an alarmingly simple question and yet one that he felt unable to answer. Simon leans over to him now, "Mate—you look a little rough. What happened to you on Saturday night anyway?" Simon had been holed up with Stacey all of Sunday and George had barely seen him.

"Fanny showed up," says George, wondering if he should confide in Simon.

"The famous Fanny. So what's the story, George, are you into her? She's a nutter but you never know, that might do you some good. Like we said at the airport—time to explore. I'm certainly enjoying it. Stacey is wicked in the sack, mate. I've never experienced anything like it. I mean the rush from the show and then two nights of... well it's like we were saying at the airport. It's time to live a little—yeah?"

George hesitates before answering. He decides not to confess to Simon how he really feels. "Absolutely. Fanny's a wild thing. An acrobat, mate. You've never seen a girl get into the positions she does. Crazy stuff..."

"Now that's more like it. Nice one, mate."

What's wrong with me? thinks George, feeling like a

pretty sad excuse for a front man. Surely he *should* be bragging about sleeping with Fanny, not just pretending to? Maybe he was destined to be like Kurt Cobain, tortured and introspective forever more.

"Thesis, you're up next. Through here please."

The band are ushered into the main studio where they are shown to four stools. George is usually required to do most of the talking in these instances, although Simon and Duncan like to join in. Mark rarely says anything unless pushed.

Kevin and Bean have been doing this show for almost twenty years and are legends on breakfast radio. They've interviewed the band before.

"Okay—firstly just want to say how cool it is to have you guys here again. The show on Saturday was truly awesome."

"Always a pleasure to see you both and thank you, that's kind of you to say," says George, turning on his trademark humility.

"We figured you guys have been partying ever since, except we've heard you're like the most sedate rockers around —so what's the deal? Did you go straight to bed with a cup of hot tea?"

"Straight to bed with something hot—but it wasn't tea!" says Duncan, jumping in before George can respond.

"So it's not all true then? You guys don't just sit around playing Scrabble after your gigs?"

"Our Scrabble games can get very heated, Kevin," says George dryly, "I've even been known to throw a few tiles out the window."

The two DJs laugh.

"We knew you had it in you, George, you're hard core. But seriously guys, the show was excellent. Any of our listeners who were lucky enough to see it will agree—you guys were awesome."

"The audience last night were phenomenal," says George,

remembering the woman in the third row. "Really, we're indebted to our fans. If it wasn't for them we'd be... well, we'd be rather lonely."

"No chance of that!" says Bean. "You seem to have a way with the ladies. I don't know what they're putting in the water over there in the UK, but the chicks here dig you."

"Not that we don't!" adds Kevin.

"Aww—it's a good thing we're on the radio so you can't see me blushing," says George, keeping up.

"We're going to take some calls from listeners in a moment and then we're going to play the new single. But what I'd like to know is how the songs get written. Do you all pitch in, or is there one head chef?" Not exactly the best time for this question to be thrown at them.

"George usually comes to me with a lyric and a chord," answers Simon. "Something like... lost sock, lost sock where have you gone... and then we elaborate on *that* lyric and *that* chord for days and days until—hey presto—we've written 'Corners and Tables'."

"Then they ask for my approval," says Duncan.

"And yours, Mark?" asks Bean.

"Rarely," says Mark, smiling, but George can hear the crackle on the line.

"And do you know when it's working? I mean, are you guys like 'Yes! This one's gonna be big...'"

"Sort of opposite really," says George, "I usually say 'no—this one's never going to work' and then everyone spends more days and days attempting to convince me. It's all rather exhausting really. It's surprising we ever have enough energy to perform at the end of it."

"You guys crack me up," says Bean. "Are you ready for some calls?"

"Bring'em on," says George, anything to end this line of questioning.

"On line number one we have Melinda from Silverlake.

Melinda, you're on with Thesis. Did you have a question?" George briefly entertains the obscure fantasy that maybe his mystery woman will call and reveal herself to him.

"Oh my God, like, yes, but oh my God, like I love you guys!"

"Like we love you too, Melinda," says Duncan.

"I was at the show on Saturday and you guys looked so cute. I wanted to know, like, do you guys like plan what you're going to wear before you go on stage, or do you just like wear whatever?"

"A hard hitting music question, boys—who's going to tackle this one?" George's heart sinks. So much for his soul mate seeking him out.

LEXI
November 24th, 2009
Burbank, Los Angeles

It's five a.m. and Lexi is considering asking Russell for a raise —as soon as they get their first client. Surely waking up this early goes above and beyond the call of duty? Plus she was right about the bean stew. When she arrived to collect him this morning, he seemed to have taken up residence in the bathroom.

"Is everything all right?" asked Lexi, praying she was not going to get particulars.

"All's well. Just finding myself a tad nervous."

"You'll be great, Russell. Just be yourself." Lexi's only role this morning is moral support, which she can just about manage at this ungodly hour. The rest of her brain is still asleep.

When they arrive at the studio, they are greeted by Mildred Cotton, a statuesque woman with a short silver bob, probably in her early fifties, wearing a long purple dress and cowboy boots. Lexi can see now why Russell was so taken with her—she's perfect for him (even though she's sworn off using that word—in this instance she will allow it). Russell grows increasingly flustered when he sees her.

"Um, how is Cherub doing? Boris has been asking after her."

"Oh, he is quite a flirt that Boris of yours," says Mildred, taking off her black rimmed glasses. "A chip off the old block, huh Russell?"

"Well, I do like to think he's only inherited my best attributes."

"Seeing as I've yet to see all of your best attributes, my dear, I'll have to get back to you on that one." Go Mildred.

"Are you ready to wow LA with your forward thinking, Mr Hazelton?"

"I am, Miss Cotton, I surely am."

"Magnifique! Well, you'll only have a few minutes with Sophie, so make it memorable, and we'll run the web address at the bottom of the screen at the close of the segment, as well as featuring it on our site. I think it's just wonderful what you're doing. A true visionary."

"Yes, he really is," says Lexi, feeling totally dispensable. "Crunch, anyone?" She picks up a bowl of what appears to be granola clusters with dried fruit, and Russell and Mildred both grab a handful, although they can't seem to take their eyes off each other. Their hands collide in the snack bowl. It's all very romantic.

A woman's head appears around the doorway, "Mr Hazleton, can we have you in make-up for a moment? We just need to powder your nose."

"Well, that's a first," says Russell embarrassedly.

"I'll walk you over there," says Mildred, and before Lexi can even say goodbye, the room has cleared out and she's left holding the granola.

She puts it on her lap and continues eating. Her mind drifts to George Bryce. She tries to push him out, forcibly, but he keeps finding his way back in. Meg had called her yesterday gushing about hearing them interviewed on KROQ, "He's such a sweetheart. He was really witty and said his fans meant everything to him. I'd love to just meet him, you know, like one time, to tell him what their music means to me." *Yeah, you and Radar3Girl and a trillion other sex crazed teenagers*, Lexi wanted to say. *And me. And me.* But she didn't. She listened to Meg at length and then rushed to her computer when she got home to see if she could find the interview.

What was George doing right now? Most likely on a plane back to London. Or screwing his harpist. Or snorting coke. Or getting a blow job from a skinny eighteen-year-old. The list was endless. Her speculation is broken by Mildred, flying back into the room, flapping her arms up and down, her dress swirling around her like a billowing sail.

"Lexi! Lexi—it's Russell—he's... he's swelling. I think it might have been something he ate. Is he allergic to anything that you know of?"

Lexi's mind races. In the short time she has known Russell, she has been subjected to a catalogue of his personal health issues, from digestive flare-ups to an irritable colon. More information than she ever wanted to recall. But has he ever mentioned allergies? Gooseberries maybe. That's right. He's allergic to gooseberries. Or was that Boris? She looks down into the bowl of granola and spots suspicious looking shrivelled green culprits, hiding behind the dried cranberries.

"I think he's allergic to gooseberries," she says, holding the bowl out in front of her, in a feeble attempt to offer Mildred some proof.

"Well, he looks like one now, and he can barely speak. His tongue is swollen. His eyes are like fountains. I'll have to call the medics."

"Can I see him? Is he okay?" Lexi is having a *Grey's Anatomy* moment and half expects McDreamy to walk in behind Mildred with a clipboard in hand.

"The problem is, Lexi, he's due to go on air in seven minutes. I'm sending you to make-up. You'll have to take his place."

Lexi snorts in disbelief, "Me?"

"Yes, you! You *are* his partner, aren't you? Who else can talk about the business? I can't have an empty slot at 5:30—it's prime real estate. Kitty here will look after you. I'm going to be with Russell."

Mildred sweeps out leaving Kitty behind, the same woman who had popped her head around the door five minutes before when life was still relatively normal. Lexi feels her armpits getting damp. It's been fourteen years since she was in the debate club and that was never filmed. She desperately tries to summon her inner Maria, who apparently is still asleep. Her only consolation being that almost everyone else is as well.

"You'll be great!" says Kitty, too enthusiastically. "Just be yourself!"

GEORGE
24th November, 2009
West Hollywood, Los Angeles

George is wide awake. He went to bed at one a.m. and he's been tossing around fitfully ever since. His head is cluttered full of thoughts, like a stack of sealed envelopes waiting to be read. Every time he rips one open—another five appear and the pile just keeps getting higher. He's already spent two hours working on a song. He's called it "Third Row," but the lyrics are clumsy and the melody has yet to materialize.

He ended up sending Fanny a text on Monday saying *Take care, love George.* He felt it was suitably non-committal but not a complete blow off. She texted back *Touring with Twisted Kale. Malcom and I have been hanging. Sebastian approves. You and I cool?* George wrote *Absolutely. Cool. Tell*

Malcom I say hello. Chapter closed. Malcom can have her. He'll know just what notes to hit.

George kicks the duvet off and stares at the ceiling. If he smoked, this would be a good time to have a cigarette. If, if, if.

They haven't even started their North American tour yet and he's feeling like hibernating back in Maida Vale. He's had enough of BBQ chipotle chicken pizzas and sandwiches the size of a small car. Even the eternally optimistic weather is starting to grate on him. It's November. He wants to get caught in a downpour.

George stretches across the bed and removes his t-shirt from on top of the digital alarm clock. He chucked it there hours ago, taunted by the red numbers brazenly illuminating the room. 5:33 a.m. One more day in LA.

He reaches for the remote control and turns on the TV. If he can't sleep or write, he may as well watch music videos. The screen comes to life. He's just about to start channel surfing when he recognizes the woman's face on the screen. The woman's face on the screen. The woman on the screen! It's her! It's his mystery lady. Third row. Orange glow. Running. Crying. The song is writing itself now. It's actually her. He catapults himself to the end of the bed so he can get closer to the telly, and he turns up the volume. She's talking animatedly, to a woman with big hair.

"You see, Sophie, at Let The Green Times Roll, we're not just committed to the environment—we're committed to help-ing people save the environment and that's the difference. We all know that our world is suffering, but what we don't all know is what we can do to help. Re-using and recycling is a start, but that's just the beginning. We're here to advise bus-inesses and individuals on how they can push past the beginning and do more, so that future generations have a better chance..."

"So you offer a consultancy service?" says the inter-viewer.

"That's correct—a green consultancy service. We put the structures and guidelines in place to help people improve their environmental awareness, cut their carbon footprint and change their habits. Empowering yourselves is possible if you find the knowledge you need to guide you. At Let The Green Times Roll, we have that knowledge."

George doesn't know what to do. If he looks away, she'll be gone again and that will be the third time. Third row. Third time. This has to be more than a coincidence. Something in the universe is bringing this woman back into his view. She's so articulate. She has a softness surrounding her, which he feels drawn to. Her skin is radiant with a scattering of freckles.

"Sorry to say our time is up but thank you very much to Russell Hazleton for coming to talk with us. Most inspiring—glad you are New in Town. Details of Let The Green Times Roll are on the screen below and on our website. Next up—getting the most from your roast. Graham is here with some exciting new alternatives to Thanksgiving turkey..."

George dives sideways to the bedside table and grabs his pen and paper. He scrawls down the website and writes in big black letters the words, RUSSELL HAZLETON. Surprising name. Very surprising morning.

LEXI
November 24th, 2009
Burbank, Los Angeles

It's all happening too quickly. One minute she's eating granola and daydreaming about George Bryce, and the next she's on television with barely any lipstick on and Russell's shoes to fill. It's going well. Really well. She'd practiced with Russell so many times yesterday, she virtually knows the material by heart. But when the camera rolls and she begins to talk, Lexi isn't just going through the motions anymore. As an ambassador for the burgeoning company, she genuinely feels enthusiastic and even, dare she say it, passionate. Russell's zeal has been truly contagious and Lexi is ready to spread the word.

The only weird part is when Sophie calls her Russell. It seems no one had thought to tell her about the last minute change.

When they cut to a commercial break, Sophie looks at her quizzically. "You're not Russell, are you?"

"No," says Lexi apologetically, her heart beating at an unnaturally fast pace. "He had an incident with a gooseberry. I'm Lexi Jacobs—nice to meet you."

"Well, you were very good on air. You'll be sure to get some interest."

"Thanks!" says Lexi, forgetting for a second why she was forced on air at all, until she sees Mildred heading towards her.

"Is he okay?" asks Lexi guiltily, trying to hide how thrilled she is with her performance.

"Oh, he's fine. What a little boy—all that fuss over a gooseberry. Kitty gave him a homeopathic remedy and he settled down immediately. No need to worry though, my dear, we saw you on the monitor and you were fabulous."

Lexi looks at her watch—it's not even six a.m. yet. At least she had her TV set to record at home. She'll have to have a popcorn party and invite everyone over to see her debut.

"Oh, it was nothing," says Lexi modestly, "I just tried to think about what Russell would want me to say. He's the brainchild behind all of this. He's the one."

"Perhaps, but you're a pretty close two. Have you ever considered a career in broadcasting, Lexi?"

Broadcasting? What did she mean—like a weather girl? Or maybe she could do one of those shows on MTV and then she might have a chance of meeting George? No—she wasn't trendy enough—was she? And old. Surely she was too old?

"Uh, no—not really."

"I doubt Russell will ever let you go, but if he does—call me."

"Call you? Okay..." says Lexi, questioning if this is some sort of sign she should be following. Did the gooseberry show up this morning to send her in another direction?

"You probably want to see the patient? He's lying down in my office."

"Yes, the patient, of course!" says Lexi, her five minutes of fame rapidly evaporating, as she obediently follows Mildred out of the studio.

GEORGE
24th November, 2009
Hollywood, Los Angeles

The band are on their way to pre-record *The Tonight Show* and George and Gabe are talking in the back of the car. Earlier that day George had given the website information of Let The Green Times Roll to Gabe, hell bent on meeting this woman once and for all, although he hasn't confessed that to Gabe. This was the ideal scenario. If Gabe could set something up, George could meet her like it was totally normal, instead of contacting her directly and being mistaken for a stalker. Gabe is dubious.

"We do our bit, George. I've got these things under control. You don't need to worry about it."

"Humour me, Gabe. I saw the CEO being interviewed and she's very impressive. Let's just meet her, okay, and hear a proposal. It's been on my mind for a while now. I mean look at all the flak U2 got for their tour this year. We need to do more to set an example for our fans."

"I don't know, George. I looked at the website. That Russell Hazleton person is a man anyway. He's got long hair, but he's definitely a man. He looked like a bit of a weirdo to me."

George is speechless, "She's not a man! I saw her on the telly this morning. I would have known if she was a man!"

"Well, I don't know—maybe he's a transvestite or something—or had a recent sex change. It is a man's name, isn't it?"

"You can't tell these days. I have a cousin called Rory, and she's a girl."

George is bewildered. Could it really be possible that after all these years, he's fallen in love with a transvestite? No. There must be some mistake. He's not that thick.

Gabe sighs, clearly running out of patience with the conversation. "Let me look into it when we get home. There's got to be companies doing the exact same thing in the UK. I'll ask around."

George takes a breath, "Gabe—set up a meeting for tomorrow. Trust me. My instincts are telling me something extremely positive could come of this. Let's meet with her before we go back and then we'll have something to compare."

"With him."

"With her!" This was madness. Why couldn't destiny be more straightforward?

"Fine, my friend. I'll happily set up the meeting in the morning, if only to prove to you that the bird's got balls!"

George laughs at the absurdity of it all, but inside his head he's imagining Russell walking into the room. He'll shake her hand. She'll most likely be ultra professional, not wanting to let on that she's a fan. Maybe she's not a fan. Maybe she was just dragged to the show by a friend? Does it even matter? What if she's married? What if... George tries to stop his thoughts from waywardly spinning. Anyway, all of this could come to nothing, but he can't risk passing up the chance of it coming to something. Someone. He can't risk missing the face of this woman again. The song is unfolding in his brain—the lyrics threading themselves together while the piano chords build in the background.

> *Third time lucky, running, crying, shining*
> *Your face on the screen, wondered where you'd been*
> *You had my heart and you didn't even know*
> *Holding my heart in the third, third row*

LEXI
November 24th, 2009
Venice, Los Angeles

Lexi is on her way back from Abbot Kinney having picked up some sandwiches for her and Russell. After the abrupt turn of events this morning, she had driven Russell home, still a bit shaky but relieved to have re-scheduled his breakfast with Mildred to dinner tomorrow night. Russell had just about recovered from the gooseberry, but not from the humiliation.

"I can't think what came over me. I mean usually a gooseberry might cause a slight rash on my forearms, but I've never had such an extreme reaction to one before."

"Maybe it was last minute nerves getting the better of you?" suggested Lexi.

"Oh, Lexi—I'm really sorry—I let us all down. And goodness only knows what Mildred thinks of me now, having so generously given me the opportunity to come on her show." Lexi was feeling a bit peeved that this conversation was all about Russell. What about her saving the day? What about some undying gratitude for her leaping into action when she hadn't even washed her hair that morning?

"Russell—please—Mildred is totally into you—it's so obvious. Anyway, situations of adversity often bring people closer together, right? She agreed to dinner, didn't she?"

"Yes, yes, I know. I'll have to redeem myself at dinner."

"Just don't order anything with gooseberries in it."

"Lexi, you really were a star today. I mean you were so professional and with no notice at all. To be perfectly honest, I was shocked." *That's more like it*, thought Lexi. *Pile it on. I need some love.*

"Russell, I just did what had to be done. It should have been you, but like I said before, it's almost certain that no one saw it."

"Don't be so sure of that. Mildred tells me they get very good ratings at that hour. I wouldn't be surprised if we heard from some small local businesses today. We could be off, off and away..."

Walking back to the house, Lexi wonders now if Russell might be right. How exciting if her appearance has sparked some interest. Just remembering being on camera makes her tingle. She hasn't had nearly enough spontaneity in her life. She opens the door to find Russell sitting at the kitchen counter with Boris on his lap, looking puzzled.

"What's up, Russell?" asks Lexi, handing him his alfalfa wrap.

"I've just had a rather odd phone call."

"Explain odd?"

"A gentleman called saying he wants to set up a meeting tomorrow morning to discuss our services."

"That's fantastic!" says Lexi, "So?"

"Well, that's just it... so nothing. He said he didn't want to give away too much information and would explain more tomorrow."

"Mysterious!" says Lexi. "Did he mention seeing me on TV?"

"I don't know. He didn't say. I arranged to meet him tomorrow morning at The Sunset Marquis Hotel at ten a.m."

"Ooh, that's right by my apartment. How cool is this, Russell? Your prediction might have been spot on—maybe this is our first client?"

"Maybe. Oh, Lexi, it's all rather fast, don't you think? I don't want to run before I can walk."

"Believe me, you'll be great tomorrow! You just had a bit of a setback this morning and it's knocked your confidence."

"I suppose," says Russell. "I mustn't let a gooseberry get in my way—not when the Climate Conference in Copenhagen is just around the corner. There are changes to be made. Global emissions to be cut, and meetings to be had! We have to start somewhere!"

"That's better!" says Lexi.

"You *will* come with me though?" asks Russell, looking concerned.

"To the meeting? Do you really think you need me there?"

"I'd like you to be there, Lexi," says Russell, letting Boris nibble an alfalfa sprout.

"Okay," says Lexi, enjoying the way this day is progressing. "I'd like to be there too."

GEORGE
25th November, 2009
West Hollywood, CA

LEXI
November 25th, 2009
West Hollywood, CA

George is nervous. More nervous than he's ever been. More nervous than when he's about to go on stage with fifty thousand people waiting to hear him sing. He even thought about what he was going to wear that morning. He tried on two different pairs of jeans and four T-shirts. He brushed his teeth three times. He's never felt the force of fate quite so strongly. He knows this is meant to be. The question is— meant to be what?

Lexi is curious. She has arranged to meet Russell outside the hotel at 9:50 a.m. She wonders why the phone guy was so secretive. The whole thing might end up to be a big anticlimax. She's wearing her Theory suit trousers with a white shirt and black flats, and she feels suitably polished. Last night Thesis had been on *The Tonight Show* and she had innocently watched it with Andrew and Carl.

"He's a hottie," Carl had volunteered, as George threw himself into "I Knew It," her second favorite song on the album.

Lexi had shrugged, "Yeah, he's not bad." She was working hard on deflating her crush. Fate had other destinations to take her to.

George has suggested to Gabe that the initial meeting be with just the two of them and then, if they're interested, they can approach the others with the ideas. Gabe is not trying to hide the fact that he has no intention of taking this any further.

"I promise you, George, we're doing fine. The tour buses all run on diesel. I'll put energy saving light bulbs in the studio. Buy home grown apples. What are they going to tell us that we don't already know?"

"Something," says George emphatically.

There is a knock at the door. George's heart starts to beat as fast as it did when he was running. Gabe walks across the room to open it, and from where he is standing, George sees a thin man with a long scrawny ponytail and red trousers. What? The man extends his hand to Gabe.

"Russell Hazleton, very good of you to contact me," Gabe quickly glances back at George as if to say—I told you so. Meanwhile, Russell seems to have a firm hold on Gabe's hand and is still vigorously shaking away.

"Hi Russell, thanks for coming at such short notice," says Gabe, opening the door wider and extricating his arm.

"And this is my partner," says Russell, moving aside, "Lexi Jacobs," and like an apparition, she appears, behind the red trousers. The third row. *You had my heart and you didn't even know.*

George moves forward to shake the real Russell's hand, which he lets go of very hastily and then he is there. Right in front of her. Skin touching skin. She has long elegant fingers. He can see the freckles scattered on her nose like confetti. He already has an urge to kiss them.

"Hello, Lexi, I'm George Bryce."

Recognition registers on her face and she looks startled. "I know," she says, "I mean, hello. Hello, nice to meet you, George." Gabe obviously didn't tell them beforehand who the meeting was with.

"Shall we sit then? Can I order you some tea, coffee, juice?" says Gabe, gesturing to a round table in the far corner of the suite with four chairs surrounding it.

Lexi is speechless. Literally. She can't speak. This isn't happening. How can this be happening? Of all the things she has imagined about the mystery meeting—this was certainly not one of them. Was she just shaking his hand? She feels lightheaded, as if any second now she might have one of those surreal out of body experiences and float above the table, observing the scene from the ceiling. Russell and her sitting at a table with George Bryce. *Her* George. *The* George. No. This isn't happening.

"I wouldn't mind some roibush tea, if it's on offer," says Russell, who she can see is blissfully ignorant of the curve ball that has just levelled her.

"Roy what?" says Gabe, "I don't know what that is. Is it an American thing? You might have noticed already that we're Brits."

"Actually," explains Russell, "It's South African—from a plant grown in Capetown. Very rich in vitamin C."

"Sounds good, maybe I'll try some. Lexi, would you like some tea? It is Lexi isn't it?"

Oh shit thinks Lexi, *I'm supposed to answer that. I need to say something.*

"No, I mean, yes, it's Lexi, but no, I don't want any roibush tea." So much for yesterday's confidence peak. Right now she sounds like a bumbling idiot.

"Me neither, Gabe. I don't want any roibush tea either, so looks like we already agree on something," says George, looking over at Lexi and smiling, hoping to make the situation less weird. He feels awful that he's responsible for putting her in this clearly uncomfortable position. He can't help but notice her neck. The small crevice where the collar bone dips inwards.

Lexi needs to pull herself together. Right now. She needs to behave like the adult woman she is. He's smiling at her. She wants to slide under the table. She tries to smile back but her mouth feels like it's made of air-dried clay.

Gabe picks up the phone and orders the tea and two large bottles of water. George wonders why the interviewer called Lexi "Russell" on the television? He's not certain where to put his hands.

"Well, what do you know, Russell, they had your roibush. Americans seem to be able to deliver on everything."

"Some of the time," says Russell.

"So down to business," says Gabe, "you're probably wondering why we asked you to meet with us today. George here is in a band. Quite a well known band called Thesis. You might have heard of them?"

"I think so," says Russell, tentatively. "Although I'm ashamed to say I'm not really that up to date on current music. I'm quite loyal to Neil Diamond."

"Forever in Blue Jeans," says George. "The Diamond's a

legend!" Russell looks elated. Lexi notes how easily he has put Russell at ease. She is very slowly beginning to reoccupy her body and allows her eyes to rest on George's face, but just for a second. He's lovelier this close up. He has a day's stubble and alarmingly blue eyes. *Oh my God*, thinks Lexi, *eat your heart out Radar3Girl.*

Gabe continues, "Well, I'm their manager, you see, and George seems to think that we might be able to use your consultancy service to give us some tips on how we could improve our commitment to the environment."

"I do," says George, sensing that Lexi has relaxed slightly. He's already thinking about how he can see her again. No wedding ring. They're leaving in a matter of hours. "I saw you on the telly yesterday talking about the business—it sounds really interesting."

He saw me on the telly? thinks Lexi. *Telly sounds so sweet! He thought I was interesting? This is too strange. From henceforth I will worship at the altar of the gooseberry...*

"I've explained to George, Russell, that we're already doing quite a lot but—"

Russell interrupts Gabe, "Do you go on tour?"

"Uh, yes," says Gabe, "I mean Thesis are up there, Russell, maybe not with Neil Diamond, but with the likes of Coldplay and Green Day. Our tours are big productions. We travel all over the world."

"How many people on the tour?" asks Russell, producing a notepad and pen from his hemp bag.

"Maybe a hundred."

"And what would you say, Gabe, that you are currently doing to support your green commitment?"

"Uh, well... we endorse Fair Trade chocolate. Some of the tour buses run on diesel. We uh, recycle..."

"What?"

"Paper... plastic bottles. That sort of thing..."

George and Lexi look at each other for a moment. He

smiles. This time she manages to smile back. Does he remember her from the concert? Of course not! This is all just some huge inexplicable coincidence. Meg is going to pee in her pants when she hears about this. Lexi is just relieved that she hasn't done the same.

George is imagining the release of "Third Row." Maybe it will go straight to number one? Doesn't every woman want a song written about her? Hopefully he and Lexi will be going out by then. If she'll have him, that is. She might have a boyfriend. For God's sake, she might not even like him. Plus going out with a musician is a nightmare. Always on tour. Mostly moody buggers. Why would she subject herself to that?

Russell is coming alive with enthusiasm. Lexi can see he's gearing up into action. *Here we go*, she thinks, *does this mean what I think it could mean?*

"Gabe, now please don't take offense, but 'that sort of thing' for a band in your position is just not good enough. You need to be reducing your carbon footprint, or in the least offsetting it. You need to be examining every aspect of the tour for energy efficiency. There are alternatives to diesel now —vegetable-based bio fuels. You need to ban all disposables at your concert venues and encourage fans to bring their own cups and drinks. Why not design a Thesis concert cup made from salvaged car tires, which you can sell on your website, while donating a percentage of the proceeds to Saving the Rainforest?" Gabe is beginning to look like he's being swiftly converted. There is a knock at the door. He stands up.

"Hold that thought, Russ, while I get your tea." Gabe sprints to the door and lets the waiter in with a tray of drinks.

George turns to Russell and Lexi, "You're full of ideas, Russell. I really respect what you two are up to," that came out a bit wrong. He didn't mean to imply that the two of them were up to anything together. But what if they were? Was Russell Lexi's boyfriend? No. No, he couldn't be.

"Thank you, George," says Russell.

"I hope you consider letting us advise you," says Lexi, experiencing a sudden burst of bravery. Surely this has happened for a reason? The concert. The gooseberry.

"I would love to let you," replies George, thinking that sounded a bit clumsy as well. Clumsy but true. He *would* love to let her.

Lexi is looking directly at George, trying her hardest not to concentrate on the few stray hairs curling irresistibly out of the top of his T-shirt. In person there is something more timid about him, very different than how he is on stage. She wonders where his ego is hiding.

"Here's your tea, Russell. South African, huh? Who knew?" Gabe sits back down at the table. "Where were we?"

"Recycled cups," says Russell, "but that's just an ice chip from the tip of a glacier. There's so much more you could do. Each and every one of us is responsible for climate change, fellas." Is Russell starting to get a bit of a British twang? Lexi wonders if he's going to leave here sounding like Noel Gallagher. Her courage is building by the second.

"Remember, being in the position you are," she says with authority, "you have a massive influence over a large demographic, many of them younger. Your music speaks to the hearts and souls of your fans, so why not let your decisive actions do the same?"

Gabe and George are both nodding their heads. Lexi takes a sip of her water. There is an expectant pause in the proceedings. Can Russell pull this off? Thesis are big time. Forget about running before walking, it would be more like climbing Mount Everest when he's only ever hiked a short trail.

George is nodding like a fool. He wants her to keep talking. He's watching her lips as they meet the edge of the glass and imagining the faint imprint they will leave behind. It doesn't really matter anymore what she is saying, he is way past needing to be convinced.

LEXI
November 26th, 2009
Pacific Palisades, Los Angeles

"Honey, just ignore St. Tropez."

"How am I supposed to ignore this, Mom?" asks Lexi, who is urgently trying to pry the puppy's teeth off the hem of her dress, while precariously balancing a pecan pie in the other hand.

Lexi's Mother grabs a can of Coke and shakes it violently around the puppy's face. It must be filled with coins or nails because it makes a horrifying racket. The dog ignores her, teeth stubbornly clamped, she continues to shake her head with glee.

"Mom, get her off—she's going to rip it!" says Lexi, also concerned that the pie might fall and crush the dog, who is not much larger than a rat.

"Stop it! Stop it! Stop it!" screeches Jeanette, while lunging at the manic ball of fluff.

"What the hell is going on in there?" shouts Lexi's dad, Al, from the other room.

"Mom's training the puppy," says Lexi sarcastically, managing finally to escape the dog and deliver the pie safely to the kitchen counter.

"Jeanie, why didn't you tell me our baby doll was home?" asks Al, appearing in the kitchen and engulfing Lexi in a big hug. The kind of hugs best given by dads on Thanksgiving.

"Looks like St. Tropez is her baby doll now. She's moved on from me, Dad," says Lexi, letting herself sink into her father's barrel chest. She inhales his familiar soapy smell and kisses him lovingly on the cheek.

"I told your mother, that dog's a lunatic. She pissed on the remote control right in the middle of *Project Runway*. I couldn't even get a season pass."

"Oh Puh-leaze Alfred! Lexi, you'd have thought the world was ending! You should have heard him rant. Poor St. Tropez almost died of shame. I've never seen such a sad little face..." she coos, scooping the puppy into her arms and nuzzling her wet nose.

"Gross, Mom—I'm not kissing you now."

"What do you wanna bet, Lex, that the dog gets the turkey today and we get Domino's delivered?"

They all laugh and Lexi feels a familiar warm sense of affinity. Despite having longed for a sibling when she was younger, to dilute the concentrated quality of her parents' attention, she wouldn't trade her family in for any other. Even as a child, when Jeanette and Al argued, they made certain to reassure Lexi afterwards that they were committed to working out the kinks.

"We're in this for the long haul..." her dad had repeatedly said.

Lexi had watched her friends' parents' marriages sliced in two through high school and even college, but Al and Jeanette had somehow managed to stay true to their word. It was a lot to live up to.

"So where's your crew? Your mom tells me we're feeding the masses today."

It occurs to her that her dad is right; she has invited everyone to spend Thanksgiving with them. Meg and Tim and the kids. Andrew and his new man, Carl. Even Russell, who it turns out has no immediate family and usually spends Thanksgiving with his vet. The vet and his wife have recently bought a time-share in Puerto Vallarta, and so Russell and Boris were planning on being alone.

"You must come over to my parents'," Lexi had offered yesterday, caught up in the moment. "We can celebrate our first client!"

"And give thanks for the blessings mother earth is sending our way," Russell had added.

"That too!" Lexi had agreed, finding it an effort to slow her accelerated pulse. She still couldn't believe that she had touched George Bryce's hand, not once, but twice in the space of an hour.

The meeting had ended with a verbal agreement that Russell and Lexi would come back to Thesis with a proposal on how they could slash the carbon output of the band, complete with ideas on how to promote and educate their fan base to do the same. They would charge a preliminary fee for this document, and if all were in agreement, a consultation contract would then be drawn up.

George and Gabe had both been incredibly enthusiastic. George had even gone as far as to say, "Look, it's likely that you'll both need to come to London at some stage to check out at our studio and meet the rest of the team. We can't really go forward with something like this without the consent of all the band. We're very egalitarian."

"Yes, of course," Lexi had agreed, holding one hand firmly on the edge of her chair, to prevent herself from jumping in the air like a ten-year-old.

"Let's not forget the carbon emissions generated by one transatlantic flight," Russell had been far too quick to point out. "We *could* do a video conference."

Lexi had restrained herself from punching him.

"Oh, right," George had replied, looking stumped.

"Or you *could* walk," said Gabe, "but I forgot—you don't do that in LA, do you?!" Russell had chuckled and with the impasse temporarily deflected, the meeting drew to a natural conclusion in a flurry of handshakes and thank yous. When George shook Lexi's hand again he had looked squarely into her eyes. "Really, really good to meet you, Lexi."

She had paused before saying, "Likewise," wondering if she should read anything into the two reallys?

But back in her parents' kitchen, today, the two reallys hover in her mind as if she had never heard them. As if the whole incident was just some warped fabrication concocted in her overactive imagination.

"The crew. Yes, Dad, everyone should be here in a minute. Mom, you better lock the mutt away if you don't want Jack trying to squeeze her in his pocket or Annabelle attempting to put lipstick on her."

"First the dog!" exclaims Al, "Now Meg's crazy kids. Then your ex-boyfriend and his lover. Let the wild rumpus start!" Al grabs hold of Lexi's hands and begins to dance her around the kitchen. She slips off her shoes and climbs onto the tops of his loafers, balancing on his feet while he sidesteps around the island, avoiding St. Tropez, who has begun to bark furiously again.

"Will you two never grow up?" says Jeanette, stirring the cranberry sauce, pretending to sound irritated.

"Working on it, Mom," says Lexi, aware that she feels truly hopeful for the first time in a long while. Could it be to do with George Bryce? She *has* been floating in some kind of weird and wonderful netherworld since walking out of his hotel suite. Or could it be her realization that finally becoming a grown-up means embracing the child she once was, rather than leaving her behind? Either way. She feels full of smiles and that's all that matters. The doorbell rings.

"Brace yourself," says Lexi, sliding off her dad's feet and heading for the hallway. "They have arrived!"

GEORGE
26th November, 2009
Virgin flight VS024, Heathrow Airport, London

On the move again. As the plane shudders to a halt on the slick runway, George watches the raindrops drive against the dirty windows. He exhales. It's been less than two weeks since they left London but he feels altered. His crash course collision into Fanny's bed. The sudden rip of the band turning on him. Or could it be that they were turning *to* him? He's still trying to work that one out. The acoustic show and finding Lexi.

Finding Lexi.

Every hour of the plane journey he had committed a different detail of their meeting to memory, until he had a collage of fragments—her tanned ankle bone; the melting tone of her voice; the arch of her left eyebrow; the way she spoke with her hands as if shaping an invisible sculpture. George wants to see her again. He wants to put the pieces together and decipher the whole picture. She must have shown up in that third row for a reason. Now he just needs to find out why?

LEXI
November 26th, 2009
Pacific Palisades, Los Angeles

Three hours into Thanksgiving festivities and Jack and Annabelle are under the dining table with three American dolls, two Transformers, a can of Miracle Whip and Jeanette's half deflated core ball. St. Tropez is passed out in the corner having managed to devour a hefty portion of pecan pie and countless greasy roast potatoes, surreptitiously dropped by the children. Andrew, Carl, and Russell are ensconced in conversation about the merits of varying brands of aluminum-free deodorant, while Tim and Jeanette are in the kitchen embarking on loading the dishwasher. Al is asleep—sprawled on the couch with his reading glasses halfway down the bridge of his nose and his hands resting comfortably on his expanding belly.

Lexi is sitting next to him, stuffed to the eyeballs. Stuffed on top of stuffed. The sun is still shining and shafts of late afternoon light decorate the carpet with luminous stripes. She is contemplating helping Tim and her mother with the dishes.

Meg appears from under the table where she has managed to extract the can of Miracle Whip from her delinquent children, a curl of white foam still hanging from the nozzle.

"I'm not on a short list for the good parenting award," she says, wiping the remaining cream away with her fingertip and licking it clean.

"Well, you should be," says Lexi, "you allow your kids to be kids, not robots. That's got to be worth something."

"Your mom's a saint letting us create chaos every year," says Meg, flopping down on the couch next to Lexi.

"She loves it. She's not getting one of these from me anytime soon, so your two are most welcome."

"Do you think that's why she got the dog, as a replacement grandchild?"

"Don't start, Meg!" says Lexi, feeling rather immune to Meg's judgements today. Who cares what she thinks. She hasn't told her yet about what happened yesterday. Part of her wants to protect it forever. Keep it close so it can't get contaminated by Meg's envy or hysteria. Meg would completely flip out and try and own George or something, as if he had belonged to her first. Isn't that what most fans feel? A sense of possession over the object of their desire? Isn't that what she felt only forty-eight hours ago? Except that now that she's met him, George isn't just George Bryce anymore—lead singer of Thesis—super cute English boy. He's become dimensional. More real. She knows how he sits with his feet slightly fidgety, crossed at the ankle. She's seen the paisley shaped chocolate-colored birthmark that appeared unexpectedly underneath his watch strap when it slid ever so slightly down his wrist.

"Don't worry, since Mr. Hilarious, I've vowed not to interfere in your love life again. I'm trusting the universe will give you what you need without my well intentioned meddling." Lexi is a bit taken aback by Meg's uncharacteristic hands-off approach.

"You are?"

"Yes I am. By the way—Russell's a hoot. I like his pony-tail. So what's this impending announcement he was talking about at lunch? I'm very intrigued."

Lexi is tempted to tell Meg about Thesis right now. Her expression would be priceless, but she had agreed with Russell that it was best to keep all details under wraps until they had signed on the dotted line. She's going to have to tell her soon though, because when Meg eventually finds out, she'll never forgive Lexi for holding back.

"I can't say just yet, Meggy. Boss's orders. But trust me— it's worth waiting for."

Earlier at lunch, Russell had stood up to make a toast, ostensibly very much at ease in the midst of such an eclectic group. "Firstly I'd like to thank Jeanette and Al for welcoming me into their family on such a special day."

"Mi casa es su casa," piped up Jeanette, already a bit tipsy.

"I am very thankful for the arrival of your spirited and intelligent daughter on my doorstep only a matter of weeks ago."

"Hear, hear..." said Andrew, taking his turn to interrupt.

"It is because of Lexi that the green times are finally rolling and we might have an exciting announcement to make in a few weeks' time."

"Are you going to marry Auntie Lex Lex?" said Anna-belle, carefully scraping train tracks into her yams with a fork. She was promptly shushed very loudly by Meg. *Even the two-year-old wants me married off* Lexi had thought, amused.

Russell was undeterred, "No, no, but it is quite a treat to meet *everyone* here and may I take the liberty of suggesting we join in raising our glasses to the greatest mother of all—

mother earth—in hopes that we continue to allow her to heal..."

At which point, Al had leaned over to Lexi and whispered, "Is that guy gay too?"

GEORGE
26th November, 2009
Maida Vale

George usually enjoys coming home. Relishes sleeping in his own bed. Drinking juice straight from the carton. Ordering a curry from his local Indian and eating all the papadoms without having to share. His flat is an antidote to his real life, which doesn't actually feel real at all. Video shoots. Recording sessions. Radio stations. Concerts. People surrounding him all day long asking him questions, checking up on him, looking after him. Yes—returning to his flat makes him feel normal again—at least while he's inside with the door closed. Except not today. Today when he walked in, he felt like he had stumbled upon an IKEA showroom. His own flat suddenly feels as impersonal as a hotel room. The grey sofa looks rigid and new. The walls are bare, because when is there ever time to get anything framed? The TV is oversized. The dark wooden floors are too shiny. His bedroom is sparse. A blue striped duvet cover and a pile of comic books on a bedside table. Something in George feels desperate. What's gone wrong? Hadn't everything he had ever wished for and was convinced would never happen come true? Almost everything.

George opens his fridge and is greeted by three bottles of beer, a tub of mouldy cream cheese and a wrinkled tomato. Luckily he was resourceful enough to have left a mint Aero bar in the bottom drawer, which he unwraps eagerly now. He collapses onto the sofa and begrudgingly decides to call his parents, whom he hasn't spoken to in almost a month. His dad picks up the phone.

"Hi, Dad."

"Well, hello there, son, we haven't heard from you in a while."

"I've been in the States."

"Oh. Well, it's been raining here."

"Really."

"Is it there?"

"What?"

"Raining. Is it raining in London?"

"It was but not right now. But I guess it might, again."

"Been busy, have you?"

"Yes. We just got back from LA. We're working on material for the next album and we've got the second leg of the tour coming up, it's been—"

"George, your mother's motioning for the phone, son. She's on her way out. See you at Christmas then." George wills himself to toughen up and not be affected by his dad's lack of interest. It's not as if he's not used to it.

"Yeah. Christmas, Dad. Bye." He listens to a muffled exchange between his parents as the phone is handed over.

"Hello, George. Dorothy from the post office saw a photograph of you in the newspaper the other day. She said she thought your hair looked like it needed a cut. I said I wouldn't know, because it's been so long since I've seen you."

"Hello, Mum."

"Are you coming for Christmas then?"

"Yes, of course. Look, I hope it's okay if Duncan comes with me. His family's in Australia and he's not going back this year. I invited him to join." George had felt sorry for Duncan in a weak moment. Now he was regretting the idea.

"I suppose that's okay. As long as it's just the two of you." He can hear the reluctance in his mother's voice and guesses she is imagining him and Duncan pitching up on

Christmas Eve with a gaggle of groupies at their heels and a wheelbarrow full of cocaine. Not that he could put anything past Duncan these days. Perhaps he should invite Fanny to join, who would likely arrive in a Christmas pudding bra. That would go down well.

"Yes, Mum. Just the two of us."

"Have you heard from your sister? She was going to give you some ideas of what to get the boys as presents."

"She can't control everything," says George, noticing the familiar clench of resentment constricting his jaw when Polly and the triplets are mentioned. "I'll get them whatever I want."

"But last year you gave them bubblegum machines when we were all quite certain you knew of their allergy to e-numbers."

"I didn't know. They're kids. Kids like bubblegum. What does she want me to get them, brussels sprouts?"

His mother sighs, "Archie bounced so hard on his bed, George, he made a hole in the ceiling. Your father spent two days re-plastering. Maybe an educational game?"

"Maybe. Look, I've got to go, Mum, that's my doorbell. I'll see you on Christmas Eve, okay?"

"Okay, dear. Goodbye then."

"Bye, Mum."

George hangs up the phone and breathes in the silence. His mind wanders to the band. His other family. The one he had fooled himself into believing wasn't dysfunctional. Was everyone sitting around now talking behind his back? His family gossiping about his puffed up self-importance? The boys complaining about his obsessive control? If so, George is ready to stop playing the victim and see, for once, if he can begin to prove them all wrong.

LEXI
December 5th, 2009
Franklin Canyon, Los Angeles

Unable to contain herself for much longer, Lexi has decided to
tell Meg about the meeting. Tim is staying with the kids while
Lexi and Meg hike up Franklin Canyon. Lexi thinks it might
be easier to break the news while they are walking, instead of
sitting face to face. Meg has been her closest confidante for so
many years of her life, but best friendships come with all sorts
of baggage—neat little make-up pouches with lots of fun
lipsticks and eye shadows, and big bulky suitcases filled with
unwashed laundry. She's pretty certain this revelation might
unearth some dirty clothes.

"So you know the big mystery client of ours?" she
begins, already feeling her heart rate building as they start the
incline.

"Have you done the deal?" asks Meg, taking a swig of
water.

"Not quite, but I couldn't really keep it from you any
longer."

"So? Tell me already!" It hasn't rained in months. Clouds
of dust are billowing around their feet.

"It's Thesis."

"Very funny, Lex. No really—who's the client?"

"It is, Meg. It's Thesis. Russell and I went to their hotel. I
met George Bryce and his manager."

"You what?" Meg stops and pulls on Lexi's arm,
attempting to get her to turn around. Lexi resists and keeps
walking.

"I met George Bryce and his manager. It's all been a bit
surreal."

"You met George Bryce. You met George Bryce and you
didn't tell me?"

Lexi can hear the fire in Meg's voice.

"I *am* telling you. I wanted to tell you before, it's only that Russell was concerned about confidentiality and—"

Meg starts walking again, pumping her arms frenziedly. "I can't actually believe this! You met George? Ever since we went to the concert, I've been wondering if he really was looking at me that night. I've even imagined what I would say to him if I ever bumped into him. And now—you've actually... met him. *You*! It's not fair. It's just like high school—it was always you who got everything!"

Lexi had been expecting this conversation to be weird, but this was even weirder than she could ever have given Meg credit for.

"I can't believe you're saying this, Meg. I thought you'd be pleased for me. This could mean that my career is finally taking off. And anyway, you're forgetting one thing. No, three things! No, four things! We're not in high school anymore. You're married. You have two gorgeous kids, for God's sake. *You're* the one who has everything." Lexi's heart is pulsating in her throat as she realizes that 'everything' is a word even stupider than 'perfect'. *Everything* is different for everyone and her definition is rapidly shifting.

"I *know* I'm married," says Meg, despairingly, "but I deserve a break from Tim, don't I? I wasn't going to leave him for George anyway—I was just going to have an affair. Being *married* is not all that it's cracked up to be."

"Exactly! Then why are you always trying to persuade me to do it?"

"Because—because... I don't know. We grew up believing in it—didn't we? Mr. Darcy? Maria and Captain Von Trapp? Ross and Rachel? You and Andrew..."

"Me and Andrew? Well if that relationship didn't shatter your illusions, I don't know what would."

"I know but at the time it seemed so romantic."

"At the time." Lexi's temples are throbbing. She can feel the sweat dripping down the back of her neck.

"It's just that George Bryce has been like a secret bar of chocolate I've been hiding away. When life gets yucky, I take him out and steal a corner." What with Lexi's appetite for fantasy and Meg's imaginary liaisons, it's a wonder George still has time to write music.

"I get it, but he's real, you know. He probably has a girlfriend. He leaves the toilet seat up. He burps."

"He does? Did he burp in your meeting?!"

"No! But he could have done."

"What was he like?"

Lexi hesitates before answering. "He seemed nice. I'm not sure yet."

"Sexy?"

"In a boyish kind of way but this is going to be entirely professional." She sounds extremely believable, after all she has herself to convince as well.

"Of course. I know I'm acting crazy. I *am* happy for you, Lex, really I am. It's an awesome opportunity. Can I meet him?"

Lexi pauses, horrified at the prospect of Meg completely embarrassing both of them in front of George. Any association to an obsessed fan would be disastrous.

"I don't even know if I'll see him again. They might not even use us."

"They will. I know they will."

But will they? Lexi and Russell have been working overtime all week beginning to compile a PowerPoint for the band, covering all aspects of how to reduce and offset their carbon footprint. Russell has even discovered a manufacturer of guitars sourced from non-endangered wood grown in sustainable forests, as well as proposing a line of recycled products for the Thesis website made from CDs, vinyl and one of a kind personal items from the band. Lexi has been loving every minute, educating herself on renewable energy sources and the most effective methods to offset carbon emissions.

Between learning from Russell and putting in her own hours of research, she's now quite the expert too. They should be finished with the presentation next week, at which point Russell will talk the band through it on iChat. Beyond that? Lexi has no clue and is trying not to speculate.

They continue up the dusty hill without speaking, quite clear there is no turning back. She knew telling would inevitably change something. When Meg gets over her shock, she'll definitely ask for details, and all Lexi really wants to do is keep them to herself.

GEORGE
5th December, 2009
Maida Vale recording studios, London

This isn't the first time George and the band have recorded at the legendary BBC Maida Vale studios, but every time he enters the building he feels as if he is falling backwards in time, caught up in a historical vortex with hundreds of other musicians who have walked through these doors. The place still smells of cigarettes smoked in 1975. In addition to four large performance spaces there is mostly a jumbled warren of rooms, overflowing with music paraphernalia and obsolete equipment. Radio One records their famous *Live Lounge* sessions in studio V, which is why Thesis are here today. They are going to sing "I Knew It" as well as a cover version of a Sugababes song, intentionally chosen to be ironic. George's flat is two streets away, and he enjoys knowing this landmark of a building is so close to him, peeling and palatial in the midst of rows of mansion block flats. Living nearby helps him feel connected to his calling.

The techs are just setting up the room for rehearsal. Simon is eating a Mexican chicken wrap and texting Stacey. Mark is reading *The Economist*. Duncan is drinking coffee, which only serves to boost his already wired state of mind.

George is toying with the lyrics of "Third Row" and has made the unprecedented decision to show it in its embryonic state to Simon, Mark, and Duncan all at the same time, as well as asking Mark to share his lyric ideas. Gabe is dashing around the studio, multitasking and ensuring everyone is on top of everything they need to be. He catches George's eye, "You okay?"

"Super," says George, "Well up for this."

"Yeah—you'll own it."

"By the way," asks George, as nonchalantly as possible, "have you heard from Russell and Lexi yet in LA?"

"Actually I did. He sent me an e-mail saying that they'll be ready with a proposal soon. You know what, mate, I've got to say I completely misjudged those two. I thought it would be rubbish, but I was really impressed with their approach. You were right."

"I shouldn't say I told you so. But I told you so."

"Yeah, yeah, yeah. I'm looking forward to seeing what they get back to us with."

"They *should* come here at some point, don't you think? To, you know, look at the studio and everything and talk to the tour manager."

"Let's check out what they come up with first, but to be honest, I wouldn't mind meeting her again anyway."

George's stomach lurches. Great. Gabe fancies Lexi. This is not on. What's he supposed to say, *hey matie, that's my future girl you're imagining naked*? No, he can't possibly reveal how much he likes her. For a start, if any of the others find out, he'll never hear the end of it. He wants things to manifest naturally now, not become a spectator sport. If he just ignores the comment, though, Gabe will assume she's fair game. He needs to think quickly.

"Yeah, well, I'm sure those two were an item," George says, fumbling to find a reason to put Gabe off.

"Seriously? Her and Russell?"

"Gabe, it was so obvious—the chemistry between them. I can't believe you didn't pick up on it. I reckon they might even be married."

"Married. Really? Was she wearing a ring?"

"Pretty certain she was."

"Bummer. I guess I'll concentrate on the bio fuel."

"Yup."

"I don't really have time for a girlfriend anyway."

"You really don't. We're far too high maintenance... and all the travelling and everything, it would never last. Mark and Anna have to work so hard on it, you know. I see a relationship counsellor in their future."

"You do?"

"Don't say that I told you, okay?" says George, snapping shut his notebook. This detour seems to have done the trick. He hopes he's not laying it on too thick.

"No, no I won't. Counselling. I didn't realize." Gabe looks concerned.

"It happens." George drums his pencil on the cover of his notebook and points across the room, "Karen's waving. Must be ready for rehearsal."

He stands and loops his arms around the back of his head, feeling quite pleased with himself, for all the wrong reasons.

LEXI
December 11th, 2009
Venice, Los Angeles

The day of the mega presentation has arrived. Russell has orchestrated the whole thing with precision, instructing Gabe to have access to two computers in London, one on which he and the band can watch the PowerPoint, and one on which they can video conference with Russell and Lexi.

"I don't really need to be in on the conference, do I?"

asks Lexi, suddenly feeling acutely self-conscious about seeing George again, even if there are thousands of miles and millions of pixels between them.

"Of course you do!" says Russell, aghast. "Lexi, we're in this together now—remember? I told you if things took off we could become partners and this might very well be the beginning of things taking off."

"I know. I know. I just don't like being on camera." Lexi takes a sip of her green tea while it is still too hot and burns the tip of her tongue. "Ouch."

"Well, that certainly didn't come across on *Good Morning LA*. Mildred said you were born to be in front of the camera. In fact, she was talking about it again only last night."

"Oooh. You saw Mildred again last night? What would that be, date number three?"

Russell raises his eyebrows, "Four actually."

"How have you managed to sneak one in without me noticing?"

"She came over here with Cherub on the spur of the moment. She's been chewing her tail, poor thing, and Mildred wanted to get my advice on cat supplements."

"A double date!" says Lexi, opening up her mail application. "I'm sure you pointed her in the right direction, Russell."

"Actually, we spent quite some time googling and we discovered that a cat's tail quivers when it's in love."

Lexi laughs. "You did, did you? Well? Was Cherub's tail quivering?"

"No, but I think mine was!"

"Russell Hazleton!"

"I didn't know it could happen this quickly, Lexi."

"I've heard tell it can happen even quicker. In seconds. Not that I have any experience of that," she hastily adds.

"We just seem to be on the same wavelength—about everything. Plus she's so supportive of the business. She's been telling everyone."

"Here's the proof," says Lexi, "we have about twenty new e-mails all making inquiries. Russell, I think it's wonderful, you and Mildred are great together."

"I can't put my finger on it, Lexi, but it's like you've been my good luck charm. Ever since you answered my ad, things have really turned around for me."

Lexi feels like crying. What's with the weeping all the time? Has she become a crier? It's got to stop. She much prefers it when she's in control of her emotions. "I have that effect on people," she says, trying to rush the moment on. "Now, what time is it in London?" Lexi checks her watch.

"It's five in the afternoon," answers Russell, "and we're set to go in fifteen minutes. I'm feeling very optimistic. I'm sure Gabriel and George will be most interested in our presentation. I've downloaded some of their albums as well and I think they're really rather catchy. Not my kind of thing, mind you, but very appealing all the same."

Lexi nods, thinking she must sneak to the bathroom and check her hair in the next ten minutes. "Yes, they are," she says. "Very appealing."

GEORGE
11th December, 2009
Camden, London

LEXI
December 11th, 2009
Venice, Los Angeles

George doesn't know where to put his hands. He is trying to concentrate on the computer moving through the slides of the PowerPoint but all he can think about is Lexi. If he glances over at the laptop, he can see her sitting beside Russell, looking very composed, one leg crossed over the other with her hands resting in her lap. Her lips look deliciously pink.

But he's not supposed to be looking at her. He's supposed to be paying attention to the presentation. When he does pay attention, he thoroughly approves. They've come up with some stellar ideas, but he's finding it impossible to stay focused. When they'd first popped up on the screen she seemed very relaxed and confident, waving a casual greeting. He had felt intensely uncomfortable and only managed to raise up the palm of his hand like he was giving a stupid stop signal. Now the final chord for "Third Row" which he's been grappling with for days has unexpectedly arrived in his head. *She's my muse* he decides. *Even a trace of her brings me to life.* He wants to get to the piano. He wants to pick up the laptop and dance it around the room.

Lexi is trying to sit still. This is the strangest set-up. She can see the whole band and Gabe on the screen in front of her, watching another computer running the PowerPoint, as Russell eloquently talks them through each slide. He has reminded her to join in whenever she wants to add something or expand on what he's saying, but she doubts she will. When the video meet-up first began she had attempted a jovial wave at the screen and said "Hello again," and then had felt incredibly foolish, as if she had made the most senseless comment imaginable. She thinks it's best to say as little as possible.

Seeing George again reminds her that they are worlds apart. Worlds and oceans. Dreaming about him is ridiculous. Anyway, he's far too cool for school and certainly too cool for her. He barely managed to raise his hand earlier on and now he looks distracted. It was different in person. He's very likely bipolar. Perhaps this whole clean cut image is just a mask. A clean living musician? It's a blatant oxymoron. Clean cut to a rock star most likely translates into shooting up heroin five times a week instead of seven. Smoking dope instead of crack. Having only the occasional orgy. Looking at him now she guesses he is totally stoned, along with the drummer who appears to be twitching. She is completely prepared to forget about any further useless daydreaming, when he turns his head towards the camera and smiles, like a fourth grader sneaking a peek at a girl in the neighboring row of desks. At this point, Lexi forgets everything else instead.

***

"So there you have it, chaps—a comprehensive overview of what is possible for Thesis. The word possible being the key here. Because of course how much difference you make in the world, and how exactly you inspire your hundreds of thousands of fans to emulate you, is *your* choice. Everything seems impossible until you give it a go, right? I dare say the four of you would have once thought it impossible to reach the heights you have achieved today. Had that thought stopped you, well, you would never have continued striving. It's when we talk ourselves out of things that the possibilities sadly disappear." Russell pauses for effect. "Questions?"

George loves Russell. He says all the right things. Of course he's not going to stop striving for Lexi. If he doesn't try, he'll never know.

Was Russell a mind reader on top of everything else? Lexi thinks she might add writing horoscopes to his repertoire. Is that what she's been doing recently, talking herself out of the possibility of love? Surely not! She just doesn't want to set herself up for disappointment anymore. Look where all her fantasizing has led her in the past. Russell's talking carbon emissions, not romance. She's reading meaning where none exists. Or is she?

"Exceptionally wise words, Russell," says Gabe, brimming enthusiasm.

"Yeah," says Simon, "I really like the ideas for the product line and the special edition items—wicked. It captures the uniqueness we always envision for the band. You've really understood that."

Mark nods in agreement, "Defo. This is the direction we need to be taking."

"Russ, is it true, mate, that the biggest problem with the global warming is because cows fart so much?" George can't believe Duncan's just said that. Now Lexi's going to think they're a bunch of adolescent plonkers.

Lexi can't believe the drummer's just said that. She's loath to quote Bradley but seriously, that's hilarious.

"Actually, Duncan," says Russell, "as ludicrous as it sounds—there is an element of truth in your question. When cows pass wind they release a gas called methane which penetrates the ozone layer contributing to harmful environmental effects."

"See guys, I know my shit!" says Duncan proudly, flicking an elastic band at Simon.

"Yup, well no cows on the tour, so that's a relief. Shall we get back to what effect *we're* having on the environment?" says George, desperately attempting to restore order.

"I reckon *your* farts might rival a cow's any day!" retorts Duncan.

Lexi wants to laugh. At this stage it's hard not to.

"Please forgive his retrograde behaviour," says George, "Duncan's renowned for lowering the tone of the proceedings." Bloody Duncan. Lexi must be appalled.

"Might I suggest if there are no further questions that you take a little while to discuss matters and get back to us," says Russell. "Once you give us the go ahead, we can have our lawyers draw up a consultation contract." *Wow* thinks Lexi, silently applauding Russell. Lawyers? She didn't even know they had any. If he's nervous, he's not letting it show a bit. Meanwhile, she's been sitting beside him mute.

George likes the sound of that. Contract means a deal. Deal means contact. Contact means he can see Lexi again—in the flesh.

"Sounds good!" says Gabe. "Great to see you both and we'll be in touch very soon."

"Yeah, wonderful, Gabe," says Lexi, not wanting to log out having barely opened her mouth.

"Cheerio then, gentlemen," says Russell and presses exit.

GEORGE
11th December, 2009
Camden, London

George relaxes back in his chair. He's glad that's over with. Now things can get moving.

"Did that chick just say 'You're wonderful, Gabe'?" asks Duncan, who obviously has no intention of maturing anytime soon.

"What?" says Gabe, looking very disconcerted. "She said I was wonderful? Did you hear that George?"

George is supremely agitated. "No I did *not* hear that, Gabe."

"She's a hottie, huh. I say let's go for it!" Duncan drums on the table with his fingers.

This is getting worse by the second. Now they're all after her. It's extremely doubtful that she's unattached. She appears to put a spell on every man she meets.

"Look guys, there's nothing to go for, those two are married!" says George, a little louder than intended.

"I mean, let's go for the contract," says Duncan. "But really? Married? That Russell has got it going on, man!"

"Who cares," says George, dismissing the fact that he's blatantly making this up. Anything to get them off her scent. Anyway, for all he knows they might well be married. "Let's get back to the contract. What do you two think?" he asks, turning pointedly to Mark and Simon. George is working on learning how to share.

"I think we should use them. It seems like money well

spent to me," says Mark. "Anyway, by all accounts things aren't going well in Copenhagen at the summit, so it's up to individuals to do whatever we can."

"I'm in," says Simon, "Russell's a dude."

"Excellent," says Gabe, "love it when a plan comes together. I'll call them tomorrow and seems fairly likely that we'll need to get them over here pretty soon to do their eco audit."

George releases a breath. Just what he's been waiting for. So, he might have to fend off a few rivals or even overthrow the current king, but he refuses to be deterred.

LEXI
December 11th, 2009
Venice, Los Angeles

Russell looks elated. "If I do say so myself, I think that went swimmingly."

"It did," agrees Lexi, "there was nothing for me to add, you were on a roll. I'd be very surprised if they didn't say yes!"

Russell picks up Boris and kisses him on the lips.

"Boris, my dear, I think you and I should take our lady friends out for a celebratory drink this evening."

Lexi is trying her hardest to hold onto excited, but just underneath the surface something more like fear is gripping the sides of the rug ready to pull. Everything is happening so quickly and her stupid juvenile crush is preventing her from even seeming vaguely professional.

"Russell, I'd love to, but I'm supposed to be meeting up with Andrew and Carl tonight."

Russell looks flustered, "Oh, right—I meant Mildred and Cherub, but of course we'd be happy for you to join us. We could make an evening of it..."

"No, no of course not," says Lexi, mortified, "that

wouldn't be very romantic now would it? I'm all set to meet up with the boys. In fact I was going to ask you about the lawyer you mentioned, because Carl is a company lawyer, you know. I think he specializes in contracts. Maybe we could use him?"

"What an inspired idea. I haven't actually talked to my lawyer since registering the name of the company, and he was most unsuitable. It turns out he had a cat phobia and spent a good portion of our meeting having heart palpitations."

"Well, that's settled then. I'll talk to Carl tonight." Lexi goes back to her computer and sits down. "Now, let's get clicking on these inquiries. If even a quarter of them turn into something, it looks as if next year could be very busy!"

Next year. Just around the corner. In her original master plan, next year would have been her fifth wedding anniversary with Andrew. They were supposed to have had two kids by now and a dog. Suddenly she remembers. George. The family dog was going to be called George. Lexi thinks how odd it is that the only thing that has managed to survive her outdated fantasy is that one single word.

GEORGE
24th December, 2009
M4 motorway, England

Duncan has his feet on the dashboard and is smoking. The open passenger window is letting in the rain and George can see from the corner of his eye that the inside of the door is getting drenched. He is already annoyed and their two days at his parents' house have barely begun. "Dunc, give it a rest, will you, and close the window. It's bloody freezing in here."

"Yes Dad," says Duncan, chucking the butt away. "Mellow out, mate. It's Christmas, we're supposed to be full of the joys of the season. How bad can it be?"

"You've met my parents."

"They're cool, George. I mean a bit conservative maybe, but they do say the apple doesn't fall far from the tree."

"Shut up. I'm nothing like them. I'm exactly the opposite to them. In fact I would venture to say my entire personality developed as an adverse reaction to the three people I lived with." The motorway is dense with cars. George changes lanes to try to get in the one that's moving. The moment he does, it grinds to halt.

"Get me a violin, mate. My dad was a fucking lunatic. He was an Aussie butcher—it can't get worse than that. He smelled like meat and carried a cleaver."

Duncan doesn't talk much about his family in Melbourne. In fact, in the seven years George has known him, he's only been back to Australia once. Perhaps there's a reason after all for Duncan's manic behaviour. Yet another human attempting to dodge his DNA, only to discover that he's shackled to it for the rest of forever.

"Did he use the cleaver outside of the office?" asks George, thinking that maybe he doesn't really want to know the answer.

"He threatened to, mate. He's a barbarian. But he did get me into drumming. He used to listen to Ozzy Osbourne. I drummed my way through my teens to drown him out."

"Ozzy or your dad?"

"Both! He thinks what we're doing is rubbish. Last time we spoke he told me I'd sold out to the sissies. Anyway, enough about him, he can fuck off. All he wants from me now is money."

George can see the exit looming. At least Duncan's dad wants something from him. George would be happy to give his parents money, but they don't even seem to think he's worthy of that. *Two days* George tells himself, hating the fact that he continues to show up at all.

LEXI
December 24th, 2009
West Hollywood, Los Angeles

Christmas Eve. The night before the big day. When she was a little girl, Lexi remembers hours spent baking cinnamon cookies shaped like reindeer. She would meticulously place a small cranberry at the end of each of their noses until she got to Rudolph, who was honored with a bright red maraschino cherry. Lexi was the only one in the house allowed to eat Rudolph.

Tonight, she has agreed to accompany Andrew and Carl to their friend Johnnie's party. Johnnie is Carl's partner at the law firm. Lexi first met him a week ago when she went with Russell to discuss drawing up legal contracts. Johnnie and Carl had given valuable advice and agreed to act on their behalf. It had all been very professional, both of them dapper in grey suits and crisp white shirts. This evening, however, is a slightly different story. Johnnie answers the door to his apartment dressed in a Santa Claus hat, a white beard decorated with silver sequins and a short red jumpsuit. He is holding a half bottle of Dom Pérignon. The room is bouncing behind him and the Scissor Sisters are blaring from all open windows.

"Merry Christmas, campers! Come on in and meet the elves!" Andrew, Carl and Lexi are ushered into the heaving throng.

"Did I mention that Johnnie's a wild cat?" yells Carl over the music, obviously noticing Lexi's slightly uncertain expression.

"No, you didn't!" she yells back.

"Have a drink!" says a Mrs. Claus, dressed in a velvet cape and long false eyelashes. A lime green cocktail is thrust into Lexi's hand.

"Thank you!" she replies, but can barely hear herself speak.

Within minutes, Andrew and Carl have disappeared into the center of the room where a large crowd has gathered to dance. Lexi guesses it will take a few green drinks until she can join them. She spots double doors leading onto a balcony and heads in that direction.

GEORGE
24th December, 2009
Stanford in the Vale, Oxfordshire

Surprisingly, his family seem to have formed a welcoming committee outside of the cottage. As he turns the corner into the lane, George can make out his parents—Mum and Dad in coordinating red and green jumpers; Polly who looks like she's put on weight since the last time he saw her; her husband, Martyn, always smiling inanely; and the triplets, with pasty white faces and identical outfits.

Duncan gets out first and high fives the boys.

"Thing One. Thing Two. Thing Three. How's it hanging, dudes?"

Thing Two glares at Duncan. "You smell like the pub. Mummy says the pub is a bad place."

"Padstow! Be polite," says Polly, tapping him on the top of his head.

"No worries. I respect a kid with the balls to say it how it is. Polly, lay one on me." Duncan leans in and kisses Polly smack on the lips. This even stops Martyn from smiling for a second, but he manages to shake George's hand, "Nice to see you, brother-in-law." George guesses Martyn has always hated him as much as Polly does.

George goes to give his parents a perfunctory hug. "Welcome home, son," says his dad. The word *home* jars.

"All right, Dad?"

"Hello dear. You *are* looking awfully tired," says his mother, patting him on the back. She smells like sage and onion stuffing.

"Well, I'll be sure to sleep a lot while I'm here, Mum," says George, beckoning to Duncan. "You remember Duncan?"

"Mr. and Mrs B.—thanks for the invite. Much appreciated." Duncan swoops in on Lawrence and Harriet who appear to be cowering. Meanwhile, George can no longer avoid greeting Polly.

They hug stiffly.

"Hello, George. Have you noticed the boys' t-shirts? I bought them off the Internet especially. Aren't they fab?"

George looks down. Archie, Padstow and Trevor are all wearing red t-shirts printed with black electric guitars and the words, "MY MUM ROCKS."

"Fab," agrees George, not daring to voice his real opinion.

As the motley group begin to shuffle inside, George feels a tug on his sleeve. He looks down to find one of the triplets (possibly Trevor? He can't always tell the difference) staring up at him with big blue eyes, not dissimilar to his own. "Uncle George?"

"Yes, mate?"

"I hate this t-shirt. Mum forced me to wear it. The label is itching my back."

George laughs and ruffles Trevor's hair. Maybe he has an ally after all?

"Don't worry, Trev. I'll cut the label out for you when we get inside." Trevor smiles gratefully. Obviously, George has not mistaken him for one of his brothers.

Once in, Harriet shows Duncan to Polly's old bedroom, now kitted out for the triplets.

"I call the top bunk!" yells Duncan.

"Polly and the boys will stay at their house tonight, Duncan, so you can have this room all to yourself. Anyway,

George likes to sleep in his old room." Harriet looks at George wistfully, "I do wish you'd come and stay more often."

Polly calls from the kitchen, obviously eavesdropping, "It's hardly worth keeping your room intact for you if you're never here. Mum could use it for her knitting circle."

When George had first moved to London for university, he used to come back more regularly and had begged his mother to leave his room alone. It was the only space in the house belonging entirely to him, untainted by anything quaint or twee. It held the worst of his memories, but the best of his dreams. Was there really any point in hanging onto it now? Wasn't it time to move on from hoping that his family would finally redeem themselves?

"You're right, Pol. Knitting," calls back George. "That could be your project for next year," he says turning to his mum, "delete me from the house. While you're at it—why don't you cut me out of all the family photos?"

Harriet shakes her head, "Don't be so sensitive, George. She doesn't mean it."

Duncan, unexpectedly, jumps to George's defense, "Sensitive and brilliant, Mrs. B. That's what makes George such a phenomenal musician. You should be very proud."

"Yes, of course we are. Now," she says, hurrying the moment on, "remember you two, no smoking in the house and dinner will be ready at six. Oh, and the boys are allowed to open two presents each tonight, so let's all meet at the Christmas tree at 5:30."

"Looking forward to *that*," says Duncan.

She leaves George and Duncan standing in the narrow hallway, their heads almost touching the ceiling.

"Regretting it?" whispers George, who is suddenly relieved to have Duncan with him, remembering how lonely he can feel in this house, even with everyone around.

"Not yet," says Duncan, "but when can we crack open your dad's sherry?"

LEXI
December 24th, 2009
West Hollywood, Los Angeles

Lexi manages to push her way through onto the balcony where those who have overflowed outside are smoking and talking. She clutches her green cocktail feeling hopelessly out of place. Who would have guessed that Lexi Jacobs, the most popular girl in her senior year, would be this familiar with feeling uncomfortable? She's contemplating hiding her drink in the jasmine and slipping away inconspicuously, when she hears a man's voice behind her.

"Come here often?" Lexi turns around to find a tall guy with blond curly hair and glasses. He's wearing jeans and a blue striped shirt. She needs to think of a cute, snappy comeback, but her mind is blank.

"Uh, not really."

"Well, I can't say I blame you. Especially if when you do, guys like me approach you with age-old pick-up lines."

She smiles, "I've heard worse."

"No! You can't have done. You're just saying that because you feel sorry for me. I'm Lance, by the way," he offers his hand.

"Hi Lance, I'm Lexi."

"Lance and Lexi, we already sound like a couple."

"We do, do we?"

"I'm not gay. In case you were wondering. It's only that a minute ago I was thinking that I might be the only person at this party who wasn't, until I saw you."

"That's very presumptuous, how do you know that I'm not gay?" Lexi takes a sip of her drink, thankful that she didn't dispose of it in the potted plant.

"I have a straidar—it's a bit like a gaydar, except opposite."

"Useful."

"Well, it *is* tonight. So who dragged you along?"

"A friend. Well, actually Johnnie's my lawyer."

"He is? I guess you got a shock when he answered the door?"

"I did! And you?"

"I'll see your connection and raise you one. Johnnie's my brother." Lance has perfectly aligned white teeth.

"Good choice, he's great."

"It runs in the family."

"Unlike modesty?" Lexi lowers her chin and raises her eyebrows. She might be out of practice, but if flirting is anything like riding a bike, she thinks she may have just gotten back in the saddle.

"Life's too short for modesty, Lexi. Tell me something you're brilliant at?" She can see sparkle lights reflected in Lance's glasses. She pauses, unnerved by how few things come to mind these days.

"Baking reindeer cookies."

"A traditional woman. I like that. I'm brilliant at dancing. Care for a demonstration?" He puts his hand on her shoulder.

Lexi is fully aware that she is supposed to have sworn off men, and in the words of George Bryce, be at a 'table for one'. However, she doesn't need her mother or Meg clambering up the side of this balcony to tell her that she'd be a fool not to give this one a try. He's promising. A far more agreeable word than 'perfect'. Anyway—it's only a dance.

"You coming?" he says, searching her face for a response.

"I'm coming," says Lexi, as she gives in and allows Lance to lead her into the fray.

GEORGE
24th December, 2009
Stanford in the Vale, Oxfordshire

The Christmas tree is plastic and festooned in silver tinsel, coloured fairy lights, and gold baubles, three of which have the triplets' faces superimposed on them wearing antlers.

Polly points them out to George immediately, "Look at these! Aren't they fun? I ordered them off the Internet."

George wonders if Polly ever leaves her house, or if she spends hours on end sitting at the computer buying cheap crap. Was this really the same girl who used to laugh at *him* for being such a twerp? Who used to boast about the pervert who approached her in the local supermarket asking her if she was interested in an international modeling career? She actually fell for it. She was even planning on meeting up with him, until their parents found out and forbade her to leave the house for two weeks and tore up his card. She cried for months and accused George of narking on her. It would have suited him just fine had she been abducted.

The triplets are seated next to the tree waiting for the go-ahead to open their presents. Archie is picking his nose. Padstow is sucking his thumb and Trevor is leaning against George's leg, having barely left his side since George had carefully cut out the scratchy label.

"So, George, you might be interested to know that the boys are extremely into music now. Archie's taking piano lessons. Pad's learning the oboe and Trevor is mastering the tambourine." Polly points to each of them smugly.

"Excellent," says George, stifling a yawn.

"Yeah and we've got a band and Dad says we're miles and miles and miles better than you," Padstow has removed his thumb to make this charming announcement.

Martyn pokes him in the ribs, "No, Paddy, Daddy never said that, did I? I said your Uncle George would love to hear all about your band. Remember?"

"I don't remember that, Daddy. I remember you said that Uncle George's band was—"

"Great! I said Uncle George's band was great!" Martyn's smile is getting wider and more forced by the second.

"Uncle George's band *is* great," says Trevor to his dad. "Mummy said their last album went to number one for lots and lots of weeks and trillions of people buyed it from their commuters."

George is beginning to grow rather fond of Trevor. "Computers," George whispers to Trevor stressing the 'P', amazed to hear that Polly says anything positive about him when he's not around.

"Yes," says Trevor, "comPuuuters."

"Of course they did, Trevor," says Martyn, defensively.

"Yeah well, I bet you rug rats rock too," says Duncan, "What's the name of your band? Maybe you could open for us at Wembley next year."

"It's called We Three Kings," says Archie, examining the snot he has carefully removed from his right nostril.

"Figures," says George under his breath.

"What was that, George?" asks Polly.

"Nothing, Pol. I said Fabulous. Fabulous name for the band."

"Well, Martyn and I thought if the Jonas brothers can do it, why not the Tabor Triplets? Right, Martyn?"

"Right, Polly," says Martyn on cue.

The doorbell rings and nobody moves.

"Are we expecting anyone else, Harriet?" calls George's father, settled in his armchair with his second tumbler of whiskey.

George's mother comes in from the kitchen wiping her hands on a yellow apron.

"I'm not expecting anyone, are you, Polly?"

"Amelia said she might drop in to say hello, but she did say she'd call me first."

The doorbell rings again.

This inertia is doing George's head in. He feels like grabbing the Christmas tree and wielding it around the room.

"Should I answer it then?" he asks.

"I'll get it," says Martyn, reluctantly standing up.

"But Mummy," whines Padstow, "Granny said we could open up two presents and she said we could do it now and we've been waiting and waiting and waiting for ages."

"Yes, Father Christmas will be here soon if we don't do it right now!" demands Archie angrily.

"Not true," says Duncan, "Father Christmas is having a pint at the pub. I saw him there earlier. He needs to chillax before his big night."

Polly shoots Duncan a furious glare.

"You're fibbing!" says Padstow.

"Mate," says Duncan, "trust me. FC and I are like this." He holds up two twisted fingers and waves them hypnotically in front of the boys' faces. "Now watch carefully. Keep your eyes on these two fingers. I'm going to put you to sleep."

Archie and Trevor are riveted, but Padstow leaps up and shouts.

"I'M NOT GOING TO SLEEP UNTIL I GET MY PRES-ENTS AND YOU NEED TO GO AWAY! YOU'RE STUPID!"

Brat thinks George, just as Colin walks back into the room followed by—oh God—could it really be? Hardly recognizable, but yes, it is, Amelia Hoffman. Polly's best friend during secondary school. One of the original Grapefruit Girls.

"Hello boys, Auntie Amelia's here!"

George had once thought that Amelia Hoffman was the sexiest girl on the planet. Not only did she have luscious breasts and smelled wonderful, but she had long thin legs and a bottom that was just on the right side of curvy. It's now on the wrong side. She's painted into black leggings and a gold sequined bustier. Amelia glances nervously around the room and finally settles on George.

"George, what a surprise! I completely forgot you were going to be here."

"No, you didn't," says Polly through pursed lips. "I told you this morning."

"Oh, did you? It must have slipped my mind."

Amelia is making her way across the room, clambering over the triplets, towards George, who forces a smile and leans in to kiss her cheek. She has other things in mind though and lunges forward, pushing her ungainly breasts into his chest, as she traps him in a hug. She doesn't smell like grapefruit anymore.

"Hello, Amelia," he pulls away.

"Georgie, you're all grown up. I always knew you were going to be a success. Remember those songs you used to play on your Yamaha? Whenever I passed your bedroom, I told Polly they were amazing. I sensed you had a raw talent."

Polly guffaws. George realizes that Amelia Hoffman might be responsible for making him feel even shittier than his sister did. She used to mock him mercilessly, until one Saturday night in June when she cornered him at the side of the house as he took the rubbish out. "I've always loved you, Georgie," she had whispered dramatically, "don't tell Polly, but I'm going to let you kiss me." Amelia had pitched forward offering him her lips, smothered in slick peach coloured gloss. George thought he was going to pass out. He could smell damp potato rinds and the heady citrusy scent wafting around Amelia's neck. This would be it. His first kiss. And with the girl he fancied the most. He leaned in to take the permission granted, but just as his lips were about to touch down, she pulled back with a look of disgust. "Psycho boy. I can't believe you even thought I was serious!"

Brutal. The memory burns.

"Um, Amelia, this is Duncan. Duncan, Amelia."

Duncan takes her hand and kisses it. "Sounds like you know all of Georgie's dirty little secrets, Amelia. I'd like to hear more."

"I wouldn't," says Polly, "anyway, the boys were just about to open some presents, Amelia. That *is* before you arrived, unannounced."

"I'll stay," says Amelia, "I love presents!"

Polly is clearly livid. "Are you sure you can stay? It looks like you're on your way to a party."

"Oh, this old thing?" says Amelia, tugging at the gold top. "It was just the first thing I grabbed."

"Could I be the second?" says Duncan with a straight face.

"I don't think so, Duncan. Amelia's married with a lovely little girl *and* a baby. Aren't you, Amelia?"

George is enjoying watching Polly bristle.

"Yes, Polly, I'm married, not dead."

"Neither has stopped me in the past," says Duncan, finding his lascivious stride.

"Well, aren't you just the naughty rock star!" giggles Amelia. George reckons he's in for a long night.

LEXI
December 24th, 2009
West Hollywood, Los Angeles

Lexi has had more green cocktails than she cares to remember. She lost count after the YMCA. She's back on the balcony now with Lance sitting on a bench underneath the jasmine plant. They've danced for an hour and she feels giddy and a bit sweaty. Unlike her, Lance seems to be entirely in control.

"You're sexy when you dance, you know that?" His arm has found its way around her shoulders.

"Oh God, I'm sure I made a fool of myself!" says Lexi, self-consciously flattening her hair back behind her ears.

"Quite the opposite. You had fun. Looked like you needed it." They are the only people on the balcony and the party seems to be clearing out. Johnnie pops his head around the French doors. "I knew you guys would hit it off. Lexi, Andrew says you've had a run of bad luck in the boy department."

"Thanks to Andrew," says Lexi embarrassedly.

"Well, I'm here to tell you," says Johnnie winking, "Lance is a keeper."

"I'll bear that in my mind," calls Lexi, as Johnnie disappears again.

Lance turns to look at her. "You? Bad luck in the boy department? I find that extremely difficult to believe."

"Do you always say all the right things?" Lexi's head is still swimming in jasmine and tequila and she's wondering if this man is too good to be true.

"Only when I'm not saying the wrong things," and before he can say anything else, he leans in to kiss her.

GEORGE
24ᵗʰ December, 2009
Stanford in the Vale, Oxfordshire

George is lying in his old bed, in his old room, staring at the black wintry sky outside his old window. The wall is a patch-work of faded blue paint, empty outlines reminding him where his beloved music posters were once taped up. He's surprised there's not a crater in the mattress—a carved out space where he spent endless stagnant years, gazing at the ceiling. What an awful night. Amelia was toxic. Duncan got too drunk, too quickly. The triplets eventually opened their presents and then Archie whined relentlessly for more. Duncan called Padstow a "fuckin wanker" under his breath, but Polly heard. And George's parents looked on disapprovingly, as ever, shaking their heads as if to say, *where did we go wrong?*

George tries to remember a time when things in this house weren't so horrible. Flashes of memories spark in his brain like worn-out film reels. Planting strawberry seeds in the garden with his mother. Watching his father tinker with the engine of his granny's Triumph 2000 on the weekends. Occasionally he'd allow George to assist, and George has never forgotten the pungent smell of the engine oil smeared on the tips of his fingers like paint. Playing hide and seek with Polly and squeezing tightly in the narrow dusty space beneath his parents' bed. He can't remember exactly when things began to deteriorate. When his grandmother died his father stopped speaking for weeks. He always looked distracted and George began to feel like a nuisance. George withdrew in response, turning inwards, while Polly came out, shouting and crying at even the most minor of disturbances. It appeared that her tactics were far more successful. His mother was always dealing with Polly while his father spent more and more time locked away. When George turned twelve, already lost in the music inside his own head, his mother tried to explain, "He doesn't mean to be so hard on you, Georgie. It's only that *his* father was always so tough on him. It's all he knows." George's grandfather had died of stroke before George was born.

"But why can't he be different?" George had asked bravely, knowing as the words left his mouth, that his father most likely asked his mother the exact same question about him.

LEXI
December 24th, 2009
West Hollywood, Los Angeles

Lexi and Lance have been kissing on the balcony for at least five minutes. She is too drunk to gauge how long is too long and the last thing she plans to do is wake up on Christmas morning in the bed of a curly-haired stranger, no matter how white his teeth are. She manages to pull away.

"I think we should call it a day," says Lexi, "Or should I say call it a night?" Is she slurring her words? Oh God, she's slurring her words! He's going to think she's a slutty lush if she doesn't pull herself together quickly.

"I'd definitely call it a night, Lexi. A *very* good night."

"I like you, Lance. Your hair is so curly and your teeth... your teeth are so white. I mean how do you get your teeth so white? You must use some industrial strength chemical?" Lance laughs.

"I like you too, Lexi. I'm going to make sure Andrew gets you home safely and I'm going to get your phone number and call you. Is that all right with you?"

"Everything's all right with me, Lance. Everything. Except I've crossed everything out of my dictionary. Everything and Perfect. Gone. For good. Promising is still there though. Promising is such a promising word. It's one of my new favorite words." Lexi picks up the blue cushion imprinted with palm trees propped at the end of the wicker bench. She wonders if anyone would mind if she laid her head down on it and went to sleep.

Lance looks at her amused and kisses her hand, "Merry Christmas, Lexi Jacobs." And then he turns and goes inside.

GEORGE
24th December, 2009
Stanford in the Vale, Oxfordshire

George is still up, lying on his bed, looking at the Thesis website. They've made some changes recently and he wants to check them out. The first thing that pops up is a video clip from the acoustic concert in LA. He clicks on it, thoughts of Lexi washing over him. Are there any angles on the audience? If he watches carefully, maybe he'll notice the glimmer of recognition in his eyes when he notices her. A seminal moment captured on film. Something he can show his grandchildren when he's 80 and regaling them with stories of his rock and roll youth.

"Your grandmother appeared like a vision..." he can picture them now, quirky little kids with scruffy hair and chocolate smudged mouths. A bit like Trevor. Unexpectedly the kid seems to have won him over. Earlier today, George had played Old Macdonald on the out of tune piano he used to practice on as a child, while Trevor had tapped along on his tambourine. Polly had walked in and caught them, smiling proudly. "Isn't he precious?" she'd asked, and both George and Trevor had replied, "Yes!" at the same time. At least she's managed to produce one decent boy out of the three. He has to give that to her.

The concert clip doesn't reveal anything. He cringes watching himself perform, so clicks off and scrolls down to the chat room links instead. Doesn't every fan contemplate if the band is ever on line? George knows that he used to do that, hoping he might inadvertently get into a conversation with Thom Yorke, about Thom Yorke. He doesn't do this often, but occasionally he will go on the message board. He's never posted anything, although he's been tempted. The first message that pops up tonight says:

```
Happy Christmas, Thesis! George's
family is so lucky to have him singing
round the xmas tree!!!! I'm jealous!! I
love, love, love Thesis SO SO much.
Radar3girl.
```

George grimaces. Radar3girl can remain in ignorant bliss. He goes on to get quite involved in an in-depth analysis of *Twelve Thousand Words* versus *Corners and Tables*. Bobsyouruncle7 thinks the first album is far superior while Dawnlicious rates "A Suitable Dawn" as one of "the most extraordinarily beautiful songs of all time."

There is a tentative knock at his bedroom door. It can't possibly be Duncan, he was drunk enough to have passed out hours ago. Polly and Martyn and the boys had left immediately after dinner. Amelia, thank God, had her own long-suffering family to return to. It must be one of his parents come to berate him about something. Why does he continually subject himself to this torture? The knock is more persistent the second time. George closes his computer and is just about to get up, when the door creaks open.

"You still awake?" Amelia's sparkling torso appears in the gap. *Oh shit* thinks George. She's even worse than his parents.

"I thought you'd gone home?" George looks at her warily.

"I did, but I realized that I'd left my handbag behind so I've just popped back to get it. Blonde moment," she says giggling, walking into the room and sitting herself down on the bed next to him, their shoulders touching. Amelia moves her hand to George's knee.

"It does bring back some memories sitting here with you, doesn't it?"

"Not really, because you never sat here with me, Amelia. I don't think you ever stepped foot in here."

"Oh, but I wanted to, George... I really wanted to."

"Whatever. It's late, Amelia. I'm sure your husband will be wondering where you are."

"Let him wonder."

"Okaay. But I'm also very tired and I'm going to—"

"Kiss me. You're going to kiss me, George, I know that's what you've always wanted. Ever since you were thirteen you wanted me, didn't you? You probably spent long nights in this very bed dreaming about me. Well here I am. All yours..." She leans her head on his shoulder and smiles up at him, revealing a red smudge on her front tooth.

What the hell? Why does he always find himself in these situations with women he doesn't want instead of women he does? Amelia must be delusional. As if he would ever touch her after what she put him through. He takes a deep breath.

"You're right, Amelia. I did always want you. It hurts to admit how very much." George turns towards her, and just as she's about to try and smooch him, he pulls away. "Psycho girl. I can't believe you even thought I was serious!"

He stands up, filled with a childish sense of satisfaction. Amelia looks suitably startled. "I should have known you'd be the type to hold a grudge. Your loss, George. I'm still the talk of the town. You know they say I used to give the best blow jobs north of Banbury."

"Tell that to your husband, not me," says George, taking in the tragic sight of Amelia, slumped on his bed in sagging gold sequins. What kind of a mundane life must she be leading? He hates to admit it, but sometimes revenge really *is* sweet.

"Do you honestly think you're above us now just because you're famous?" asks Amelia bitingly. "Well, news flash, George Bryce, you're not *so* wonderful. Keane are much better than you." And with that stinging insult, she huffs out of the room, closing the door firmly behind her.

LEXI
December 25th, 2009
West Hollywood, Los Angeles

Lexi is finally back at home after a long day at her parents' house and a drop in at Tim and Meg's to deliver gifts. Her father had cornered her by the ham and asked her if she'd consider auditioning for *The Amazing Race* with him. "Your mother is begging me to choose her, but her sciatica would drag us down." Meanwhile, her mother had bought her a lacy black camisole and an Italian cookbook. Both presents screaming, *if only you had a man to appreciate these.* Lance had already texted her first thing that morning, "Have a cool yule, Lexi. Quite the unexpected gift—meeting you..."

Meg had forgiven her for being in the same room as George Bryce and was newly invigorated by the appearance of Lance. "I told you it was all going to happen for you if you opened yourself up to it. The universe was listening."

"Maybe you were right," Lexi had said, "but don't marry me off just yet. It's only been one kiss." Actually she thinks it was far more than one, but the problem is, Lexi doesn't actually recall all the details of their night together because of the lethal green drinks the elves were passing around like lemonade. She's already called Andrew to see if he can fill in the picture, but he's not picking up. She'll just have to wait for him to get home. She checks her phone again now. Russell has texted, "May the joy of the season rejuvenate you as you recycle love around the planet." He has attached a picture of him and Mildred ladling out soup at a local homeless shelter. Russell really is an inspiration. Lexi, on the other hand, has spent the day embracing consumerism and now feels hugely guilty for it. She should have given her father homemade jam instead of cashmere socks. What kind of role model for the company is she? She's definitely going to make some steely New Year's resolutions and stick to them, but for the time being she makes herself a mint tea and settles down with her laptop.

GEORGE
25th December, 2009
Stanford in the Vale, Oxfordshire

It's after midnight and the run-in with Amelia has left George edgy. He decides to get a glass of water then maybe sit in the garden for a little while and stargaze, something he can't do much of in London. As George passes Polly's bedroom he hears muffled noises from inside. He opens the door slowly, hoping to find Duncan awake so they can plan their getaway the next day. Instead, he finds Amelia Hoffman crouched on the floor between Duncan's legs, determined to prove one of her well-earned credentials. Duncan has Bob the Builder stuffed in his mouth. When he sees George, Bob drops and Duncan grins. Amelia is still on task.

"Busy, mate."

"I can see that!" says George, slamming the door a little too loudly as Amelia bolts upright. He's now stupidly woken his mum, who rushes out of her bedroom bleary eyed.

"Is everything all right?"

"Yes, Mum, great, everything's okay. Duncan was just having a nightmare," says George herding his mother towards the kitchen and shutting the door. Wait until Duncan hears who Amelia Hoffman *actually* is. An original grapefruit girl. Then the nightmare will be real. George hopes that Amelia will finish up pronto and slip out quietly. If his mother finds out, all of her worst fears about the band's depraved lifestyle will be confirmed. And on her best John Lewis sheets.

"Tea, Mum?"

"That would be nice, George, thank you."

"Happy Christmas," he says, filling the kettle. His mum's maroon toweling dressing gown reminds him of when he was a very little boy. Hiding in the folds of her long skirts. Holding on tight to the tie around her waist.

"Happy Christmas to you too, George. We're all glad you came. It's good to see you in person and not just read about you in the newspapers." In the past, George might have heard that as an accusation, but tonight he can see in his mother's eyes that maybe she actually means it.

"I'm sorry I can't get here more often, Mum. Our life is so busy, it's just hard..." George's voice trails off.

"You used to dream about this, didn't you? I'll never forget all the piano lessons and that guitar from the charity shop falling to pieces. It was all you wanted."

George thinks of Stardust, stashed carefully away in his empty flat. "I still have that guitar, Mum."

"I told your father you were talented. He just didn't want me to encourage it because he was so worried about your future." George reckons that his mum has had to spend her entire marriage making excuses for his father.

"I know, Mum, I know," he hears the front door close with a barely perceptible click and hands his mother the mug of hot tea.

LEXI
December 25th, 2009
West Hollywood, Los Angeles

The Thesis website appears on the screen. Lexi's been re-searching their current product line this week, in preparation for the introduction of the new 'green' items. Everything is moving forward now. Carl and Johnnie have drawn up the contract and Thesis Ltd have agreed to all the terms and conditions and signed. Gabe and Russell have spoken a few more times since, and made a plan for Russell and Lexi to make a trip to London in February. London in February?! So exciting! She's never even left the States.

Since the video conference, Lexi has been stubbornly pushing thoughts of George Bryce into the background and concentrating instead on the thrill of developing the business. He has returned to where he belongs; a face on a video screen; an image on an album cover; an unattainable boy whose world she could never fit into. Just today, Meg had thrust last month's *Star* magazine under Lexi's nose, opened to a picture of George and that weird singer, Fanny Arundel, stumbling out of an after party the night of their concert. George is hanging his head, while Fanny is holding up two fingers to the camera. Lance, on the other hand, is a real person. Maybe even a prospect for her. Just like Russell had said—it's about being open to possibility. It would help if she knew what his profession was, but with those clothes and those glasses, he wasn't going to be a musician, was he?

Without warning, the Thesis home page begins to play.

It's the acoustic concert. Her concert. For a moment she is transported to the third row. Hearing George's voice sends shivers down her spine but then she imagines going on a date with Lance. A quiet dinner by the beach. Maybe a moonlit walk afterwards. Hmm... Perhaps juggling work and a relationship is not so unthinkable after all?

GEORGE
25th December, 2009
Stanford in the Vale, Oxfordshire

George is ready to leave. They have consumed one extremely large, extremely dry turkey and pulled twenty Christmas crackers. They are currently all seated by the tree again, wearing crumpled paper crowns, while the three boys play "God Rest Ye Merry Gentlemen" on their instruments of choice. He had only agreed to stay after lunch because of Trevor.

"Uncle George, you have to wait and see me rock out," Trevor had pleaded, waving his tambourine and jumping up and down excitedly.

"Okay, I'll wait," George had said, stuffing his Christmas presents into his duffle bag—a grey striped tie from his parents ("Your mother and I thought you might need to look respectable sometimes") and Michael Jackson's unauthorized biography from Polly and Martyn ("We still can't believe he's gone!").

He'd broken the news to Duncan about Amelia that morning, when Duncan had slunk into George's bedroom looking sheepish.

"Fuckin' hell! A Grapefruit Girl? Why didn't you tell me before? That's legendary, man."

"Do you have no discretion?" George had asked, "you *did* know she was my sister's married best friend?"

Duncan had looked unfazed. "Discretion? Never heard of it, mate."

George had shook his head. Really, who can blame Duncan for wanting to rebel in such a suffocating environment?

And now the two of them are perched on the edge of the beige chintz settee listening to the cacophony that is the boys' performance. It might be worth it for the smile on Trevor's face though. Archie and Padstow look mostly bored.

When the song comes to an end, Duncan stands up, clapping and hollering. His red paper crown flutters off his head and lands on the floor.

"You aced it, dudes! I knew you were going to put us out of business." The three boys beam and Polly looks over at George, and for a second she actually appears a bit vulnerable. Her usual smug expression is replaced with a searching stare, as if she's asking for his approval. George continues the applause, "Future *X Factor* winners. Simon Cowell better watch out," he says.

"That's just what I told Martyn," exclaims Polly, back to her familiar self-satisfied tone.

Later in the afternoon, George and Duncan throw their bags in the boot of the car and say their goodbyes. Trevor has glued himself to George's side. Before he closes the car door, George leans down and says, "Hey Trev, maybe when you're a bit older, I'll get your mum and dad to bring you and your brothers to one of our shows?" Trevor's eyes widen, "When I'm five?"

"Yes, when you're five."

"Yessss!" says Trevor punching the air with a grubby fist.

As George drives away, Polly and the boys waving them off, he turns to Duncan. "So..." says George, "Amelia tells me she gives the best blow jobs north of Banbury."

"I've had better," says Duncan with a straight face, "south of Banbury."

The two friends laugh as the car accelerates and his parents' cottage shrinks in his rearview mirror.

LEXI
December 31st, 2009
West Hollywood, Los Angeles

New Year's Eve. The most overrated night of the entire year. It never improves. Even in her heyday, when Lexi was the most sought-after girl in school, New Year's Eve was always a disappointment. Andrew inevitably got so drunk he could hardly talk and midnight came and went with a ridiculously wet kiss, which felt more like a lick from a basset hound. Not that she'd ever been licked by a basset hound, but she'd always had a good imagination. She's already decided to do absolutely nothing tonight. No parties. No champagne. No sequins. No Dick Clark. She's going to get into bed at 10:30 and wake up ready to face the new year. New job. Possibly a new man. New Year's resolutions (cut out sugar, only use reuseable water bottles, cardio three times a week, read more) —perhaps she should even think about moving? Wasn't it time to separate from Andrew again? Lexi ponders all of this as she sits in a café in West Hollywood with Andrew and Carl, eating eggs over easy and hash browns. Her phone vibrates in her purse and she dives to find it.

"Must be lover boy for the third time in the last half hour," says Carl. "Obviously he just can't get enough of you, Ms. Jacobs!" Lexi smiles. The day after Christmas, Lance had left for a trip to San Francisco to visit his parents with Johnnie. He's not due back until tomorrow, but he's been texting daily and called once. They'd only talked for a few minutes, but he'd been extremely charming and persuaded Lexi that they should go out on a date the night he returned. She hadn't needed much persuading. His latest text says "Very much looking forward to the new year. Especially tomorrow night..."

"What's he saying now?" asks Carl, who is already like

part of the family. Lexi holds her phone protectively to her chest, "None of your business."

"Come on, don't be so coy. We know he wants your body."

"Maybe so, but I'm still not telling you."

"Oh, I just love the first few weeks of a new romance," says Andrew nostalgically.

"That was us only like a month ago," says Carl, scooping a spoonful of scrambled egg from Andrew's plate.

"Was it only a month? It feels like a lifetime." Carl hits him playfully with his napkin. "A lifetime of love which I wouldn't trade for the world," says Andrew, leaning in and kissing Carl's cheek.

"Get a room, will you?" says Lexi, realizing that both Andrew and Russell seem to have met their soul mates on the very same night, while she's spent the past month as a voyeur of two of the sweetest budding romances. It was enough to make anyone ill. No wonder she had resorted to believing that George Bryce had locked eyes with her. Desperate tactics in desperate times. But now everything was going to change.

Carl had filled in a lot of the blanks about Lance. He was a structural engineer. Thirty-five years old. Never been married.

"I don't know what you did that night, Lexi, but Johnnie says Lance is completely smitten by you."

"Smitten!" exclaims Andrew. "Who wouldn't love a man who uses the word smitten?"

Lexi isn't sure what she did either, thanks to the cocktails coloring the entire evening in a misty green stupor, but she's sure she was fabulous and all arrows are pointing to Lance being fabulous too. Who cares about being alone on New Year's Eve? She is transitioning into a capable, independent career woman, who just might have met a very suitable, mature, self-assured man. Alone is the new together.

It's her own choice. For the first time in a while, she feels completely on top of things.

GEORGE
31st December, 2009
Soho, London

New Year's Eve. The most overrated night of the entire year. It never improves. Endless kissless midnights as a teenager. It really shouldn't be allowed. One night imbued with the expectations of a thousand birthdays. Someone should make it illegal. The band are performing on the Jules Holland special tonight and George is hoping to play straight through from one year to the next. Bring it on. Where can Thesis go this year? Every year he reckons the dream can't get any bigger, but it always does. Thinking about the band's success is mind-boggling. It's like not only buying a winning lottery ticket once, but then buying one again and again and again. Only to find yourself surrounded by cash and wondering why you still feel needy.

George is sitting in a bar in Soho with Simon and Stacey and Mark and Anna. Is there such thing as a fifth wheel? If there is—he's feeling it. Stacey has been suctioned to Simon ever since they got together in Vegas. He was never worried about the Yoko effect with Anna, she sits back and lets the boys do their thing, but Stacey could be a problem. George picks up his beer. It's 5:00 p.m. and the party's started early.

"George, are you listening to me?" asks Stacey. She has a loud nasal voice.

"Sorry, Stacey, what was it you were saying?" George is pretending not to hear her. "Loud in here, isn't it?"

She rolls her eyes, "Like you're not used to noise!"

"What?" he cups his hand to his ear innocently.

"I was saying that I've been telling Simon my ideas for styling you guys. I mean you're not college kids anymore, you could be totally updating your look." George turns to Simon, who instead of jumping in and defending the unpretentious ethos of the band, is staring at Stacey with an idiotic grin. His usually unkempt red hair has been slathered in gel and looks like an ice sculpture.

"Have you been styling Simon?" he asks sarcastically.

Stacey strokes the underside of Simon's chin, which is beginning to show a thatch of red stubble. "As a matter of fact I have. We're working on a goatee, aren't we, babe?"

"Yes, we are," says Simon compliantly.

"Mate, it looks like you have a swan on your head, and a ginger fucking swan at that."

"Oh, you're funny, George," says Stacey bitchily as she turns to Simon and kisses his nose. As loud as it is in the bar, George swears he hears her say, "No wonder he can't get a girlfriend. He's so uptight."

It never fails to astound him how quickly the feelings come rushing back. One damn comment, a sideways glance, a tone of voice, and it's like some bloody trapdoor opens and he's sliding down into the thorny abyss, fifteen years old, feeling like shit. How much more successful does he have to get in order to keep that door padlocked shut? Why does he care what a girl like Stacey thinks of him?

George stands up and leaves the table. He has that urge again to be in open space, to run away. Simon follows after him and grabs his arm. "Come on, George, ease up. She's just trying to be helpful." They push through a crowd of young Londoners, drinking early, every one of them wanting to put something behind them and start afresh. Some of them recognize George and Simon and nudge their friends, or do a double take, or just outright stare. George keeps moving through the crowd until they are outside. The early evening air feels sharp and cold. He leans against a brick wall to avoid the throng of people coming in and out.

"I'm fine, mate, you didn't have to follow me. Just needed some space is all." George knows that he and Simon are overdue a conversation since LA, but now is not the time.

"George, it's me you're talking to. I know you're not fine." George isn't sure how to respond.

"Sim, honestly. It's all good. You know, New Year's Eve— it's never been my favourite time of year. I should be writing. I've got a lot in my head."

"George, look, I get it. Stacey and I have been talking about it. It must be very difficult for you having to see me with her."

"What do you mean?" George is incredulous. Is Simon joking?

"Look, mate—it's okay. She told me about what happen- ed in the make-up trailer in Las Vegas. She's cool with it now, but she just wants you to be too." George's head is swirling. What happened? She was the one who kept positioning her tits so they were right in front of his face. She told him he had eyelashes like Brandon Flowers. He just smiled.

"Nothing happened!"

"Yeah, but she says it was obvious you were into her. I mean let's face it, who wouldn't be—she's awesome. But she chose me and now you're struggling with that. Clearly."

"I'm not struggling."

"You know me better than anyone, right?"

"I thought I did."

"Well, I think this is it, George. I know it's only been a few weeks but I think Stace is the woman for me."

"THE woman?" George is appalled. This is catastrophic. Stacey could destroy them if she had her way. "I thought you said you didn't believe in that stuff?"

"I didn't. Until I met her," says Simon, starry-eyed. "I'm done with spending my time on sandwiches. Us, you and me, the band, we'll always be everything but I need more."

George is trying to take it all in. Isn't this what he's been wanting as well? Why else has he been weaving a future in his imagination with Lexi? So why does he feel so angry with Simon? So abandoned? As aggravating as Stacey might be, at least she's here. Lexi is still really just a figment in his mind. A projection of what he hopes for. In reality she might end up being as irritating as Stacey. She might have bad breath. She might laugh like a horse.

A young guy with an earring and thin twitchy lips approaches them.

"You guys are sick. I saw you in November and I met my girlfriend at the gig. I owe you one, can I buy you a beer?"

Simon looks up, "Cheers, mate—we're good. Thanks for the support though and glad we could be of service." *That's just great* thinks George *I'm making it happen for everyone but me.*

Another guy stumbles over. He has a tattoo on his neck and thick black glasses. "I know you twats," he blurts out, pointing an accusing finger at them both. "You're a bloody fucking joke! Call yourself musicians? You should be ashamed of the mediocre shit you force us to listen to."

Idolized in one moment and stabbed in the throat the next. George is just grateful Duncan isn't there, or else this idiot would be on the ground with a mad Australian fogging up his lenses. Simon smiles, "No one's forcing you to listen to us. Turn over."

"I'll bloody well turn you over, you posh wanker!" The lunatic lurches forward but fortunately twitchy lip guy steps between them and George and Simon inch back towards the door of the bar. They are confronted by Stacey, pushing her way out, looking worried.

"There you are. I missed you, babe," Stacey leans in protectively to Simon and he rubs his hand over her bum.

"I missed you too, babe-a-licious."

George feels wretched. He hasn't said anything to Simon to try and deter him. Maybe it's best. Let people go their own way and make their own mistakes, right? But this isn't just any mistake. This could affect him and the future of the whole band. On the other hand, if he says something he risks alienating himself even more from his best mate. Stacey already has a tight hold. He needs advice. It's usually Simon he turns to. He knows exactly what Duncan will say. Mark most likely approves, and Gabe, forever the diplomat, never likes to take sides. George wishes he had someone objective to ask. Someone like Lexi. He can see it now, calming him down, making him tea, kissing him gently. George looks around him. Strangers are closing in on him again as the pavement outside gets busier. He feels trapped. Imagining Lexi just isn't doing the trick anymore. He needs to find out who she really is and he needs to do it soon.

LEXI
January 15th, 2010
Tree People Park, Los Angeles

Lexi is at the Tree People park, an environmental nonprofit organization in the Santa Monica mountains, promoting healing cities through sustainability. Russell is running a workshop for fifth graders on fashion recycling and trash to toys. He is standing on a bench carved out of a tree trunk, modeling some of his ponchos made from used aluminum foil and discarded single socks. Mildred is commanding a small camera crew with authority, as she is considering giving Let The Green Times Roll a weekly spot on *Wake Up LA*. It's a good thing that Lexi went to bed early on New Year's Eve, because over the last two weeks she's hardly slept at all. Between dates with Lance and the momentum at work picking up at a rapid pace (it seems that the new year is inspiring lots of people to turn over a new leaf, literally, and go green), things have been a little hectic. Three days ago there was a massive earthquake in Haiti devastating much of the country, and along with thousands of helpless others, she has been glued to CNN.

Mildred strides over wearing a long flowing silk top adorned with yellow and black dragonflies, large round sun-glasses obscuring most of her face. "What's it going to take to persuade you to get back in front of the camera, young lady? I know Russell is divine, but you mustn't let him have all the limelight."

Lexi looks up from her iPhone where she is tackling her ever-expanding Inbox. Inquiries have been piling up.

"Oh, Mildred, you're sweet, but I have far too much to do behind the scenes at the moment. Thanks to you of course."

"I'll accept that excuse for now, but just don't forget how good you were."

"I'll try not to," says Lexi, flattered by Mildred's sudden interest.

"There's more to you than meets the eye, my dear. It's obvious to everyone else but you." Lexi can feel her cheeks redden. She can manage compliments about her shiny hair, her smooth skin, her cute outfit, her efficient time-keeping, but Mildred's comment touches a different part of her. A part that is waiting and wanting to be seen again. She hadn't rea-lized that Mildred had given her any thought at all since her TV debut.

A sudden burst of laughter erupts from the fifth graders. Russell has a sock on each hand and is recreating a scene from *Star Wars* using a broken umbrella as a makeshift light saber.

One of the children is waving her hand wildly.

"My mom won't let me play with trash. She says trash spreads germs and germs crawl into your bloodstream and then you wake up with an infection which scratches, or even worse, you wake up dead."

"Well, technically," says Russell, "you can't actually wake up, if you're dead."

"Still," says the girl. "She won't let me."

"I bet you use a lot of hand sanitizer in your house then?" says Russell knowingly.

"She keeps it on a key chain," the little girl looks very impressed.

"Excellent. Your homework, Ellen, is to collect all the empty hand sanitizer bottles you can over the coming months. I want you to paint them every color of the rainbow and erect a sculpture in your bedroom. Tell your mother you are working on celebrating the earth, while she works on eradicating germs, which by the way, with moderate exposure, can be very beneficial for boosting your immune system, but that's another lesson."

Ellen beams.

"My genius..." says Mildred proudly to Lexi and wafts back to the action.

Lexi is left feeling distracted. She looks out over the tops of the trees bordering the descending dusty trails. She has another date with Lance tonight, her fourth in two weeks. They are taking the shuttle up to the Getty to see the photography exhibit and drink a glass of wine as the sun sets. She thinks she's beginning to remember the meaning of the word romantic again. Lance is chivalrous, intelligent, attentive, good looking, motivated. All the boxes checked. All the boxes. So there are no sparks dancing in spirals above their heads when they kiss, but the kisses are nice all the same. Lexi reminds herself that spirals are totally unhelpful. Anyway, it's early days and they haven't even slept together yet. She'll know when the moment is right. He's not putting any pressure on her, unlike her mother and Meg who begin every conversation with "Soooo....." Lexi feels acutely observed since meeting Lance. Every time she's with him, she imagines the two of them on a stage at the Hollywood Bowl, surrounded by stadium seating—her mother, father, Meg, Tim, Andrew, Carl, Johnnie, even Jack and Annabelle, all sitting in the front row, eating popcorn, praying for a happy ending.

GEORGE
15th January, 2010
Abbey Road Studios, St. Johns Wood, London

Fanny's warm breath tickles his ear. She smells like Marmite. "I've missed you, George. We need to hook up again soon." George has a ghoulish vision of actually being hooked up above Fanny's bed, pinned to the wall like a Damien Hirst. He scratches his ear to try and distance her lips from his skin.

"Want a Twiglet?" She holds out an open packet.

"No thank you," he says, hoping she'll stop talking.

"Go ahead, George, indulge. I'd like to have a lick of your Twiglet right now, right here." George almost spits his tea out.

"Bryce—are you with us? Second verse—in C minor. You come in strong with the line 'Let's hope that hope helps Haiti's heart and hope that hope heals every part' and then Guy slides in on bass." George nods, feeling like he is in a school assembly and has been caught whispering to his neighbour. He wants to say, "But sir, it wasn't me really!" Fanny crunches on her Twiglets innocently.

"Yes, Miles, sounds great. I'm with you."

Miles Freeman is an iconic eighties producer who has gathered the cream of the music crop here today to record a charity single for Haiti's earthquake victims. He seems immensely proud of the dreadfully saccharine lyrics he has concocted. The room is buzzing with talent, but at this moment they are all a bit like sixth formers, shuffling their feet, waiting for the bell to ring so they can go and have a smoke.

George is here because he can't stand the helpless feeling he gets watching the news. The force of impotence is stifling and the divide between those who have and those who haven't appears to be expanding on a daily basis. He is compelled to watch how the country crumbled in minutes, one structure falling in on the next like children's building blocks.

Except it wasn't a game. It was all real and here on the other side of the world people are getting on with their lives—eating Twiglets, worrying about the weather, watching Arsenal play Tottenham. It's meaningless. So he agreed to make the cheesy single in hopes that the proceeds would actually go somewhere. Do something. Not end up lining the pockets of some corrupt government officials.

"Miles, sweetie," Fanny raises her hand and waves it dramatically in the air, "I think I should duet with George on that line. We make beautiful music together."

Tinchy Stryder sniggers from the front row. Someone else wolf whistles. It really is feeling like school now.

"We'll discuss, darlin'," says Miles in a thick Irish accent. "Let's take five and come back for first rehearsal."

George moves away from Fanny as quickly as possible and weaves his way through the crowd of his peers. It's still difficult to believe that he belongs here. He half expects that at any moment someone very official, wearing a uniform with a shiny badge, will tap him on the shoulder and escort him out of his life, finally revealing him to be a genuine impostor. Looking around the room he wonders if every one of the 'stars' here feels the same way? Underneath the peacock tails were they all trembling just like him? Matt Bellamy from Muse strides over and shakes George's hand. "Congrats on the Brit nomination, mate. We're in good company now."

George is half tempted to ask Matt if he too feels like a fraud.

"Cheers, Matt, the boys and I were saying the same. You guys are tearing it up. Everyone's talking about your shows."

"Oh, well—it's not an easy job is it, George, but some-one's gotta' do it. You touring soon?"

"States in the spring. I'm preparing myself for the bacon blur."

"The bacon blur?" Matt looks confused.

"Yeah, you know the drill," says George, "one large American breakfast blurring into the next."

"Well, good luck with that." Matt pats him on the shoulder and makes a beeline for Dizzee Rascal. George is feeling noticeably more vulnerable without the rest of the band. Simon was supposed to be with him today but Stacey had insisted that they keep their private reservation on the London Eye. When George had questioned Simon choosing to go on London's biggest tourist attraction, versus being part of the charity single, Stacey had intervened.

"George, it's like totally hard to get a private reservation. We have the pod all to ourselves and it will take weeks for me to book that again. You can represent the whole band, can't you?"

"That's not the point, Stacey. It's the principle of it. Do you know how many people died in Haiti? Do you have any idea what the survivors are going through? This is something we can actively do to help."

"I know, George. It's like totally horrible but don't give me a guilt trip. I'll buy the friggin single. I'll wear the friggin t-shirt. I've been waiting forever to go on the London Eye and Simon promised me, didn't you, babe?" Simon had nodded obediently, a response George was becoming a bit too familiar with. Thinking back on the exchange makes his skin crawl. "Love is blind" is taking on a whole new meaning. In Simon's case, love is not only blind but scarily ignorant and selfish as well. The sex better be damn good to justify her.

George looks around the busy studio, hoping Fanny doesn't creep up on him again. He'll see most of this lot at The Brits in a month's time. Thesis are up for three awards this year, British group, British single and Listener's Choice album. He knows the right thing to say, "It's great just to be nominated," which is true, but it's still even greater to win. One more month. He can wait. He'll have to. Not just for the

Brits, but to finally see Lexi again. Gabe announced yesterday that Lexi and Russell would definitely be visiting in February.

"I thought it would be fun if they came to the Brits ceremony with us," he suggested, "as a kind of highlight of their trip. I'll add their names to our table. You good with that?"

George feigned disinterest. "Fine."

Gabe had no clue how fine it actually was. George isn't exactly counting the days, but he's close to it. By the time the Brits roll around he might possibly have confirmed that Lexi Jacobs is the woman he could love... the anonymous 'you' in "A Suitable Dawn"... the shining light in the third row. He just has to talk to her first.

LEXI
February 3rd, 2010
Venice, Los Angeles

"How many times a week does he work out, Lex? He's totally rocking that lycra," says Meg appreciatively, appraising Lance from a distance. Lexi and Meg are waiting in the parking lot while Lance and Tim rent bikes for their first official double date. There isn't a cloud in the LA sky and the beach stretches before them like a silky white oasis.

"Yeah, he's not leaving much up to the imagination, is he?" responds Lexi, who hadn't known where to look when Lance arrived to pick her up that morning.

"Mr. Armstrong at your service," he'd said, presenting her with a single red rose hidden behind his back. Lance tried really hard. His effort grade was off the charts.

Meg keeps staring. "Why make us wonder? If you've got it flaunt it, right? I wish Tim would work out a bit more. He's going to need a training bra soon if he's not too careful. Tim—" Meg shouts across the parking lot, "will you get me a bike with a cushy seat. You know I'm a bit sensitive down there."

"Really, hon? I wouldn't remember," says Tim, even louder.

"Very funny," says Meg scrunching her nose up at him.

"You're not still punishing him, are you?" asks Lexi, hoping to deter Meg from any further inappropriate yelled exchanges.

"Not exactly," replies Meg, adjusting her helmet. "We just don't have time anymore. Once the kids are in bed we're like, should we watch *Mad Men* or have sex? *Mad Men* always wins."

Lexi still hasn't slept with Lance. Lance is being extremely patient, although it is starting to feel a bit like when she was first dating Andrew in high school. She remembers her mother once trying to talk to her about sex when she was a teenager. "Boys like to compare it to baseball, sweetheart. I like to compare it to shopping. At first you browse. Then you touch. Then you try. And finally you buy. Going all the way is like when the saleslady runs your credit card. It's a very important transaction and not one to be taken lightly..." When Lexi had first started sleeping with Andrew, every time he ejaculated, she could hear the sound of a receipt printing.

Lexi looks over at Lance. He flashes his blindingly white smile. She's leaving for London in two weeks and suddenly wonders what she's waiting for? Is she scared that if the sex isn't good then she'll run away? Find an excuse to leave him behind just like she always does, incurring yet again the wrath of her mother and everyone else in the audience? Lexi reminds herself that she's changing. Making choices for herself and not for her mother or Meg or anyone else. What is it that Johnnie had said? *Lance is a keeper.* Well, if she doesn't run that credit card soon then she'll never find out.

The boys come over leading two bikes for the girls.

"Your carriages await, fair maidens," says Lance in a mock Shakespearean accent.

"Why thank you, kind sir..." says Meg and hops onto her bike while mouthing to Lexi, "He's too cute!"

"Isn't *your* trip across the pond pretty soon?" asks Tim, as the four of them cycle their way out of the parking lot and onto the bike path. A stocky woman boasting a very small bikini and not so small biceps whizzes by them on roller-blades.

"The thirteenth," says Lexi. She still has trouble fathoming that in a few weeks she and Russell will be on a flight to London on a real business trip. A couple of months ago she'd barely even heard of Thesis, and now they are about to initiate her into a world she'd never even envisioned.

"Lucky! You're going to London to meet George Bryce, again. It's not fair."

"I told you," says Tim proudly, "he's your free pass. I'd do that for you—one night—but only if he can guarantee me a night with Scarlet Johansson."

"I thought you were meeting with a band?" calls Lance behind him.

"She is," shouts Meg, "and George is the lead singer and *I* love him. Too bad he's going out with that skank, Fanny Arundel. I saw another picture of them today at some Haiti benefit. She is *out* there."

Lexi doesn't feel a thing when she hears this. Good sign. Her ludicrous crush is losing power rapidly.

"I don't know a thing about pop music," says Lance. "I'm an opera kinda guy. Have you ever seen *Madame Butterfly*, Lexi? I think it's playing in San Francisco at the Opera house. We should take a road trip and stop off in the wine country on the way."

"Rein it in there, buddy," shouts Tim, "you're giving me a lot to live up to."

Meg cycles to try and catch up with Lexi. "The wine country? Are you kidding me? He is SO romantic." But Lexi hasn't heard any of them. She is picking up speed, the wind rushing in her ears, while the ocean streaks past her in a crayon blue blur.

GEORGE
3rd February, 2010
Maida Vale, London

George clears his throat. The restaurant is noisy. A local pizzeria chosen specifically because his parents don't like to go into the West End.

"All those people squashed on the streets together. It makes me nervous," muttered his mother, when George had suggested somewhere on Regents Street. They have insisted on driving to London for his birthday, and much to his dismay, have brought Polly with them.

"The boys were dying to come, but they have a spelling test tomorrow and Martyn thought it would be too stressful for them."

"Spelling?" asks George, "they're like three or something. Isn't it a bit early for spelling?"

"Actually, they're four, George, and their nursery teachers have indicated that they all have an extremely high IQ."

"They must have inherited that from Martyn's side of the family." George knows he's being juvenile, but he can't resist.

"Now... now... you two," chimes in their mother, who was always pretty hopeless at keeping the peace.

"He started it," says Polly accusingly, glaring at George.

"Well, dear, just ignore him."

"She does ignore me, Mum." *Come on!* thinks George. *Stop trying to get their sympathy. Why can't I just shut my gob, unless it's to eat garlic bread?*

Polly is prickling and her cheeks are quickly becoming red and blotchy, "Just because you're in a band you think we should be falling all over you? You always wanted to be the centre of attention. You and all your horrid moods. You could never get over the fact that I had Mum and Dad to myself for two whole years before you were born."

George is speechless. Why does everyone think he wants

what they have? He's not even sure what he wants, so how the hell do they know?

"Polly, you have no idea what you're talking about," says George, struggling to find a less pathetic comeback.

"What, so you think you're the only one with anything meaningful to say? Well, I'll tell you something, little brother, fame is fleeting, but family isn't. Where will the band be in forty years, George? You're not the Rolling Stones." Polly picks up her glass of red wine and downs it in one gulp.

The table is silent. The restaurant is alive with noise and activity, while the four of them sit there like discarded wax figures in the basement of Madame Tussauds. George wants to stand up and walk out, but his mother looks as if she's going to burst into tears and he can't bring himself to do it.

His dad speaks for the first time, "George, Polly just means that sometimes you're hard to reach, son." That's ripe coming from him. "We're here, aren't we? We're trying. Even Polly. Isn't that right, Pol?"

Polly is busy pouring herself another glass of wine.

"One of the reasons I came tonight was because I wanted to tell you in person about my special news."

George wriggles uncomfortably in his seat. What now? She's probably pregnant with sextuplets. The waitress interrupts Polly's imminent headline, arriving just in time with the pizzas. Her long dark plaits dangle in front of George's face as she carefully places his in front of him.

"I saw you at the 02 in November—you were brilliant. I was right at the front."

"Lucky you!" snaps Polly. "Now if you don't mind we're trying to have a family dinner."

"Thanks very much," says George, but the poor girl is so mortified, she can't get away fast enough.

"Polly, that really wasn't necessary." George has lost his appetite.

"I think it was necessary, unless we want to spend the entire evening talking about you."

"It *is* his birthday, dear," says their mother, for once coming to his defense.

"I know that, Mum, but I was right in the middle of my announcement."

"Announce away," says George, mentally noting that perhaps it is finally time to cut all ties with Polly. What is he hanging onto? The hope of one day their relationship improving? He blames his sister for souring everything in the family and she obviously blames him. The truth is a destination in the middle that he just can't seem to reach. *Destination in the middle. That's a lyric* he thinks. Could even be a song title. Maybe even the title of their next album. *Destination in the middle. Couldn't get there if I tried. Destination in the middle. Through a forest of your lies.* The words begin to bounce around his brain. He needs a napkin. He fumbles in his back pocket for a pen, so he can scribble them down. Polly looks disgusted.

"You're not even listening to me, are you? You didn't even hear what I just said."

George falters, "Yes I did."

"What are you doing?" asks Polly, appalled. "You're not going to give your autograph to that waitress, are you?"

"That might be nice, dear," offers their mum. "You *were* a bit brusque with her."

"No, no," says George, wishing he could sprint back to his flat and get this song written. The verses are suddenly flapping around his head like trapped birds beating their wings against a window.

"So will you or won't you?" asks Polly emphatically.

"Will I or won't I what?" replies George, completely lost.

"George, are you high on drugs? You're acting very strangely." His mother puts down her fork and stares at him accusingly across the table.

"No, Mum, I am not high on drugs!"

"Will you or won't you perform at my wedding?!" says Polly, raising her voice.

"Your wedding?" says George, even more confounded. "You mean you and Martyn aren't married?" He could swear he attended some hideous event seven years ago. He has an image of a marshmallow with Polly's head balancing precariously on top.

"I knew you weren't listening. We *are* married, you idiot, but we are renewing our vows in August in honour of our seventh anniversary. The boys will be performing and we all hoped you might want to play a few songs, to help us celebrate."

She's even more of a loony than I thought, decides George. Does she honestly believe that he would consider it a privilege to play in front of her and bloody Amelia Hoffman and all the other maniacs in their village? Plus, renewing their vows? It's the worst thing he's ever heard.

George looks up from his napkin. His parents are staring at him, waiting for a response. Polly is tapping her fake red nails on the side of her wine glass. He feels as if every table is holding their breath, waiting for him to respond.

"I can't," says George. The words feel like lead on his tongue.

"Typical," says Polly. "You mean you won't?"

"I can't because we'll be on tour in the States. I can't just leave. I'm sorry, Pol."

His parents both look crestfallen, but what's new about that?

"You're not sorry!" says Polly, scraping her chair back and standing up. "You're not even sorry one little bit. And here I was trying to hold out an olive branch on your birthday. I don't know why I bothered. Don't worry about your nephews. I'll break the news to them. It was Trevor's idea anyway."

George stares down at his pizza, focusing on the greasy pools of oil. His parents are both silent. Why couldn't *he* be the one to scrape his chair for once and walk away? So much for liberating himself from Polly or proving his family wrong. Yet again, she's won the round and he's the eternal disappointment.

LEXI
February 10th, 2010
Brentwood, Los Angeles

Lance and Lexi are fooling around on his bed.

"You're driving me crazy, Lexi Jacobs," says Lance in a husky voice. He has this habit of using her full name, which ever so slightly reminds her of being told off by her mother when she was ten. "Tidy up your room, Lexi Jacobs, haven't I already asked you?"

Tonight is going to be the night. She's leaving for London in two days and doesn't want to wait any longer. Just an hour ago they were sitting at her parents' dining table eating cheese and grapes and playing footsie under the table. Her father was going into great detail about the auditions for *American Idol*, and Lance, to his credit, was trying his hardest to appear fascinated.

Her mother had been begging for the last few weeks to meet Lance, and Lexi had finally buckled, giving in to that old part of herself that wanted to please her. Of course he was above and beyond Jeanette's expectations. She could barely contain her excitement when she saw his smart blue blazer and handsome square jaw. Before long she had dragged Lexi into the kitchen, placing her hands firmly on her shoulders.

"Now you know how much your father and I love you and we would never tell you what to do, my angel."

"Yes you would," said Lexi, wondering if this dinner was a mistake.

"It's only that we have noticed you looking a bit lost for the last few years. Well, the last ten years really. But that's beside the point. You seem much better now. The job is super and Lance is divine. Divine, Lexi with a capital 'D'. I'm just saying that it's not all the time you meet a nice man like him. And he's got hair and a career and a good sense of style. So just don't..."

"Don't what, Mom?" Lexi had asked, hoping her mother wasn't going to run upstairs and unpack the wedding dress.

"Don't think you don't deserve this, darling. That's all I'm saying. You deserve to be happy."

Lexi allows Lance to slip his fingers under the elastic of her lacy underwear, trying her hardest not to think about her mother or her Visa card. *I deserve to be happy*, she tells herself, wriggling out of her panties.

Lance sighs. "You're so sexy, Lexi," and before he can say 'Jacobs', she covers his mouth with her lips, surrendering each second just a little bit more.

GEORGE
10th February, 2010
Camden, London

George and the boys are in the studio playing. Mark has presented them with lyrics to a song he's been writing called "Never Anyone" and the four of them are messing around with a hook and experimenting with melodies. George, un-used to working with someone else's words, feels like he's being force-fed, but is trying as hard as he can to rise above the judgement and stay with the process.

He puts his hand up to momentarily pause everyone.

"Mark, I'm really into the first verse. It flows and I'm there with it. But when you say 'break me, rake me, desiccate me' in the chorus—it's just not working. Anyone else feeling that?"

"It's too aggressive," says Simon.

"I wanted to convey how it feels to be at the mercy of someone else," says Mark. George has no intention of asking if this song has been written about him.

"Yeah," says George, "but that comes with a yearning, doesn't it? Something softer. It could be simple..." he sings quietly into the microphone, "Break me, rake me, undertake me..."

"That actually works better," says Mark magnanimously.

"It does," agrees Simon.

"Bingo baby," says Duncan, pointing his drumstick in the air.

George brushes his hair away from his eyes. He thinks he might finally be learning how to share.

LEXI
February 13th, 2010
Los Angeles International Airport

Lexi and Russell are waiting in line to check in at British Airways. Russell is visibly nervous and has twitched his way through most of the car journey while plying himself with Rescue Remedy, virtually sucking the dropper dry.

"Do you think Mildred will remember to give Boris his ginkgo tablets?" asks Russell worriedly. "They help with his melancholia."

"Melancholia, are you kidding me, Russell? It's going to be party central at Mildred's house. Boris and Cherub are going to be living it large. Relax."

"I'm just not so sure if this is a good idea, Lexi."

Lexi glances to the left, "You think that line would move quicker?"

"Not the line—the whole journey." Russell looks at Lexi forlornly. "Maybe you should go without me?"

"Russell, you are *not* abandoning me at the gate. No

gooseberries here, may I remind you. This is huge. Thesis are our first clients and this trip is essential for client relations. Human contact in business is irreplaceable. It can't all be done over a computer screen."

"But the environmental impact of a transatlantic flight is monumental. I'm wracked with guilt. I haven't slept in days. Surely, I should practice what I preach?"

Lexi is exasperated. "Russell—as far as I can tell you have arranged planting a whole rainforest in Peru to offset the carbon emissions of this one flight. Plus you've packed like two pairs of underwear and a tank top in an organic hemp backpack to diminish luggage weight and help with fuel consumption. You're an eco saint. In fact I bet when we land in London the Queen of England will be waiting there to knight you, right at the baggage claim. Be prepared. "

Russell breathes in deeply. "Okay, but I'm going to miss Boris and Mildred."

Lexi pats his arm reassuringly, "They'll be fine. You've lived the majority of your life without Mildred. You can manage a few days without her now, and Boris is in good hands."

"I know, I know. But I don't want to live any more of my life without her, Lexi. I've decided that when we return, I'm going to ask for one of those good hands in marriage." Russell straightens his shoulders.

Lexi smiles. "Really? That's great news, Russell. I'm so pleased for you." And she is, truly. Maybe soul mates aren't actually mythical creatures after all? Was Lance her soul mate? She knows what her mother would say, "Ish Pish—anyone can become your soul mate if you work hard enough at it. Stick with them. *Your* problem, honey, is that you find fault and bail out too quickly." Or was her problem that she'd spent her entire life believing every word her mother had said?

The woman in the pristine blue suit with her hair coiled in a tight bun beckons Russell and Lexi to move forward.

"Welcome to British Airways. Passports and tickets please. Will you be travelling to London with us today?"

"Yes, we will," says Lexi, turning to Russell and nodding reassuringly.

GEORGE
13th February, 2010
Primrose Hill, London

George walks briskly up the hill. It's a crisp night and a cold breeze snaps around his ears. This is one of his favourite spots in London. When he reaches the top he can stand and survey the skyline—the tip of St. Paul's Cathedral. The neon arc of the London Eye. The iconic post office tower—a futuristic anomaly erected in the 1960s. In the summer, this park is heaving with picnickers and kids kicking footballs, and dogs frolicking around the trees, but on a winter's night it is a quiet haven. The old fashioned street lamps illuminating the pathways remind George of Sherlock Holmes. Men with capes and pipes behind all the lit windows of the surrounding houses. Mysteries being solved. Hot pots of tea being drunk. George often comes here to write. Now at the top of the hill, he shoves his hands into the pockets of his jeans and blows a chilly curl of mist from between his lips. When he was a boy he used to pretend that he was Sherlock Holmes, scouring the woods with a plastic magnifying glass for clues, teaming up with an unlikely Luke Skywalker when Watson had a head cold or had overslept.

A man bundled up in a North Face jacket walks by with an oversized poodle and nods at George. It's a relief. George knows the difference between an "I know who you are!" stare and an average "You're just another bloke in the park" one. These days he enjoys feeling like just another bloke in the park. The headlights of a plane glide noiselessly above him, reminding him that Lexi is on her way. He suddenly feels very small. How did it happen that he's had to concoct such an elaborate fantasy about one woman he barely even knows, in order to believe that there is hope for his love life—hope for his heart? In a few days he might be right back where he started from. Disillusioned. Downtrodden. Depressed. A whole dictionary of 'd' words.

His phone vibrates in his back pocket. He pulls it out. Fanny again. He's had two missed calls from her in the last week and now a text. "Call me Georgie boy. I need to see you." He can't face fending her off at the moment. She's most likely following the macabre orders of Sebastian, her dead lover, who has instructed her to not give up her pursuit. Fanny and all of her ghosts will have to wait. He'll be seeing her at the Brits on Tuesday and can come up with some excuse then. Right now he has far more important matters to attend to.

LEXI
February 14th, 2010
BA Flight 282, somewhere high above Canada

Lexi is too excited to sleep. She's eaten five small packets of chili flavored pretzels and drunk a mini bottle of cheap red wine. She's also played poker, scoops and hangman on her iPhone and has watched *School of Rock* and *The Titanic*. Russell is breathing heavily next to her, wearing a purple silk eye mask and sheepskin slippers, which he had sneakily produced from a side compartment of his backpack declaring, "It always helps to bring home comforts when you travel." Lexi had half expected him to pull Boris out of the other pocket.

She has now found an infuriatingly obsessive moving map on her screen and has been gazing intently at the teeny weeny little airplane crawling its way over Canada, currently hovering just above some place called Goose Bay. Only five more hours to go, which wouldn't be too awful if every hour didn't feel like three. Lexi can't wait to see London! She only wishes she had more time to sightsee. As it is, the business has had so much interest in the last month that she and Russell have discussed hiring another employee when they return. They might even have to consider expanding to a small office space because conditions are getting rather cramped in Russell's house. The first deposit has come through from Thesis for the design work they've begun on the product line and the business is beginning to build some capital. The business is actually a business now, no longer a grandiose idea floating aimlessly in Russell's eccentric brain. It has legs and feet and a body, just as she had first envisioned. It has room to grow and Lexi knows she has played a direct role in making that happen. It feels really satisfying.

Lexi lies back in her seat and closes her eyes. Russell is making soft whistling noises as his head flops forward and then snaps up again. Lexi's mind wanders forty-eight hours back to her first sleepover with Lance. It had been very... nice. He had been extremely... attentive. But just as things were hotting up, George Bryce had appeared. Uninvited. On stage. Singing. Staring. Sitting. Turning to smile. She had tried to push his blue eyes and black floppy hair out of her mind and concentrate on Lance's smooth and toned chest. But George hadn't left. In the end, Lexi had no choice but to allow him to stay, and the lovemaking had gone from being nice, to being really, really nice. She'd often read that fantasizing about another man when having sex was completely normal. But did that include the first time you have sex with someone? Lexi opens her eyes again and checks the moving map. The plane is beginning its journey over the Atlantic. She's positive George's cameo appearance in the bedroom was just a minor setback. She'll see him this week and be reminded that he's completely untouchable, unlike Lance, who is definitely access all areas.

GEORGE
14th February, 2010
Camden, London, 2:00 p.m.

This is it. The womb. The pulse of transformation. The simultaneous beating hearts of frustration and fruition. George is addicted to the recording studio. Whenever he begins to question his career path, he only has to return to the studio to be reminded that he was born to make music. It is not a choice anymore, but an imperative. He needs to be here. The creative process is his class 'A' drug. It lures him in every time. Taunts him with a curved tail and venomous tongue and then wraps him up in an endless embrace, pumping him full of the most delicious elixir.

They are here today laying down the first track of "Third Row." He has managed to coax Simon away from Stacey a few times over the last two weeks. Along with Mark and Duncan, together they have delicately shaped George's lyrics into a quiet but lush love song, with murmured verses and a bold chorus dipping and soaring in unexpected moments. George is slowly becoming accustomed to the new world order.

"It's a beaut, isn't it?" says Duncan.

"What's the inspiration?" asks Mark, cradling his bass guitar as if it were a sleeping baby.

"Just a thought... you know... about what if..."

"So it's not based on a true story?"

"A bit of both, I guess. Fact and fairytale blended into one."

"She's not real then, mate? This chick in the third row?" Duncan brushes his cymbals.

George hesitates. Is she real? Of course Lexi is a real person, but is the Lexi of his imagination actually just a fictional character?

Before he can answer his own question, Gabe throws open the door.

"I'm loving this, boys. Loving it. By the way, reminder that Russell and Lexi from Let The Green Times Roll will be arriving today. I've scheduled them to come and meet with us and tour the studio tomorrow, and then they're joining us at The Brits on Tuesday."

Well, there's his answer. He'll find out soon enough. He just has to figure out how he is going to get Lexi on her own over the next couple of days. The Brits are always madness. If he can just have an hour with her. A conversation. A connection. Surely then his intuition will be confirmed or not and he'll know if this is fate or fabrication.

"That bloke Russell's a beast," says Duncan. "Can't wait to meet him and his hottie eco sidekick in the flesh."

"Grow up, Duncan. Don't embarrass us, for God's sake," says Simon.

"Oh, what are you, Mr. Mature all of a sudden now you've got a ball and chain?"

"No," says Simon calmly, "I just think it's not cool to talk about women so derogatively."

"Excuse me—that's a big vocab word for you, Ginger-nuts. Did Racy Stacey teach you how to pronounce that one?"

"Fuck off!" says Simon.

"Get used to it," says Mark. "He's been talking shit about Anna for years."

Duncan shrugs. "Only my opinion, but I reckon hitching yourself to one piece of arse when there's a stadium of tight buttocks to choose from is a big mistake." George is beginning to feel claustrophobic. He wants the music. Only the music. In a few weeks they'll bring in a producer to start working with them on the new material. Right now he needs his lips pressed closed to the microphone, the notes cascading in his ears, the chorus cleansing this discord away.

"Let's get back to work, boys," volunteers George. "It's Valentine's Day, after all. We're lovers, not fighters, right?"

"Yeah, about that," says Simon hesitantly. "I was going to

wait, but I wanted you lot to know before anyone else. I mean, Duncan has completely ruined the moment, but that's not exactly unusual."

"Let me guess!" says Duncan, "You've discovered a rare variety of relish, a tantalizing pick-me-up for any bland baguette?"

"Very amusing. You missed your calling, Dunc." He pauses dramatically. "I'm going to propose to Stacey tonight. I'm gonna get married!"

George deflates. Damn it. Stacey is not right for Simon. She's possessive and insecure. A mate with no soul. What can he say?

"Congratulations, Sim." He walks over and pulls his best friend in for a hug. He doesn't want to let go.

"Good on you, Simon," says Mark, nudging George out of the way, "Anna will be chuffed. She'll have someone to complain with."

Simon laughs, "I know it's quick and everything but Stacey's incredible. I've never met anyone like her before."

"Thank God," says Duncan.

"Duncan, mate, I don't expect you to understand, but just don't dis her, please."

The moment has gone. George can't possibly lose himself in his lyrics now. What's the point anyway, writing songs that trick people into believing in love at first sight? Think of all the poor, pathetic girls who will hear this and fantasize that it might have been written about them, while George meanwhile will probably still be sitting alone in his flat eating Crunchies and holding a grudge against Amelia Hoffman. Isn't he simply perpetuating the vicious cycle? Prepping thousands of unsuspecting teenagers for ultimate heartbreak? Are Simon and Stacey really in love? Or has she just targeted him like a parasitic tick attaching itself to a dog. It's obvious to George that she has an agenda.

"Look, mate," says Duncan, "I'd love to be dancing in the

hallways over this, but I'd be lying if I said I was thrilled. What's happening here? Before long we're all going to be changing nappies and shit like that. We're not even thirty yet."

"Ease off, Dunc. It doesn't have to affect the band, does it?" says George, knowing this is his own wishful thinking.

"Can we stop talking like I've just been handed a death sentence?" says Simon, picking up his guitar. "I'm getting married and I'm friggin' happy about it. Now let's finish laying down this bloody love song."

LEXI
February 14th, 2010
Hyde Park Corner, London, 2:00 p.m.

Russell grabs Lexi's wrist as the driver accelerates in a sea of swerving cars, taxis and big red buses, all seemingly merging into the same two narrow lanes.

"Good gracious. I don't remember so many cars the last time I was here," he gasps.

Lexi is alert with curiosity. She doesn't feel tired at all. She is still struck by how weird it is to be driving on the other side of the road with the steering wheel where the passenger seat should be. It's as if she's been transported into an opposite universe, where everything is unexpected.

"You've been to London before?" asks Lexi, surprised. "You never said."

"Well, it was many moons ago in 1975. I hitchhiked across America then hopped on a cargo ship from New York. I spent a very memorable summer in this fine city working."

"What were you doing?" asked Lexi, realizing she knows almost nothing about Russell's previous incarnations.

"Well, my dear, you might find it hard to believe, but I was a model for a brief stint of time."

"A fashion model?" asks Lexi, amazed.

"No—an artist's model for a life drawing class in Soho. I

stayed in a youth hostel and Don McLean played a free concert in Hyde Park. I was in the front row. Look," he says, pointing out the window, "that's where the concert was!"

Lexi looks out over a massive expanse of green in the middle of such a bustling metropolis. It's a wondrous sight and helps to clear the image of a naked Russell being sketched by a room full of English hippies.

"Here we are," says their driver, pulling up outside a modern glass and concrete block, harbored among statuesque buildings clearly hundreds of years old. A doorman dressed in a tailored black coat opens the door of the car and offers his hand to Lexi. She accepts, feeling horribly underdressed in Gap jeans, Uggs and a comfortable cardigan.

"Welcome to The Metropolitan, madam. I trust you had a pleasant journey."

Lexi is enchanted. Everyone is so polite. "Why yes, thank you," she says, hoping to sound suitably genteel.

Once inside the lobby, they are greeted by a short girl wearing purple jeans with thigh-high boots. She has spiky black hair and glasses, "Hi, I'm Becca. You must be Russell and Lexi. I work with Gabe and the band."

Lexi shakes her hand, "Nice to meet you."

"How was the flight?"

"Long!"

"Yeah. What's up with that? Someone needs to move LA closer to London, right?"

Lexi laughs. Becca doesn't look more than twenty, but she is just one of those uber-cool girls who make you question what the secret is.

"So, I don't want to overwhelm you before you've even unpacked, but this is your itinerary. It's kind of bonkers, lots to fit in, but the lads are all chuffed that you're here."

Lexi takes the envelope.

"Most kind of you," says Russell.

"You must be knackered. Why don't you check in and get settled and we'll have a car here to pick you up first thing."

"Great. Thanks," says Lexi, beginning to feel a little lightheaded.

"And by the way, George has told me about your plans for the website and everything, and I think it's awesome."

"It's the earth that is awesome, Becca," says Russell, sweeping his hand in the air. "We are merely attempting to protect that awesomeness and hoping everyone else will do the same."

"Cool, well, I'm on board, Russell," says Becca, revealing a silver stud in her tongue when she smiles.

Lexi wonders how close Becca is to George? He's obviously surrounded by witty, trendy girls like her. How silly was she imagining that he might have been gazing at her during his concert? Crazy really. She's relieved to have moved on from that puerile scenario and can safely say she feels almost nothing at all when she thinks about him now. Almost.

GEORGE
15th February, 2010
Camden, London

LEXI
February 15th, 2010
Camden, London

There are at least eight people in the room and everyone's talking. Even so, every time George so much as glances at Lexi, it's as if the world goes quiet.

Lexi has never experienced anything like this ever. She only has to glimpse the back of his head and her stomach tightens. The word 'butterflies' has taken on a whole new meaning. She has them. Not just a handful, but a forest of translucent, colorful creatures fluttering against her rib cage and rising up into her throat.

He has to curb an impulse to walk towards to her. To take her hand. To lead her out of the room. He keeps telling himself there is nothing more that could happen to confirm to him that this connection is real.

She has to stop herself from turning around and running out of the door. She wants to gulp cold air into her lungs and freeze this melting feeling. This is not convenient. This should not be happening.

He needs to see her alone.

She needs to be sure that she is *never* alone with him.

"Lexi, what are your thoughts on the subject?" Russell is talking to her. Everyone in the room has stopped to look at her, except George. He is looking at his feet. They have just finished walking around the recording studio and now they are meeting with Gary, the band's tour manager, to discuss the potential to carbon neutralize the upcoming "Under the Radar" tour.

"Solar energy panels," Russell continues, "I was saying how we are advising all of our clients that solar panels are the way of the future, isn't that right, Lexi?"

"Yes, yes," says Lexi, endeavoring to recover. "Harness the resources we do have rather than exploit those already depleting. The sun is—" George looks up from his shoes and catches her eye. *Oh dear God. This is torture.* She can't think straight.

"The sun is..."

"Hot," offers Duncan. "Like you."

Shit! thinks George. Duncan's getting started. He needs to stop him.

"What?" says Lexi.

"Duncan says you look a little hot. Maybe you need some fresh air?" George walks over to her and takes her arm.

"No, I'm fine. Just the jet lag, I think." Lexi can feel his fingers lightly resting on her sweater. Her cheeks feel like they're burning.

George is close enough to smell her and thankfully there isn't even a hint of grapefruit. Rose petals. She smells like rose petals.

"Some air might be a good idea," says Gabe, getting in on the action. "The journey this direction can really knock you out."

Russell nods in agreement, "Don't concern yourself, Lexi. We'll save the important parts until your return."

Before she can resist again, which would undoubtedly call even more attention to herself, George is leading her out of the room and into the corridor. She doesn't know what to do. She's exhausted. When she and Russell finally made it up to their rooms, Lexi had opened her door to find practically a garden full of long stemmed red roses. There must have been a hundred of them. A small white card was propped against one of the vases. *Happy Valentines Day Sexy Lady, from your not so secret admirer xoxoxoxoxo.*

Lexi wasn't sure whether to feel elated or smothered. She had spent the night lying awake, until she could no longer bear the smell of the petals and thought she might gag.

George opens the door of the studio and leads Lexi outside. The street is teeming with people. In LA you would only ever see this many people in a shopping mall or at the airport. There is a biting breeze and the sky looks like thick grey felt.

"Sorry about Duncan," says George, beginning to walk. Lexi falls into step next to him, starting to breathe, finding it easier to concentrate now that they are outside. So much for avoiding being alone with him.

"It's fine, he's very entertaining. I don't know what's wrong with me... the jet lag must be fogging my brain."

"Yep—that can do it," says George, trying to work out what's next. He can't just say to her, *I hardly even know you but something out of our control is bringing us together.* Or could he? What he really wants to do is kiss her. That's what he should do. Just kiss her. But that could backfire. She might think he was some sex-crazed rock star and be disgusted. How is he ever going to get this right? The one thing he does know is that he can't let her leave London without something happening between them. Something concrete, rather than this intense chemistry driving him to distraction.

"Your studio is great," says Lexi, trying to hold onto a coherent thought.

"We like it," says George, noticing that Lexi is about two inches shorter than he is. Perfect kissing height. "So is this your first trip to London?"

"Yes, it is."

"Cool. It's the best city ever—in my humble opinion. I mean LA is good too but—what have you got planned while you're here?"

"Other than business? I don't know, I thought maybe Russell and I could take one of those buses that drive around Buckingham Palace and the Houses of Parliament—try and really embrace the whole obnoxious American tourist thing."

George laughs. "Go for it. You should get to Abbey Road studios and take a picture of both of you on the zebra crossing —that would be hilarious."

Lexi notes the word *hilarious* and how when it leaves his lips, it doesn't bother her at all.

"Maybe we will."

"How long have you and Russell been together anyway?"

"I've been working with him since last year, but I'm positive he's been campaigning for the environment since birth. We're not together though, I mean like a couple together—if that's what you mean? I wasn't sure..." Lexi trails off embarrassedly. Of course that wasn't what he meant.

"Together together? No—I didn't mean that but... good. I mean good that Russell is so passionate about his cause. I love that." This is going well.

"I know. He really *is* inspiring. And passionate about lots of things. Especially his cat." Lexi is beginning to feel as if she can say anything to George.

"Really? I don't like cats," says George, pushing his hands into his pockets to prevent them from trying to hold hers. "My parents used to have one when I was a kid. They give me the collywobbles."

"The whatie wobbles?"

"The collywobbles—you know—like the creeps."

"Or the heebie jeebies?"

"Or the heebie jeebies."

"Collywobbles—I like it. I'll have to use that one when I get home."

"You do that. Let me know how it works."

Lexi laughs, "Will do. So let me see, you don't like cats but you have parents. The picture is widening. I bet the parents must be very proud, even if their cat gave you the wobbles."

"You forgot the colly."

"Huh?"

"Before the wobbles."

"Got it. Sorry."

"Forgiven. Proud parents? That's another conversation. My family is strange." Lexi notes his reference to *another conversation*. He's already anticipating more.

"Oh God—my parents are strange too..."

"What about the rest of you? Any brothers or sisters?" asks George.

"Nope—only me."

"Might be a lucky escape. I have a sister, but she's always hated me."

"I can't imagine anyone hating you."

"You're too kind, but really, she does. She thinks I'm pompous, which I probably am."

"Maybe she's jealous—I mean it can't be the easiest thing in the world having a brother who gets so much attention."

"Have you been e-mailing her?"

"No! I'm just imagining what it might be like *being* her. My parents were a bit too obsessed with me. I would have loved a brother... or a sister."

"Ahhh—I'm getting sad. Did *you* have a pet at least? One that you liked?"

"My mom has one now—a yappy little dog called St. Tropez. That's how weird she is."

"A hint of irony perhaps?"

"No irony. She honestly thinks it's a chic name to call a dog." Lexi notices a girl wearing headphones and a wooly hat look over her shoulder as she passes George.

"It might be the way of the future. You should get a gold-fish and call it Liverpool." George hopes the girl who just walked past isn't going to backtrack and try to talk to him. He doesn't want this rhythm ruined. He doesn't want this to end.

"I could do that," says Lexi, feeling suddenly like the world is effortless.

"Yes, you could. I could get one too and call it San Diego. They could be pen pals, or Facebook friends I guess."

"How would they write to one another?"

"They wouldn't. They'd just transmit silent messages through the water. Like dolphins."

They both walk for a little while without talking—transmitting some of their own silent messages.

"We should probably get back," says Lexi, admitting to herself that this is exactly the opposite of what she would really like to do.

"Probably," says George, as they turn around. "Although there are still lots of animals we haven't talked about yet." Lexi loves his quirky sense of humor. How easily he makes her laugh without even trying.

George wants to kiss her. He should just kiss her. Here. Now. Or else he might never find the moment again. Why do the bloody films make it look so easy?

"Thanks for the fresh air," says Lexi, needing to savor the sweetness between them. Knowing that anything more is surely unfathomable.

"You're welcome. How are you feeling now?"

"Better."

They are almost back at the studio entrance—a nondescript black door with no indication of what lies behind.

George takes a deep breath. *This is it, do it! Don't talk, just lean forward and kiss her.*

They both stop in the street and Lexi looks up at George. He has grown a beard since the last time she saw him and his hair is a bit longer. He looks like a nervous teenager, not a famous rock star.

I'm doing it right now, he tells himself.

Get back inside, she tells herself.

He pitches forward slightly.

She tilts her chin.

Don't kiss me, she thinks. *Please kiss me,* she thinks.

The space between them momentarily closes and their lips are on the verge of touching, when the door flies open.

They both jump backwards. Quickly.

Gabe and Russell are standing in the doorway.

"We were just checking up on the situation," says Gabe, looking quizzically at George, who has started to cough.

"Are you okay, Lexi? Or am I asking the wrong person?"

Lexi pats George on the back. "*I'm* okay but I think George might be choking on his gum. He was just showing me some of the sights of Camden town."

George holds up his hand. "I'll survive," he says, darting back into the studio. He can't believe he's fucked that up. Fate has been so good to him, delivering Lexi into his eye line on three different occasions, and now he can't even manage to kiss her.

Lexi composes herself and smiles at Gabe and Russell.

"Making progress?" she asks, trying to sound interested.

"Lots," says Russell, "why don't we fill you in?"

They all head back indoors.

Oh my God. Oh my God. Oh my God. Lexi's whole body is churning up with desire and confusion. She wants to giggle and cry at the same time. She attempts to steady her thoughts and her heart, both swirling around in ecstatic, jet-lagged euphoria, while a bossy voice inside of her begins to transmit loud and clear, *Hello missy! He's not a happiness option. He's a famous singer, who lives across the world from you, dating a slutty pop idol. Get with the program, honey.* Lexi knows this is true but somewhere in the background she can hear another voice. A relaxed, chilled out voice. The voice of a girl sitting cross-legged in the grass, threading a daisy chain. *Or write a new program*, this girl says, pulling one delicate green stalk carefully through another. *He's completely lovely. It's all up to you...*

GEORGE
16th February, 2010
Maida Vale, London

Somehow The Brit Awards seem to have receded into the

background overshadowed by Lexi landing, but George wakes up knowing today is the day. This is the third year they have been nominated. The first year they were up, they won 'British breakthrough act' and the second year they won 'British single'. Tonight there's a chance they might get the album award. The band are performing "Under the Radar" and George has calculated that despite yesterday going horribly awry, Lexi is in London for the next forty-eight hours and he'll be sure not to miss another opportunity. Surely she'd be inclined to kiss him after seeing him perform in front of thousands of people? He needs to stop thinking and start acting.

After they went back inside yesterday to continue the meeting, he had caught Lexi's eye a couple of times. She didn't look away immediately. That had to be a good sign. He shook her hand when they all said goodbye. He made sure to not let go too soon. Gabe had scheduled a magazine interview that afternoon and then there was a dinner with a new producer they were considering using for the latest album.

The journalist from *NME* was a pretty Asian girl with a Scottish accent.

Halfway through the interview she asked, "You've been linked recently to Fanny Arundel. You're both making a big impact internationally. Do you think you might ever perform together?"

"Unlikely," George had replied cagily. "She's a friend. Our directions are extremely different. I'm not sure Fanny's looking to break new ground right now—she seems to be great just where she's at."

"And Thesis *do* want to break new ground?" She had raised a provocative eyebrow.

"Well—we want to explore uncharted territories with this new album. Not a concept album exactly, but more like a book of short stories. Most importantly we don't want to disappoint our fans."

"It seems your fans are rarely disappointed. Rumour has

it that you're quite a perfectionist during the recording process."

George had chuckled. "Is that a polite way of saying control freak?"

"You tell me."

"It's hard to know when a song is ready to fly. I suppose it's a bit like being a parent who doesn't want to let their kid go to nursery school, so they keep calling it back to tie their laces just one more time."

"So you're saying that your songs are like your babies?"

"Of course. I get attached. I think a lot of artists do."

The journalist had clicked off her recorder at that point.

"Brill. I've got some good stuff here and your manager is giving me the hand signals. Thanks, George, and best of luck at the Brits tomorrow."

They both stood up.

"You and Fanny just friends, huh?" she had said, sliding her recorder back into her bag. "Are you looking for any more friends?"

George had paused for a second. She was pretty fit. Seemed intelligent. She was in the industry, but not too far in. He should have taken her number. Any normal bloke in his position would have.

"We've got a Facebook page," he'd said jokingly, remembering how Lexi's soft palm had fit neatly in his hand.

"I get it. Well, if you change your mind, here's where to find me." She'd pulled a card from her bag and handed it to him.

George looks at the card now and tosses it into an empty kitchen drawer. He rinses out his Oscar the Grouch mug and boils the kettle. The band are being collected at one p.m. and being taken to Earls Court for a final sound check and run-through before tonight's ceremony. This morning he's told Gabe he wants to join him to meet with Russell and Lexi at the graphic designer's office in Paddington. Gabe wants all designs signed off before they go to production and he wants last minute input from Let The Green Times Roll. Having been initially so reluctant, he has now embraced the ethos whole-heartedly.

"Do you think it's unprofessional if I ask Lexi out?" Gabe had asked George yesterday after the meeting. "She's not with Russell. I checked. I don't know why you thought that."

"Extremely unprofessional," George had responded quick-ly. "Don't even consider it."

"Yeah, yeah, you're probably right," Gabe had said, look-ing downtrodden.

George pours his tea reassuring himself that he should not feel guilty for deterring Gabe. He's not trying to mislead his friend, but occasionally destiny goes a little off track. George is merely assisting in its redirection.

LEXI
February 16th, 2010
The Metropolitan Hotel, London

Lexi is spinning. The combination of the electricity of a new city, the adrenaline of working and the memory of being very nearly kissed by George Bryce, has left her on a permanent high. She has spoken once to Lance and thanked him for the roses but tried not to linger on the phone, suddenly feeling like she needs a bit of space. "I can't stop thinking about you, Lexi Jacobs." Well, *she* can't stop thinking about George Bryce. It's not that she has any illusion that something of any substance might possibly happen between them, but the thought that something could, something might, is making her crazy. Lexi gave in and called Meg last night after coming in from a delicious dinner with Russell at a restaurant next to the Thames. Not being able to talk about it with anyone was becoming agony.

"Are you flippin' kidding?!" Meg had screamed down the

phone. "George Bryce tried to kiss you? I'm freaking out right now!"

"Please remain calm. I need you to be calm and think about me for a second. Just breathe. You can do this."

"Okay. Focus. Focus!" Meg had shouted. "Are you absolutely sure he was going to kiss you?"

"Yes. I'm sure. At least I think I'm sure."

"And were you going to kiss him back?"

"I don't know! I didn't have time to think about it. It just kind of happened, or actually didn't happen."

"Okay, Lex," Meg had said, sounding less hysterical, "I mean you know I would be the first person to say jump his bones, despite being absolutely consumed with envy, but you've got Lance now."

"I've got Lance now and he's wonderful. But maybe I don't feel as strongly for him as I should?" Lexi had glanced around the room at the wilting roses, making a mental note to call housekeeping and have them removed.

"Lance is a total catch, Lex... you're just being swayed by the allure of a skinny English rocker with a sexy new beard and a beautiful mind. Who wouldn't be? But he's a player, right? He has to be! He'll probably give you chlamydia and you'll feel disgusted with yourself afterwards. *And* you're working with him. *And* you've got a boyfriend now who is a total sweetie and you don't want to jeopardize that. I want to say go for it, I really do. But I just can't. I'm team Lance all the way. You *can't* do anything."

Lexi knew Meg had a point. Not just one point, but many. She'd stayed silent on the other end of the phone. The daisy chain was wilting.

"Sweetie, you'll just be a disposable item to a guy like George Bryce. Don't forget what your business is there. It's all about preservation, not throwing things away."

Meg can be astoundingly lucid and insightful when the situation calls for it, and Lexi hangs onto those wise words as she gets dressed for this morning's meetings. She had ducked into Selfridges department store yesterday and picked up a cute black skirt and a pair of ankle boots to wear to the awards ceremony tonight, along with Meg's purple leather jacket. Lexi already loves London. All the women look so stylish, but not in a plastic, overpriced way. She could imagine living here. Renting a small flat. Walking through the park to work every day. Taking the tube. Wearing knitted hats and gloves in the winter.

Luckily the meeting this morning is only with Russell and Gabe and the graphic designer. That's fine with her. She needs to stay well out of temptation's way. George will be so busy tonight, he's bound to hardly notice her at all.

GEORGE
16th February, 2010
Paddington, London, 10:00 a.m.

LEXI
February 16th, 2010
Paddington, London, 10:00 a.m.

There are about ten of them packed into the lift. George had been standing right next to Lexi but a group of businessmen crowded on at the second floor and he was jostled into the opposite corner. The suits are debriefing a meeting they must have just had and Russell is explaining to Gabe the perils of petroleum. George can't even catch Lexi's eye.

The big guy behind Lexi keeps jabbing her with his elbow as he gesticulates to his colleague. His cologne is overbearing and every time he inadvertently touches her, she tenses up. It's not as if she isn't tense already since coming face to face with George in the lobby, who was not scheduled to be at this meeting. His hair was slightly damp and it took everything in her power to stop herself from imagining him in the shower.

George follows the numbers moving up. Their appointment is on the fifteenth floor and the businessmen have pressed 14. One of them suddenly says, "Crikey, forgot I was supposed to deliver the portfolio to Morton. I need to get off at 10." Lexi is standing near the front. When the doors of the tenth floor open, she steps out to let the man through. Another woman squeezes on.

Lexi is plotting various strategies in her head to avoid being too close to George. She must not sit next to him in the meeting. She must direct all of her attention to Gabe. It is a relief when they arrive on the tenth floor and she has to step off the elevator for a moment to let the guy out. Another woman darts in front of her and the doors start to close. Lexi presses the button on the wall, but the doors keep closing. "I'll see you up there," she calls through the gap, quite content not to squash back into the airless space.

It happens so fast that he doesn't even think about it. It's as if something instinctual propels him forward just as the lift doors are closing. George pushes his way through the narrowing gap, like fleeing the jaws of a snapping crocodile, he gets out just in time. Lexi is looking at him with her mouth partially open and a questioning look in her eyes. He clears his throat, "Couldn't stay... get claustrophobic..."

Lexi is stupefied. How has this happened again? Running from temptation has never been so impossible. Usually she just shoves the chocolate chunk cookies into the cupboard behind the pasta strainer. George is tenacious. He must be one of those types that need a challenge. He can challenge himself elsewhere. She is *not* going to be his disposable paper bag.

"Couldn't stay... get claustrophobic..." he says comically, and she tries not to smile.

"I don't need an escort, you know."

George nods, "Honestly, that bloke's aftershave was killing me."

"Old Spice?" She really shouldn't even be engaging him in banter, in fact she should just tell him right now that she has a boyfriend.

"Very Old Spice," he responds. Lexi presses the button to call the elevator again. The two of them stand next to each other in the windowless hallway. *This is it*, George tells himself, *You probably have one minute. One minute to finish what you started. One minute, Third Row, Destination in the Middle—* the songs for the new album are lining themselves up one after another and it's as if everything is crystallizing in this single moment. He stops thinking. He moves towards her. Here it is. His kiss.

He's getting closer. She could move away. She s*hould* move away, but every cell in her body is tingling, anticipating his lips. When their mouths finally touch, the kiss is soft and tender and deliciously deliberate. He tastes like mint and his beard is slightly scratchy against her chin. His hand slides around her lower back and she forsakes every resolution she has ever made. Ever.

It is so freeing not to be thinking and just to be kissing. At last. This kiss is like his music translated into action. For all the love songs he has ever written—he himself has felt so little love. For all the hearts he is responsible for making throb—his own heart has stayed so still. Until now. George could kiss Lexi forever. And ever.

Neither of them can say who pulls away first. Lexi feels completely unbuttoned, despite remaining fully clothed.

George smiles triumphantly, "I've been meaning to do that for a long time," he says, still close, almost whispering.

"You have? How long?" She flashes back to the concert at the Avid. Remembers him on stage. Staring.

"Really, really long," he says, and this time Lexi knows she *can* read something into the two reallys.

GEORGE
16th February, 2010
Earls Court, London, 4:00 p.m.

George is sure that tonight's performance will be a standout one. The venue is crawling with people setting up and preparing for the most high-profile music awards ceremony in the UK. Adrian Carter, one of the event organizers, seems surprisingly cool and collected as he shows the band to their dressing area. "You're on for your final rehearsal in thirty minutes. In the meantime, please do let us know if there is anything you need." What could George possibly need, now that he has the memory of kissing Lexi to carry everywhere with him like a secret charm?

Earlier that day, when the doors had opened, George and Lexi had stepped back into another lift, this time with only a few people in it. He'd held her hand tightly for the next five floors and reluctantly let go, just as they reached the fifteenth floor.

Gabe and Russell were waiting.

"What happened to you?" asked Gabe.

"Nothing," said George. "It felt as if there was about to be a situation in there." Little did they know that there *was* a situation soon after. The most blissful situation George could imagine.

"Yes, it was getting a little cramped, wasn't it?" said Russell. "I find in those circumstances, hatha yoga breathing helps."

"I'll keep that in mind," George had said.

After the meeting, as they said goodbye, he'd mouthed "talk later" but he wasn't sure she'd understood. What now? She's going back to LA. He's here with a million commitments and then they're starting their tour. He'd tried calling her hotel that afternoon, but no one had picked up. He'll just have to wait until he sees her to get her phone number. This feeling he has, this feeling like some wild and extravagant blossom is unfurling deep inside of him, surely she must be feeling it too?

LEXI
February 16th, 2010
Metropolitan Hotel, London, 4:00 p.m.

Lexi left Russell an hour ago at the Science museum, mesmerized by an exhibit on renewable energies. She's stopped at Selfridges again to buy a smoky grey eye shadow and a lipstick called 'dare me'. She can't make any sense of what has happened today, only that in the hours since George has kissed her, she feels ridiculously alive. And all she wants is more.

GEORGE
16th February, 2010
Earls Court, London, 4:15 p.m.

Simon comes up to George and puts his arm around him. "I just wanted to say thank you mate, for being so supportive of my relationship with Stacey. I know you two didn't get off to the best of starts, but she likes you and she's agreeing to a clean slate. Come on, she knows it's you and you only for Best Man—you'll do it, won't you?" First Polly's bloody second wedding and now Simon marrying Scary Stacey and they all seem to want George on the sidelines cheering them on.

Anyway, things will be different now. Lexi will be with him. He won't be alone.

"I can't leave it to Duncan, can I, mate? I'll do it—just don't make me wear a penguin suit."

Mark is sitting shuffling a pack of cards. "You could, you know, wear a penguin suit. I mean like a real one with a beak and everything. Should I run the idea by Stacey?" Mark is way more talkative since the band have been working on his song. George realizes now how important that was to his self-esteem.

"Good luck with that," says Simon, looking nervous. "Oh yeah, George, and Stace says she's got a bunch of friends she could set you up with."

"Not necessary," says George.

"Why's that?" asks Duncan, who is already on his third bottle of beer. "You saving yourself for our Fanny? I saw her down the hallway just now. Not a scratch of make-up. Could pass for fifteen. She's ripe for the picking, G Whizz. If you're not biting anymore, I will."

"Help yourself," says George, knowing it's unlikely that he can avoid seeing Fanny for the entire evening.

"I would, but she seems to think she's not finished with you. She told me it was extremely top secret urgent that she talks to you pronto. Shall I send her in?"

"Very funny," says George, looking forward to a life with a woman who is psychologically sound. "She has a direct line to the underworld or something, Dunc. She talks to her dead boyfriend, Sebastian. She's completely mad."

"Just my type," says Duncan opening up another bottle of beer. "I'll convince her tonight. After we've won."

George needs to tell Gabe to supervise Duncan. He doesn't want him off his head before they've even rehearsed.

LEXI
February 16th, 2010
Metropolitan Hotel, London, 4:00 p.m.

Lexi walks down the long, minimalist hallway with a growing excitement about tonight's festivities. She's decided she's not going to tell anyone about the kiss. Or the hand holding. Or her heart, which feels as if it has been lit by a thousand flickering candles. Not even Meg. It's hers to savor for a little while longer. She'll be back home in a few days. Back to reality. Back to Lance. They've only been dating for six weeks. It's not like they've even discussed being exclusive, except they see each other every weekend, so she knows that they are. But for right now all she wants to do is continue this adventure while she can. This might be the first time in her life she has actually rebelled and it feels exhilarating. Sliding her key in the slot, Lexi plots out her next hour. She's going to run a hot bath and shave her legs. The door swings open.

"Surprise!"

Lance is lying on the bed wearing the tiniest pair of black briefs, an over-enthusiastic smile and nothing else. *Oh dear God.*

"Lance! What... what are you doing here?" She throws her bags down on the floor and looks around the room, flustered, wishing someone could wave a magic wand and make him go away.

"What does it look like I'm doing? I'm surprising you!"

"Well, holy crap, that worked. You really *have* surprised me."

"Good. That was the intention. Are you happy?" he rolls off the bed and walks towards her for a hug. She can see the bulge growing in his underwear like a balloon inflating. She wants to scream.

"I'm just a little taken aback, that's all. I don't really like surprises." He pulls her towards him. He smells like pretzels.

The only word running a marathon of circles in her head is *George, George, George.*

"Let me see what I can do to rectify that. I raided the mini bar. I've opened up a bottle of champagne. You've got to agree that London is one of the most romantic cities on earth." He has no idea how very much in agreement she is. He tries to kiss her and she wriggles away.

"I'm sorry, Lance. It really is good to see you," she lies, "it's just that I'm not feeling great. I've been a little queasy all day. It must have been something I ate."

"Here, gorgeous," he says, leading her towards the bed, "sit down, I'll give you a foot massage." Now she wants to scream even louder than before, as he unzips her boots and starts kneading the balls of her feet.

"How's that? If I'm not wrong, there's an acupressure point right about here that helps with nausea." It would have to be a pretty big point to help tackle what Lexi is feeling.

"That's helping a bit, thank you," she says, withdrawing her foot. "So what's the story? I'm very busy with work, you know."

"No story. I just couldn't stand another second without you and it happened that the firm needed me to fly to Paris to meet with another engineer for that bridge project, so I thought I would kill two birds with one stone and make a little pit stop. I know you're busy. I'll only bother you after hours," he says, winking. Lance has definitely killed more than two birds with his stone.

"Paris? When are you leaving?" she doesn't want to be too obvious but she needs to know.

"Thursday morning and I was hoping you would come with me to celebrate."

"Celebrate what?" asks Lexi, glancing at the digital clock next to the bed.

"Our engagement."

"Excuse me?" Has he just said what she thinks he's said?

"That is if you'll say yes." Lance falls dramatically to one knee, and now because his briefs are obscured, he looks as if he's naked. He slips his hand under the mattress and pulls out a large, glinting diamond ring.

"I love you, Lexi Jacobs. I only realized how much when you got on that plane and flew away from me. I know it hasn't been long but you're everything I've been searching for in a woman. Kind, beautiful, sexy, intelligent, responsible. Will you do me the honor of marrying me?"

Her heart stops beating for a second and she closes her eyes. All her candles have been blown out. This cannot be happening. When she opens them again, Lance is still balancing in front of her holding the ring. She starts to speak but is drowned out by an extremely loud knocking.

"Lexi! Lexi, are you in there?" Russell is hammering insistently. "Lexi, are you there?"

"Yes!" she calls, leaping up from the bed and running to the door, anything to try and get away from the question at hand.

"Did you just say yes?" asks Lance. "Was that a yes?"

Lexi throws open the door and comes face to face with a very traumatized-looking Russell. His linen trousers are ripped at the knee and he is holding a napkin to his chin. Lexi can see blood seeping through.

"Russell! What happened to you?"

"I was mugged by some terrifying yobos outside the tube station. They ripped my fanny pack from around my waist and threw me to the ground. It was dreadful."

"Oh you poor thing!" says Lexi, guiding Russell into the room, "Come and sit down."

Lance begins frantically pulling on his jeans.

"Lance, my goodness, what are you doing here?" asks Russell, who is rather shaky on his legs.

"I'm proposing to Lexi, Russell," says Lance, "in fact I

was right in the middle of it." He holds out the diamond for proof.

"I *do* choose my moments, don't I?" says Russell, accepting the glass of water that Lexi has poured for him, "What did she say?"

"Well, the last word out of her mouth was—yes," says Lance, looking hopefully to Lexi, who is feeling bizarrely suspended in time, wondering how long the three of them can survive her silence. She just doesn't know what's supposed to happen next. Is this the happy ending that everyone is waiting for?

GEORGE
16th February, 2010
Earls Court, 7:00 p.m.

LEXI
February 16th, 2010
Earls Court, 7:00 p.m.

George has managed to manoeuvre Lexi away from the table, pretending that he wants to introduce her to someone. She had arrived separately from Russell, and George had begun to worry, speculating that maybe she wasn't going to show. She looks amazing in a short black skirt, ankle boots and a leather jacket. Her hair is the colour of walnut wood.

"Hi again." Everyone is eating before the show begins and he has to lean in to be heard above the noise. He puts his hand on the back of her waist, finding it difficult not to touch her.

"Hi," Lexi is trying to remove Lance from her mind. She left him at the hotel eating a club sandwich. "Are you sure I can't come with you?" he'd said.

"Definitely sure—it's business."

"You look very spectacular." George is close enough so that she can feel his breath.

"Have you seen Lady Gaga yet?"

"Oh her.... Boooring."

"You nervous?"

"I will be if I don't get your phone number soon."

"How many girls have heard that?"

"Only the ones I kissed today. Care to see the list?"

"Not really. But now that you mention it, I might ask if Fanny Arundel is on it."

"Ask away."

"Is she your girlfriend?"

"Absolutely not. The questions are starting. Does this mean we're getting serious?" George has never been more at ease with a woman.

"That depends. I do need to talk to you about something."

"I'm about to get a bit busy being a rock star. Can I see you alone later?"

"I'm not sure that's the best idea..."

"Trust me—it is." There is something about Lexi that is both reassuring and intriguing. He knows that underneath her poised exterior he'll discover a more fragile layer. He's ready to explore.

"Why should I trust you? I hardly know you..."

"But we do know each other, Lexi, don't we? Don't tell me you're not feeling the connection too?"

"I am, George. I am. But it's kinda' freaking me out because there are things that you don't know. It's complicated." The glint of the diamond ring flashes before Lexi's eyes.

"I *do* know, Lexi. I've been wanting to tell you. I—" Gabe skids to a halt in front of them. "George, where the hell have you been? They need you backstage—now. Everyone's waiting."

"Okay, I'm coming," he steps away from Lexi. "I'll see you after the performance. I'll finish the story then."

8:15 p.m.

George is in his element. No dancers. No fancy light show. No gimmicks. Just him and the boys doing what they do best with nothing to hide behind. Tonight they are singing "Under the Radar"—one single gem. One chance to confirm that they've been nominated for a reason. He's singing to a roomful of fans and peers, but really he's only singing to one person and this time he knows exactly who she is.

How could I have left you
Tried so hard to forget you
You slipped under the radar
I'll start looking today

The static in my brain
Slowly driving me insane
Searching for a name
I never even knew
Try and end this
Searching
I've missed the crucial clue
never ending searching
for you, you, you

You slipped under the radar
I was looking away
I was looking away

He wrote this song three years ago, long before he was even aware of Lexi's existence. The best part of singing these lyrics tonight is knowing that they are no longer true.

Lexi can hear glasses clinking, but mostly just a hushed silence as George holds the room enrapt. This should really be one of the most exciting and magical nights of her life—in

London at The Brits, sipping champagne, watching George Bryce on stage singing in his incredibly sexy voice, actually knowing for sure that the one woman he wants to be with tonight is her.

Instead Lexi is consumed with a guilt that is making her fidget. How can she be so fickle? So careless? So selfish? No men for months and then two arrive at the same time, both offering her completely different directions. She wishes now for the girl she once was, the all-American prom queen with her future laid out neatly before her, like a laundered outfit hanging on the back of a chair. Or does she? *These are not real problems*, Lexi reminds herself. *Think of what other people in the world are suffering through and here I am whining about being wanted by two different men.* Lexi looks up at George on stage, singing beautifully, sounding dreamy and vulnerable. As usual, his lyrics are talking to her. All she has to do is try and work out exactly what they are saying.

9:25 p.m.

"And the Listener's Choice award for best album of the year goes to Thesis!" The table erupts. George takes a deep breath and looks around at the boys. Duncan's eyes look disturbingly glazed. Stacey has wrapped herself around Simon's neck. Mark is kissing Anna. He catches Lexi's eye instead. She smiles. He wants to kiss her again, right now. He can't wait to tell her everything—how he saw her running, how he saw her in the third row, how he saw her on the television, how he wants to continue seeing her every day of his life. He doesn't. He smiles back. He walks with the rest of the band to the stage. He accepts the award from Lily Allen and says graciously into the mike, "The Listener's award means the most to us. If *you* weren't listening, you wouldn't be hearing, so thanks for listening, hearing and voting. Cheers!" He hands the microphone to Mark, who is customarily reserved in these situations. "Thanks to our fans and families," says Mark, holding up the award. "We love you all!" The audience clap and holler. Duncan tries to grab the microphone, but thankfully the music kicks in and they are ushered off stage quickly before he can say anything.

Lexi watches George accept the award. Before she knows it he'll be pulling her away again, trying to talk. Trying to kiss. She resolves to tell him everything about Lance. She realizes that's her only choice.

10:05 p.m.

The awards are over and the mood is effervescent. It has been a memorable ceremony and George was blown away by Dizzee Rascal's duet with Florence. Robbie Williams wound up the evening with a medley of old trusties and Lexi had asked, "Who's that?"— a reminder to George to be grateful that they are known on both sides of the globe. There will be a slew of all night parties to choose from now, but George's only intent is to slip away with Lexi. Maybe they'll take a taxi to the Embankment and walk along the river, or perhaps he'll take her to his favourite spot on Primrose Hill.

Lexi feels slightly relieved ever since making the decision to come clean to George and a few glasses of crisp white wine have helped take the edge off. They'll talk. She'll explain her dilemma. He'll understand. Won't he?

The night has been incredible. Jay Z was amazing and Fanny Arundel gave a performance that made even Lady Gaga look tame, wearing nothing but iridescent underwear and twenty lollipops sprouting out of her beehive hair.

Russell appears to have recovered from his earlier trauma and has been chatting to Gabe most of the evening. George is sitting across the table from her and keeps catching her eye and grinning. She can't believe that she has wasted so much time imagining George to be the arrogant, womanizing rock star that he obviously isn't. It appears that Duncan is the one member of the band who is fully embracing that stereotype. He has stood up and is swaying back and forth like a precariously unstable tree.

"Sooo," says Duncan, holding an empty glass above his head. George is worried about him. He has managed to circumvent Fanny for the entire night, but he saw Duncan falling all over her backstage. He's definitely high on something, most likely supplied directly by her.

Duncan waves the glass in the air, "I'd like to say bottoms up and tits up to us all for being such talented fuckers!"

"Hear hear!" says Simon.

"And congratulations to us for getting engaged!" pipes in Stacey, who is even louder when drunk.

Lexi only has to hear the words 'engaged' and her stomach drops.

"Hear, hear, hear!" repeats Simon boisterously.

"Are we making toasts?" Fanny Arundel, in her outrageous ensemble, has suddenly appeared at the table, licking one of the lollipops previously balanced in her hair. She drapes an arm theatrically around George's shoulder.

"Want a lick?" she says, sliding the lollipop seductively down her tongue.

George is horrified. He needs to get her away immediately. "The show is over, Fanny," he says, hoping she'll get the hint.

Lexi considers Fanny to be one of the most intimidating creatures she has ever seen, even though without her comically high shoes, she's probably not much taller than five feet.

"My show's just beginning, Georgie. Don't you want everyone to toast *our* happy news?" All George wants to do is take Lexi's hand and run. Everyone at the table is listening.

"You're pissed, Fanny."

"Oh—not pissed, George—not in my condition. I've been trying to reach you for weeks but you've been so very, very busy. I just thought you might like to toast this as well..." She pats her stomach several times while tilting her head to one side and smiling. George feels the blood draining from his face. He bites down hard on his lower lip.

"That's right, Georgie," Fanny says holding out the slimy lollipop, "you're going to be a dada."

George closes his eyes tightly.

Lexi opens hers wider.

"Splendid!" says Russell. "This calls for more champagne!"

10:20 p.m.

How wrong Lexi was, thinking that George might be the one to break her heart, when in fact Fanny has done the job for him, grinding her spiky heels in and twisting them around ruthlessly. Everyone is moving and making noise around her but she can't really take any of it in. George has hurriedly moved Fanny away from the table and is talking to her as intently as he was talking to Lexi only two hours ago. Apparently there is a lot they need to fill each other in on.

Lexi needs to leave. She turns to Russell, "You go on to the after parties. I'm going back to the hotel to see Lance."

"I'm not so sure about that," says Russell, sounding a bit lost. "The atmosphere appears to have soured slightly."

"That's rock and roll for you," Lexi says lamely.

"I think I prefer *our* line of work."

"I agree. Shall we go then?" Lexi takes one last look over at George, who is still entangled in a heated conversation with Fanny. Even though they've only shared one kiss, it now feels far too much to walk away unscathed. And besides, her imagination has been busy with him for months, despite having convinced herself she had lost interest. Since first seeing the video, George had always been there in the shadowy corners of her mind, composing lyrics, slipping off his shirt, sliding his hands under hers. Lexi thinks back to the giddy exchange she'd shared with George outside the studio. The easy rapport between them. The thwarted first kiss. The actual first kiss. Was that really only this morning?

Gabe walks towards them both looking extremely anxious. "We did promise you an unforgettable evening!" he says self-consciously.

"And I'd say you delivered on that, Gabriel. Luckily, all we have to do is consult on the band's environmental issues rather than their love lives. We'll leave that up to you," says Russell.

"Yes, indeed. Well, thank you both for being here and let's talk before you go."

"Of course," says Russell.

"And Lexi," Gabe takes her hand and squeezes it, "Congratulations."

"Thank you," says Lexi, mystified, as Gabe walks away. She follows Russell through the auditorium towards the exits. People are still making their way out, tripping and laughing and singing drunkenly. Lexi, in contrast, feels somber.

"That's odd," she says, "why would Gabe be congratulating *me*?"

Russell looks flustered, "Oh dear, Lexi. I think I may have spoken out of line. I mean the Chablis was flowing plentifully tonight and I unintentionally let it slip about your engagement. It's only that I think poor Gabe is rather interested in you and I didn't want him to get the wrong impression."

Lexi sighs, "But I'm not engaged, Russell."

Russell looks surprised. "Lance said you accepted?"

"That wasn't a *yes* for *him*. That was a *yes* for *you* knocking at the door. I told him after you left, it's just too soon. I can't..." In fact, the exact words Lexi had said to Lance were, "I can't rush into marriage... we need to slow things down. It's early stages. We're just mixing in all the ingredients. The cake is nowhere near ready to be baked."

"No cake?" Lance had said pathetically.

"Not yet."

Lexi had hoped this would give her a bit more breathing space—a chance to see George again and make a decision. But none of that mattered now. George was gone. Off into the bleary sunset with a deranged girl/woman who was carrying his baby.

She remembers again the concert and how foolish she'd felt when Meg and the girl next to her had both said they thought George was staring at them. How could she have been so naive? The same feeling of shame envelops her now, except this time it is blacker and far more corrosive.

Lexi crosses her arms tightly in front of her chest. "It doesn't matter anyway," she says to Russell, as they walk away from the massive building and into the crisp London night. "Let them think I'm engaged." Perhaps this might even work in her favor. If George hears the news, she will have managed to detonate her own device, without even any planning involved. Russell is looking around for a taxi. The tears begin to fall from Lexi's eyes, and it is so cold outside that she imagines each teardrop freezing, forming glistening, frozen crystals on her skin.

GEORGE
17th February, 2010
Primrose Hill, London, 6:30 a.m.

George is back in his spot on Primrose Hill watching a pale orange sun trying to break through a misty sky. He's been up all night. There is nothing suitable about this dawn. He is all alone. Again. The night had unfolded like a suffocating dream. What was he to do? Fanny might well be pregnant with his child, after all, he was the moron who had slept with her.

"Come on, Fanny, how do you know it's mine?" George had insisted on asking last night, as soon as he had veered her away from the demolition she had already caused. He couldn't bear to look at Lexi. Was there any amount of damage control that could fix this?

"Because I know. I don't sleep around with just anyone, George. I'm very selective. I tried to explain to you—Sebastian and I chose you. Don't you understand?"

If George could have ripped out every lollipop from her hair and shoved them down her throat, he would. He'd never felt so full of fury.

"No, Fanny. I don't understand! I didn't choose you. I didn't choose this."

"Well, you might have thought of that before you fucked me in Vegas."

George had attempted to control himself, "That's questionable, isn't it, Fanny? You see because I don't even know if that actually happened."

"Well, it did in LA."

She had him there.

"But we used a condom," he had said in an angry whisper.

"It must have had a hole or something. It happens, George. Sebastian wanted this for us."

"What?!"

"I've been trying to let you know. I've already had a scan. We're having a boy. It's Sebastian's last chance at rebirth. He's coming home..." It was then that George knew it was a losing battle. Sebastian might be getting a final chance to give life another go, but George's number was up.

"Fanny, I need some time to let this all absorb," George had said, shaking his head. "Let me call you tomorrow, okay?" George hadn't known what the hell he was going to say to her, but he needed to get to Lexi and he couldn't wait a moment longer.

"Fine, but you better call me. We have a lot to discuss. I want to give birth on the beach in Devon... I'm thinking about doing a live Internet feed for our fans." This had to be the most atrocious conversation he would ever have in his life.

"Wow. Yeah... a lot to discuss." George had turned around then and looked towards their table. He wished with every fibre in his body that he could press rewind. The room was clearing out and everyone had dispersed. Lexi was gone. The only person left was Gabe, standing back dutifully, waiting to assess the wreckage.

George walked towards him looking stunned.

"You all right, George?" Gabe had put his hand protectively on George's back.

"Not exactly."

"We'll figure it out."

"No we won't, you don't know the half of it." He had looked around at the empty table. "Where's Lexi, Gabe? I need to talk to her."

"Lexi? Why? I wouldn't have thought you'd be in the mood to talk business."

"It's not business."

"You too, huh?"

"Gabe, I think I'm in love with her." It was the first time he'd spoken the words out loud. He pictured a caption above his head, bold black letters and lots of tiny red hearts.

"Okaaayy..." said a shocked Gabe, "didn't see that coming. But guess this is the night of the unexpected. So you can add this to the list—turns out you were right—she *is* engaged."

"Excuse me?" George had said, beginning to feel numb.

"Not to Russell. She has some high flying boyfriend who swooped in and proposed to her this afternoon. He gave her a big rock and everything."

"But..." And that was where it had ended. There was nothing to follow the but. Nothing that George could have said to explain how something so intricately configured and cared for in his imagination for the last four months could, without warning, disintegrate into a pile of papery ashes.

The sun is fighting its hardest to break through the early morning fog. George speculates he doesn't have much more fight left in him. What's left to salvage? Lexi thinks he's an arsehole. He *is* an arsehole. Lexi lied to him. Even if she broke off her engagement, why would she entertain a relationship with him? Destiny was crueller than he thought. Crueller than his mocking sister. Crueller than the most savage review. This was his fate. This bench. This cold morning. Fame but clearly not love.

LEXI
February 17th, 2010
Metropolitan Hotel, London, 6:30 a.m.

Lexi wakes up in Lance's arms. His left leg is wrapped around her, trapping her beneath it. He's fast asleep and breathing with his mouth open. The events of last night begin to fuse together, revealing a picture she would like to tear up into a thousand ragged pieces. Lance starts to stir. Lexi looks down at him and wonders if she really could love him one day as much as he loves her. Perhaps once she gets some urgently needed distance from George and London and all the dreadfully confusing events of the last forty-eight hours, perhaps then she will arrive at some clarity. He opens his eyes slowly.

"You're back."

"Yes, I am."

"I wasn't sure if I should have left."

"You shouldn't have. I'm glad you stayed."

"I don't do things in half measures, Lex, but I'm willing to be patient. All I want is for us to be together."

"I know."

"So—we still are—together?"

Lexi takes a deep breath. If destiny brought George into

her life then it also brought her here to this moment with Lance. Maybe this is really where she belongs? "Yes, we are."

"Lance and Lexi?"

"Lance and Lexi *Jacobs*."

Lance kisses her cheek, "Jacobs for now, until I can persuade you to take my name." Lexi smiles but inside she feels agitated. Take his name? She hates the idea of changing her name. She won't do it. Even if they eventually get married. And honestly she doesn't even know if she wants to get married at all. To anyone. Ever.

"Shall I run us a bubble bath then?" says Lance, pulling a t-shirt over his broad shoulders.

"Okay," says Lexi, noticing her clothes from last night thrown on the floor in a wrinkled heap, a reminder of the mess that is George Bryce. Her heart feels horribly bruised. The lyrics of "Under the Radar" are still in her head, floating around like nomadic helium balloons.

> *how could I have missed you*
> *left someone else to kiss you*
> *you slipped under the radar*
> *I was looking away*

GEORGE
17th February, 2010
Camden, London, 9:00 p.m.

Nothing was on the schedule for today. What could have been a euphoric day off with the woman he loves, has instead turned into one long empty hour after hour—most of them spent walking aimlessly around north London. George has eventually ended up at the studio, where he is now at the piano feebly attempting to write something. Anything to release this slow building pain. He called Fanny at 12:30. He'd reached her voice mail, "Hi, it's George. Look, I hope you're

feeling okay and everything. We need to talk about this...
this... situation. I'm sorry I didn't return your calls. Call me."
It's not that he wants to speak to her. He wouldn't care if he
never speaks to her again, but he knows that he needs to do
the right thing. The press will have almost certainly picked up
on it by now. No doubt *The Sun* has a headline along the lines
of **FANNY KNOCKED UP! GEORGE COCKED UP!**

He's thought about Lexi all day but he hasn't tried to
reach her. It's useless. There is nothing he can say to remove
himself from this mangled wreck, and if she really did get
engaged yesterday, that means it must have happened after
their kiss. The exquisite kiss that he thought was going to be
their glue.

George puts his fingers to the keys but can only play
jarred notes—jagged fragments of sound, mirroring the sharp
edges he feels inside. He closes his eyes as a landslide of
random words enters his mind. He doesn't hear the door
open. It takes him a few minutes to realize someone is watching.

"Where the hell have you been, mate? Should have
thought to come here five hours ago." Duncan looks like a
walking zombie. His eyes are bloodshot and the veins on his
forehead are popping out.

"I don't want to talk, Dunc."

"I'm not an idiot, I know that. Well, actually I am a
bloody pillock, mate. I've really made a balls of it this time."

"Welcome to my world." George sits back on the piano
stool.

"I'm just going to come right out with it, George. I think
I could be the father of Fanny's baby."

"Say again?"

"I didn't want to squeeze in on your action in Vegas,
George, but after she left your room, she was roaming the
fucking hallways in her fucking underwear. I was coming
back from the casino. I doubt even a nun would have turned

her down. She told me she'd been with you, but she rocks my bloody boat, mate. I'm sorry."

"Sorry?! I don't care that you slept with her. I don't even fancy her."

"I know. Gabe sort of let it slip about you and Lexi. She's got it going on, George. I think you should go for it."

"Yeah, except Fanny's announcement was a bit of a buzz kill, Duncan. And I found out she's engaged."

"Fuck that. You can change her mind. Look, George—what I'm trying to say is Fanny's my kind of crazy. If we both shagged her then there's a fifty-fifty chance. It's you or me."

"Or whoever else she bumped into that night."

"She says it's only been the two of us and I believe her. And something else, mate, my package was not wrapped, so I reckon all bets are on me."

"But she told me she knew for certain I was the father."

"Yeah well, lurking beneath those lollipops are brain cells. I called her on that. She said she'd decided that you were better father material—you know, being all sensitive and thoughtful and everything. And she's got a point. On top of it, that dead Sebastian dude wants you to be the dad. Fuck him! Since when does a corpse have so much say?"

George looks at his phone. It's 9:30. What should he do? Nothing's changed. Or has it?

"George, go get your girl, mate. If the kid's mine, we'll both end up with our lady loves. We can have one of those tests they do in the films to find out whose boys hit the jackpot first. No offense, but I think I can guess the answer."

Duncan's right—a paternity test. Lexi's leaving in the morning. Even if she's not interested in his story about Fanny, doesn't she owe him an explanation too? He stands up feeling like Colin Firth in *Bridget Jones*. He'd been forced to watch that film with Polly ten times one Christmas.

"No offense, taken, Duncan," he walks over and gives his friend a hug. "Thanks."

"You don't have to thank me for shagging the woman of my dreams. I just want to be sure you get to do the same thing."

LEXI
February 17th, 2010
Metropolitan Hotel, London, 10:00 p.m.

The fact that George hasn't even attempted to contact her today is only further confirmation that all of her worst fears about him were true. But then again, he's probably heard about her 'engagement', so why would he bother? Lexi feels emotionally depleted. She has spent the day with Russell and Lance wandering through antique markets buying second-hand scarves and sipping scalding coffee. Tomorrow morning she'll be on a plane back to normality. To Andrew and Carl. To Meg and Tim. To her peculiar parents and their even more peculiar dog. She can put this all behind her. One day, she's sure she'll look back and laugh about this week—tell her grandchildren about the English rocker who very nearly stole her heart. She'll only being lying slightly.

London is arctic tonight. As she steps out of the taxi the icy air shocks her. She is looking forward to the warm LA sun on her cheeks. She and Lance have just come from dinner at The Wolseley, a posh art deco restaurant in Mayfair where they ate oysters and hand-cut french fries. They drank nice wine. He gave her nice compliments. He told her nice stories about the nice bridge he is designing in Paris. It's time for her to get accustomed to 'nice' again and for once, try to be satisfied. As he steps out of the taxi behind her, he grabs her waist and twists her to face him. He is wearing a navy cashmere overcoat and a silk patterned scarf.

"Surely you must have mistaken me for a dapper Englishman, my dearest?" he says in a bad fake accent.

She manages a laugh, "Why yes—I thought you were Colin Firth. You mean you're not?"

"Let me kiss you and you can make up your own mind," Lance plants a very wet kiss on Lexi's cold lips. She can't get the hallway out of her mind. She can't stop recalling how kissing George had felt like arriving home—to a place she never even knew existed.

GEORGE
17TH February, 2010
the corner opposite The Metropolitan Hotel, 10:00 p.m.

George had jumped on the tube, pulling his old black beanie almost over his eyes to ensure that he wasn't recognized. As he'd sat in the carriage, speeding forward towards the next station, he couldn't stop focusing on the sign in front of him, "Obstructing the doors can be dangerous." He wasn't buying that. Opening doors could hurt just as much. If he'd obstructed the doors to his heart, he wouldn't have been sitting there then. He wouldn't have been on his way to try to convince the woman he loves to leave her fiancé and choose him and his unborn exorcist baby instead.

He'd vaulted off the tube at Hyde Park Corner and began running towards the hotel. He is nearly there. The temperature outside is plummeting and the sky looks like a sheet of cold dark metal, but the blood is rushing through him and he's feeling pumped. *If I can step out and sing in front of 20,000 people—I can bloody well have this conversation. I'll just say to her—Lexi—I love you and I think you love me too. Let's not let all of these misunderstandings obstruct our doors.* Yes! That's what he's going to say. He'll just go straight to her room and—

The black taxi pulls up exactly as he skids to a stop opposite the entrance of The Metropolitan. He sees her get out of the cab, astounded that there is even a thread of luck left with his name on it. He's just about to cross the road when he spots the bloke climbing out of the taxi behind her. Except he's not a bloke. He's not even a guy. He's a man. He's a man with an expensive coat and curly blond hair. He's probably wearing a gold Rolex and his boxer shorts most likely have a crease down the front.

George stops himself. He's breathing rapidly, metamorphosing instantly into the spotty, awkward teenager hiding beneath his crafted façade. He can hear Polly and Amelia sniggering at him from behind his bedroom door. He doesn't cross the road. He stays absolutely still and watches as this man spins Lexi around, making her laugh. He continues to watch as he pulls her in closely and kisses her passionately. Just like a film. Just like Colin Firth. It's Lexi on the big stage now. It's Lexi who is vivid on this freezing night. Irresistible. Untouchable. Out of his league. George has obviously cast himself in the wrong role.

SIX MONTHS LATER

LEXI
August 10th, 2010
Venice Beach, Los Angeles

It really is the sweetest thing she has ever seen. Boris and Cherub are under the floral arch with Mildred and Russell, and they are both licking their paws. Boris has a bow tie fastened around his neck, and Cherub's collar is a forest of freesias—most of which Boris has attempted to eat. Russell and Mildred are all in cream. Organic cotton of course. Lexi listens carefully as they exchange their vows.

"I promise to love you forever, Mildred, my precious dearest. I promise to cherish you and Cherub with tender love and care in this lifetime and beyond. And I promise to eternally honor our earth so that you and I may continue to live joyously upon her while she thrives." Mildred presses her hand on top of Russell's.

"I pledge, my darling Russell, to walk with you and be inspired by you. I pledge my love to you and Boris through every minute of every day. I pledge to support your quest to heal the wounds of this earth. I pledge to make certain that from here on out, your life is gooseberry free..." The congregation laughs, but Lexi also feels increasingly familiar tears in her eyes. She looks down the aisle at Andrew and Carl, Meg and Tim, and her mom and dad, and she feels blessed to have them all in her life. She has thought a lot about love in the six months since London. She still hasn't come to any sage conclusions, other than those that billions of people have reached before her. It is unreliable. It is heavenly. It is the most bewildering feeling in the world. It can come in disguise. It isn't easily found, and it is equally difficult to shake.

Lance and Lexi had stayed together for three months after returning from London. They had continued their nice conversations and their nice dinners and their nice sex life. They had even started watching *Mad Men*. Occasionally a Thesis song would appear on Lexi's iPod while on shuffle and she would feel her heart shift to the left a little, as if trying to make room for the pain. When the song ended, her heart moved back into its correct position. At the end of April, she deleted the album from all of her playlists. Lexi couldn't help but feel that Lance was biding his time, waiting for the right moment to pounce on her again with the shiny ring. Since coming back from London she had been battling a pervasive numbness in her chest—a fear that never again would she watch those neon colored spirals dance above her head in abandon, the way they had when she was with George. After Lance's second trip to Paris Lexi sat him down and said, "Let's talk."

"Let's not," he'd said, looking nervous.

"I'm so sorry, Lance. I thought I could do this. You're so good to me, but I'm just not ready to settle." Lance had attempted to put up a fight but eventually surrendered, packing up his Clinique shaving lotion, his brown Top-Siders and his book of love sonnets. He bade her a sad goodbye, not fully comprehending that 'settle' hadn't just meant settle down; it had meant that Lexi had decided she wasn't yet ready to 'settle' for anything less than spirals.

A month later she heard from Carl that Lance was dating Aurelie, the French engineer he had been designing the bridge with. She hadn't seen red, or even blue. He deserved to be happy and she deserved to stop hearing from her mother how she had sabotaged her own fairy tale ending.

Russell and Mildred are now exchanging eco friendly wedding bands made from recycled silver. It's a miracle that either of them has found time in their hectic schedules to fit in the wedding at all. Business has been booming for Let The Green Times Roll in the last few months. Having a high profile band like Thesis as their first clients, as well as all of

Mildred's contacts behind them, has rocketed LTGTR off to a remarkable start. Lexi made certain when they arrived home to shift all of her attention to working with new clients and hiring new employees, handing over the Thesis account solely to Russell.

Had she imagined that George was going to show up at her hotel in London and sweep her off her feet? Had she fantasized that he would reveal that Fanny's pregnancy was a false alarm and that he couldn't live without her? Yes—she had imagined all of that. When it hadn't happened (because she wasn't Bridget Jones and never would be) she had tried to move on.

Occasionally she'll hear Russell on the phone to Gabe. One time he hung up and said, "Gabriel sends his regards," but for the most part she has remained successfully disconnected. What she can't ignore is that Fanny's baby must certainly be due any day. The news only got worse after she left London. Meg soon reported back to her that according to *The Star*, the baby might not even be George's—it might be Duncan's instead. Yuck! So she wasn't far off about the threesomes and the orgies. The whole band were probably having sex with Fanny at once.

Meg leans over to her now and passes her a crumpled Kleenex. "Don't get carried away, remember that marriage is totally overrated," she says, scowling at Tim. In the grandest of best friend style, she has adapted her views accordingly, and has long since stopped hassling Lexi to conform.

"I remember," says Lexi, accepting the crumpled tissue and holding it very tightly in her hand.

GEORGE
10th August, 2010
Hospital of St John and St Elizabeths, London

George is waiting in the hallway outside the delivery room.

Fanny and Duncan had wanted him to join them in the room but he had declined. Apparently Sebastian's spirit is also in the birthing pool, holding her left hand, while Duncan holds her right.

"That guy's bloody useless," Duncan had quipped when he had appeared in a towel to update George. "He would be a lot more helpful if he wasn't fucking dead. I'm getting all the abuse, while she just smiles at him like an idiot."

George still can't believe this is happening.

His phone had rung at 2:30 that morning.

"Georgie my boy—bring it on! She's fucking mooing like a cow! We're on our way to the hospital. Get over there now, mate!" He could in fact hear some horrific farmyard noises in the background. If Fanny sounded in labour anything like she did when she was snoring, then they were all in for a long, loud night.

George had rolled out of bed and slipped on jeans and a shirt. They had been touring the States for the last seven weeks—and this was their first time home in a while to play some festivals, before heading back out on tour in September.

The weeks following the Brits were like a dank fog. His life, which had momentarily been bathed by Lexi in a shimmering rainbow light, had disintegrated rapidly into a series of relentless dark storms. George had walked away from The Metropolitan that night convinced, not for the first time, that he should really give up on his dream of being loved by anyone intimately. He had spent the next few days locked in his flat writing some of the most depressing songs he had ever penned. Gabe finally persuaded him to come out with the boys. Two weeks later Simon handed him a ticket to Vegas where he was forced to return to the scene of the crime, as well as being forced to bear witness to Simon and Stacey's ludicrous nuptials at The Real Elvis Wedding Chapel. Simon had Stacey's name tattooed on the inside of his arm and George's lyrics became even darker.

Starting the North American tour had helped.

The weirdest turn of events though had been Duncan's transformation. Since finding out about Fanny's pregnancy, he had become uncharacteristically sentimental. While George was gutted at the prospect of being the father of Fanny's baby, Duncan was jubilant. He pursued her hotly, indulging her belief in Sebastian's existence, as well as indulging her rampant sexual appetite, which by all accounts had gone into pregnancy overdrive. She soon loosened her grip on George, but the fact remained that he might still be the father of the baby. The three of them had eventually agreed amicably that there would be a paternity test after the baby was born. Fanny had apologized to George for trying to mislead him. "I don't like being ignored, Georgie." George knew he was the only one to blame and until today, had remained emotionally incarcerated.

The hospital smells like plastic. He nibbles on his cuticle. His mother, who has very recently learned how to text, sent him a message ten minutes ago, "Well?"

Last week she had phoned to say, "George, your father and I are not finding this situation very pleasant. This morning in the co-op Sharon Hillway was gossiping about us behind the shortbread display. We are trying to be supportive, but please let me know if I am going to be a grandmother, before I have to hear it in the post office from some old biddy who has been reading about you in the newspapers." George is strangely touched by his mother's concern. He wonders if she's been knitting booties. He texts her back now, "No news yet."

The noise from inside is beginning to reach a fever pitch. It sounds as if Fanny and Duncan are both chanting ancient Buddhist prayers, and every so often she screams, "Whooo-peeeeeeeee!" George stands up in pressing need of some fresh air. He takes the lift down to reception. He hasn't stepped in a lift since February without thinking about Lexi. In fact he thinks about her all the time with a weighty regret. These days the image that revisits him the most is the very first time he saw her—running. He still wants to know what made her cry that day and he wonders if she's ever cried over him? He's asked Gabe not to talk to him about her. He's made a choice to let her go. Let her get on with the life she is meant to lead. Without him complicating matters. Without him spoiling it for her.

As he approaches the entrance to the hospital, he sees a swarm of photographers like a cloud of bees waiting to sting. George should have guessed. Fanny's 'people' probably called the press the second she went into labour. At least George and Duncan had dissuaded her from the live Internet feed from the coast of Devon. It occurs to George that this is a sign of things to come. If the baby really is his, then this will be too.

Every time he takes his kid out for an ice cream, they'll probably be hounded by these piranhas. *His kid out for an ice cream. His kid.* George turns away from the entrance and heads back towards the lifts. *This isn't what was meant to happen* he thinks to himself. *I'm not ready to be a dad, especially not with Fanny as the mother.* A disarming panic begins festering inside him. He thinks of the grandchildren he was planning to have with Lexi—the sweet little tearaways with tousled hair and their granny's sparkling green/grey eyes. Their faces fade into nothing, replaced in his mind by a zany toddler with Fanny's pouty lips and a creepy man's face.

The lift doors open. George really does feel cornered now. He couldn't leave even if he wanted to. As he approaches the birthing wing, he hears something different. It's no longer the Fanny and Duncan show, instead he can hear a baby's extremely ear-piercing cry. He nods to the nurses at the desk who point him down the hallway. Duncan, still wearing only a towel, is standing outside the door of the room cradling a small writhing bundle. George feels choked up, but he doesn't know if it's emotion or bile or both.

"How is he?" says George, moving towards them tentatively.

"Bloody brilliant, mate," Duncan tenderly kisses the forehead of the little squirming human. "But the best bit is, I think I've talked Fanny into retiring Sebastian. That tosser's royally past it, and his prediction was completely wrong. We've got ourselves a baby girl!"

George smiles and looks down at the crying baby. Her face is wrinkled and red, and her mouth is wide open.

"How's Fanny?" asks George.

"Incredible," says Duncan, who is most definitely in love. George recognizes the symptoms now. "She's having words with the dead dude, while they stitch her up. He's getting off easy, I reckon," says Duncan, as the baby's cries reach an even higher pitch.

"She's certainly got some lungs on her," George says, trying to grab hold of her tiny hand.

"She bloody does, doesn't she? She already takes after her mother," says Duncan proudly.

"Sounds that way," says George, desperately hoping that the one parent she doesn't take after is him.

LEXI
August 22nd, 2010
Pacific Palisades, Los Angeles

Thirty-three. Lexi can't decide if she is pleased to put thirty-two behind her or not. As a teenager she would take the opportunity of a birthday to reflect back on the year before and check off all the cool stuff that had happened—honor roll, yearbook editor, debate captain, beach volleyball finals, valedictorian. Thirty-two has been more like a trip to Disneyland at the height of summer. It began with high anticipation but before long she was waiting and waiting in hot, sweaty lines. There were rides. Some of them, like Space Mountain, were stomach-churning and whiplash-inducing and others were magical journeys, like flying over London with Peter Pan. She has definitely encountered her fair share of characters and eaten more cotton candy than she cares to remember. She has listened to certain songs as many times as hearing 'It's a Small World' and she has wished occasionally that she could remain in one single moment until the end of time. But ultimately the year is over, and the day has ended, and the only thing left to do now is go to sleep in the car, remember the best bits, erase the worst and look forward to the next time. It's only that Lexi suspects that nothing will ever match up to that Peter Pan ride again.

Tonight she has requested a quiet dinner with her parents to celebrate her birthday. Work has been wonderfully challenging but also exhausting these last few months, between setting up the new office space, inducting two team members, keeping Russell on task and liaising with clients, she finds she is always busy and takes her laptop to bed with her. Not such a bad thing considering her laptop is endearingly loyal and gives her plenty of warning when battery power is low.

She pulls up outside her parents' house and turns off the ignition of her car. The house is dark except for a light in the kitchen window beckoning her inside. It scares Lexi to think of her parents dying—to imagine being the only one left without a sibling to share the sorrow. It occurs to her that one day this big house will be hers to move into. Will she live there by herself? Maybe she'll become an eccentric old lady with ratty grey dreadlocks and bowls full of goldfish.

Goldfish.

Liverpool and San Diego.

George.

When is he going to stop interrupting her thoughts?

Lexi gets out of the car and walks the path to the door. The night is balmy and the air smells like ocean and honeysuckle. She opens the front door to a sudden explosion of sound—"SURPRISE!!!!!"

***

Lexi is still stunned half an hour into the party. At least this surprise is far better than the last one. Lance in his black briefs is by no means a treasured memory. There must be more than forty people crowded into her parents' living room, drinking red wine and eating baked brie. Andrew comes over and hugs her tightly. They have been talking recently about him moving in with Carl and Lexi has been contemplating not getting a new roommate, but living alone instead.

"I'm going to miss you, roomie," he says, squeezing her again.

"You're not leaving the country," she says, attempting to deflect the surge of emotion she feels when she thinks about how much Andrew and she have been through.

"No, but I've become accustomed to our squabbles and your foibles."

"Mmmm, squabbles and foibles... sounds like a cartoon strip."

"Or a yummy new recipe 'Honey—I'm making squabbles and foibles tonight!' "

"Or the names of your future children, 'Squabbles! Foibles! Time for dinner!" They both crack up. Andrew, being Lexi's first true love, will forever hold a sacred place in her heart, unlike her second true love, whom she is trying to hide in a dusty attic.

Lexi's mother comes over with a tray of potstickers.

"Are you two ever going to get back together?" she asks innocently.

"NO!" they both say in unison.

"Ha! You thought I was serious, didn't you?"

Lexi transfers her hug to her mother, almost capsizing the tray. "I love you, Mom."

"I love you too, honey, and I'm extremely proud of you."

"You are?" says Lexi, heartened by her mother's capacity to expand her view of Lexi's happiness.

"Of course I am. You're wonderful!" There it is. That confidence boost from her mom. No longer her sole navigation device, but she still drinks it up. "Look at all the great work you've done over the last few months. Even your father has started to use rechargeable batteries in his remote. Who would have thought?"

Meg rushes over, "Am I missing a group hug? Russell and Mildred were just telling me about their adoption process. I never realized getting a new cat was so complicated."

"I know, they're obsessed!" says Lexi, grabbing a potsticker and thinking about George again the minute she hears the word cat. Goldfish. Cats. Grapefruits. Babies. Kiss. The list goes on.

Lexi's mother moves away with the potstickers, Andrew close behind.

Meg takes Lexi's hand, "Look Lex, I'd really rather not be talking about this, tonight of all nights, but I want you to hear about it from me and not read about it on line."

Oh God thinks Lexi. *Something's happened to George. Is he dead? Is George dead?* Meg carries on, "The news came out today—I read it on *TMZ* just before we left. George is *not* the father of Fanny's baby. Duncan is. Not that it makes a bit of difference, because I know he's a prick and we hate him now. But I just thought you'd want to know..."

It takes a second for the news to register. He's not dead. He's not a father. He's not with Fanny. She's not with Lance.

"Are you okay, Lex? You look a little hot. Maybe you need some fresh air?" Those were the exact words George had said to her that day in the studio. The day he had led her outside. Led her astray.

"Yeah, I'm fine, Meggy... I just need—" Lexi's sentence

hangs in the balance. Unfinished. Incomplete. Waiting patiently for an ending.

GEORGE
22nd August, 2010
Stanford in the Vale, Oxfordshire

Oh, oh, oh squeeze me tightly
Myyyyy Graaaapefruit Girls
Myyyyy Graaaapefruit Girls

Even having to sing at Polly's second wedding cannot mar the
feeling of longed-for relief George has been experiencing
since getting the test results back. He isn't a dad. He doesn't
have to deal with Fanny for the rest of his life. He only has to
be Uncle George. Duncan and Fanny are ecstatic. Neither of
them wanted George to be the one. They named their daughter Sabine, at the final request of her mother's dead lover. The
lunatics are running the asylum.

Talking of lunatics, George cannot fathom that here he
is, fifteen years later, singing "The Grapefruit Girls" to the
grapefruit girls. He wouldn't believe it if he'd read it in a
book. Polly's posse, commandeered by Amelia Hoffman, are
sitting front and centre in the local church hall. They are all
gazing up at George adoringly and singing along. Meanwhile,
the triplets, dressed in two-foot tuxedoes, are accompanying
him on the tambourine, triangle and recorder. Polly, bulging
out of her original dress, is also beaming from the front row,
while Martyn and George's parents are all tapping their feet
enthusiastically.

I wanted you, wanted you, wanted you
I needed you, you needled me

The Genius of the moment is lost on everyone but George.

Last week, just days after Sabine's arrival, George had picked up the phone to hear his usually stoic mother sobbing.

"George... Polly's at the hospital." George had not spoken to Polly since his disastrous birthday dinner.

"Okay, calm down, Mum. What's happened to her?" He was walking home when he'd taken the call. He remembers having to sit down on the curb. He remembers a queasy swell rising in his gut.

"Not to her. It's Pad. The boys were at a friend's house. He's fallen off a trampoline. I think he was unconscious. Your father's gone with them to the A&E and I have Archie and Trevor here with me now, but I'm just so... so frightened, George. I don't know what to do."

"It's okay, Mum. It's okay."

George had stood up and gone home and found his car keys. He had driven straight to his parents' cottage in record time and spent the evening making his mum tea and taking turns playing Connect Four with Archie and Trevor. When it was time to put the boys to bed, George had been assigned tucking in duty.

"Uncle George?" Trevor had asked, staring up at him with questioning eyes.

"Yes, Trev?"

"If Pad doesn't get better, we won't have enough people in our band. Will you and Duncan be in our band?" George had laughed and ruffled Trevor's dark curls.

"He'll get better, mate, don't worry." It turned out, after an MRI and three x-rays, that Padstow had broken his leg, grazed his face and suffered a minor concussion. He was predicted to fully recover and be just as capable of creating mayhem as he was before. Trampolines and all bouncy surfaces were banned. George and his mother had hugged in the kitchen, while the other two boys slept, glaringly incomplete without their brother. George had stayed in the empty bed.

As he plays the final bars of "The Grapefruit Girls," he changes the lyrics slightly to suit the occasion,

All those hours
Lover's powers
Myyyy Graaaapfruit Girls
I thought love would never win
Until Polly and Maar...tyn

Everyone in the church halls rises to their feet simultaneously applauding and whistling their appreciation. George stands up from the piano, takes a small bow, salutes his nephews and blows his sister a kiss. He hops off the stage, leaving Archie, Padstow (left leg in a bright blue cast) and sweet little Trevor to bask in the glory. George's parents rush over to him. His father pats his back fervently, while his mother gives him a hug.

"Very, very nice, son. Very impressed. Looks like those piano lessons paid off."

"Thanks, Dad," says George, realizing that his father truly doesn't have any idea quite how huge Thesis are.

"George, dear, that was special. Look, it made me cry! It means so much to your sister and to us. Thank you." His mother wipes her eyes with a small white handkerchief produced from her sleeve, and George has the unusual feeling, for perhaps the first time ever, that his parents are proud of him. Despite having played at the 02, Glastonbury, Madison Square Gardens, The Hollywood Bowl, he has an inkling that this gig at the church hall might go down in his history as one of the more momentous ones. He has spent so long searching for his parents' approval. Who would have guessed that it would be Polly eventually leading him to it?

Talking of Polly, here she is in a synthetic cloud of white, holding two glasses of champagne. She hands one to George. "So, George... what do you think of your talented nephews? Do you reckon they might be following in their uncle's footsteps?" George accepts this as a backhanded compliment.

"Blew me away, Pol. In fact I'd say they totally upstaged me."

"They *are* good, aren't they?" says Polly, who having experienced some real life drama, is now able to brag about her boys with a little more humility.

"Yes, they are. You're lucky," says George.

"I thought you thought *you* were the lucky one?" asks Polly.

"I've changed my mind," says George, realizing what a steep learning curve he's been on over the last few months. He's almost afraid to look down.

"It doesn't always have to be a competition, does it? Why can't we both be lucky?" She holds up her glass of champagne and George holds up his.

"To luck!" he says, chiming his glass with hers.

"And love," says Polly. "Who knows, George, maybe one day you'll get married too?"

"Maybe not," says George, wondering wistfully if Lexi is married yet.

"You *never* know," says Polly.

"Yeah, Pol, I guess that's right, you never do," and it occurs to George that his sister, whom he used to categorize as one of the most clueless people alive, has just made one of the truer observations of them all.

LEXI
September 4th, 2010
Hollywood Bowl, Los Angeles

Lexi has run all the way from a parking lot on Hollywood Boulevard. She is having difficulty catching her breath as she now sprints up the steep hill to try to reach the entrance to The Garden Boxes. The concert has started. George's muffled voice fills the sky amidst the stars and the tops of eucalyptus trees. She tries to breathe.

When Russell had told her about the tickets last week, she'd made up a feeble excuse. "Oh damn, I've just joined a book club and that night is the first meeting. *Eat, Pray, Love.* Damn!"

Russell had looked at her strangely, "It's only I thought you'd want to come along with Mildred and me, maybe bring Meg. We're taking a picnic."

Thesis were finishing off their North American tour and were playing the Hollywood Bowl on Saturday. Russell had been sent four VIP tickets, compliments of the band. Somehow George's and Lexi's almost love affair had eluded Russell, so he had no idea why Lexi might not want to be there. At this point, it also wasn't crystal clear to Lexi herself why she didn't want to be there, except the thought of seeing him again petrified her, like driving onto the off ramp. Unthinkable. So why was she thinking about it? Russell had held out the two tickets. They looked harmless enough. "Just take them, Lexi, in case you change your mind. We're invited backstage afterwards. I'm sure the band would like to see you. Gabe often asks after you."

Lexi had pocketed the tickets guiltily as if they were contraband. They had sat in her bedside drawer for a week. Would George want to see her? Surely she had just been the fleeting flavor of the month. He'd never contacted her again, but it is likely that he had heard about her engagement and felt equally slighted by her. She would never know the answers unless she asked him. As the week went on, the idea of asking him grew bigger and bigger in her mind, until it was no longer an idea but an imperative. She'd go to the concert. She'd see him backstage. She'd ask him if... she hasn't yet decided what she's going to ask him, but she's sure it will be obvious at the time. Then she can truly move on. End of story. Closure.

Lexi reaches the entrance now and thrusts her ticket at a woman with a flashlight who directs her to a box not far from the stage. It's a balmy September night but when Lexi looks up at George, she feels every inch of her begin to tremble. His beard has gone and his hair is shorter. He's singing "A Suitable Dawn."

> *Your fragile heart*
> *So torn apart and I'm*
> *Here now, here now*

She tries to block out the words. Mildred and Russell are thrilled by her late arrival, welcoming her into their private box where they are eating brown rice sushi and drinking organic red wine. There are seventeen thousand fans behind her, all of their eyes fixed on the stage. Every one of them caught up in the moment. Caught up in George and the band.

"What happened to *Eat, Pray, Love*?" asks Mildred, raising an eyebrow and pouring Lexi a glass of wine.

> *And I hear you, hear you*

Lexi takes a needed gulp, "I thought I'd do that here instead."

GEORGE
4th September, 2010
Hollywood Bowl, Los Angeles

The sky is studded with stars. Seventeen thousand people are chanting "Theeesis! Theeeesis! Theeesis!" George and the boys walk onto the stage and the crowd explodes into an exultant cheer. The lights are bright. George can't make out a single face and that is exactly how he wants it from now on. He picks up his guitar and says into the microphone, "Good evening, Hollywood," and the audience scream even louder. The atmosphere is evangelical.

A few weeks ago Gabe had come to George looking concerned. "George—I know you've got a lot on your mind and I don't want to add to it." At the time they were waiting for the results of the paternity test.

"Don't tell me, another woman has stepped up to say she's preggers with my kid? I'm turning into Wayne Rooney."

Gabe had chuckled, "No, no. Not yet. But I'm just putting some things in place for the west coast shows. I have to send Russell and Lexi some comp tickets. I can't just ignore the fact they live there and we're still doing business with them."

George had already thought about this. He had imagined playing "Third Row" while Lexi and her "man" husband were snogging in the third row.

"Not a problem, Gabe. I'll be very grown up about the whole thing. I won't start blubbering on stage. In fact, maybe we should change the projector images and put photos of Sabine up instead. You know, rub the whole baby thing in her face?"

George is so grateful to Gabe for being a steady hand and for being the only one of his closest mates who is still single. The rest of them were falling like dominoes.

"I'm sure she'd find that very amusing!" Gabe had said. "So I'll go ahead and send the tickets?"

"Send the tickets," George had said, understanding that the Bowl concert might well be his chance at closure. Soon after that conversation, he had heard the news about the baby, and then there was Padstow's accident, and finally Polly's second wedding. George had come away from all three events with an odd sensation of freedom, like some ancient padlock inside of him had finally rusted and dropped off. Maybe this is what growing up feels like? Waving goodbye to his inner adolescent would be a welcome relief.

So here he is on stage, three songs into the set list, and he doesn't even know if Lexi is there, or who she is with, but he *does* know that there is something that he needs to do. One song that needs to be sung before the book can be closed. He takes a swig of water and sits down at the piano. "How's everyone doing?" The audience roar their approval. "Good. Good." He glances around the stage at the rest of the band. Duncan flips a drumstick in the air and catches it effortlessly. He's been immaculately behaved since becoming a father. He even seems to have cut back on the alcohol consumption for the time being.

George clears his throat, "Well, this is a new song. It's actually the first time we've played it live." More cheers and whistles. "I'd always imagined that the person I wrote it for would be here when we did. I don't know if she is. Here. But I *do* know she's in this city somewhere, so if she opens her window wide enough—maybe she'll hear it. Alrightee then... too much information?" The audience cheer and clap. "Here goes... it's called 'Third Row'..."

LEXI
September 4th, 2010
Hollywood Bowl, Los Angeles

It is impossible to block out the words now. She doesn't have to imagine any more if George might be singing to her. Lexi sits very, very still and allows the music in. She can smell the sharp fresh scent of eucalyptus in the air and she can feel a delightful disbelief unfolding inside of her, as George's voice sings everyone their story. The one he's been waiting to tell her.

We've been discovered

But I'm still wanting to be found
While these nights spin round and round
House lights up and down
Different stage in every town
Lookin' for the light in the crowd
Tryin' to be heard in a world full of loud

Correct me if I'm wrong,
 you've been waiting for this song,
 so love before you go, it's time I told you so
I'm not searching for the exit
need the entrance now
Buy me a ticket, find me a seat
next to you I will feel complete

Third time lucky, running, crying, shining
Your face on the screen, wondered where you'd been
You had my heart and you didn't even know
Holding my heart in the third, third row

Life takes us
twirls us around
searching for someone
We wait to be found
Spinning around, round, round

Third time lucky, running, crying, shining
Your face on the screen, wondered where you'd been
You had my heart and you didn't even know
Holding my heart in the third, third row

Lights up brighter I can see who sees me
now my lucky number's three
seen those eyes before
I want to know more, want to know more, know more

One, two, three
Come to me
Come to me
Come to me

When the song finishes and the audience are on their feet shrieking, Russell looks at Mildred and at Lexi, who is trying unsuccessfully to conceal her tears. She has stopped trying to fight it and has officially become a crier.

"Oooh, I wonder who the mystery lady is?" he asks inquisitively. Mildred rolls her eyes at her husband and pulls Lexi in for a hug, "You dippy dodo—the mystery lady is right here!"

GEORGE
4th September, 2010
Backstage Hollywood Bowl, Los Angeles

Singing "Third Row" to a stadium full of thousands has left George hovering in a state somewhere between exhausted and elated. There is always a loss when they perform a new song for the first time. Like a painter selling a treasured canvas, they are giving up a piece of themselves to the audience and it never truly belongs just to them again.

He had dreamt of that moment. Dreamt of giving "Third Row" to Lexi. Releasing it into the atmosphere like an unexpected gift. He cannot avoid feeling deflated, despite the celebrations sparking off around him. The backstage after party is revving up as he walks into the room. A small group of LA girls in skinny jeans and tight tank tops with breasts that put the Grapefruit girls to shame, are crowded around Duncan, *oohhing* and *ahhhing* over a video of Sabine that Fanny has sent to his iPhone. He has already insisted George watch it four times that day. Duncan's grin is contagious, but

George wishes he were still under the cool stream of the shower—his refuge directly after a show.

Of all the people he doesn't want to see, Stacey is suddenly next to him holding a bottle of beer.

"You're not drinking, George?"

"Not yet."

"The show was awesome tonight."

"Even though you don't approve of our outfits?"

"I'm working on it. I've got my sights set on the next tour," quips Stacey, who is wearing a Thesis t-shirt bedazzled with red sequins.

"I wish you were joking."

"You know me, I like a project. You'll come around eventually."

"Unlikely," says George, hesitant to be bombarded by the overflow of enthusiasts and so-called Hollywood actors who come to the LA shows, most of whom he doesn't recognize. He's about to excuse himself from Stacey, when he sees Gabe heading towards him followed by Russell and a tall woman with a silver bob and long black dress. He peers beyond them hopefully.

"George—look who I found dancing in the aisles," says Gabe, subtly shaking his head, indicating to George that, no, Lexi is not with them.

George clasps Russell's hand, "Russell—what a pleasure, mate. We're so glad you could come along."

Russell looks flustered, "I told Gabriel that we didn't need to bother you, George, but he insisted. The concert was tremendous. Can I take a moment to introduce you to my lovely wife, Mildred."

"Of course," says George, turning to Mildred, "great to meet you."

"Delighted, George. Russell speaks glowingly," says Mildred, shaking his hand and gazing at him intently. "I believe you are looking for someone?"

George is confused. He's never met this woman before but she's staring right into him, as if she knows his deepest thoughts.

"Looking for someone?" he repeats.

"In the third row?"

George falters, "Do you mean? Is she?"

"Still there? Yes. But maybe not for long so I suggest you—" before Mildred can complete her sentence, George has disappeared.

LEXI and GEORGE
September 4th, 2010, 4th September, 2010
Hollywood Bowl, Los Angeles

Lexi sits watching a gang of burly roadies pack up the equipment, hauling amplifiers and long coils of electrical wire noisily off the stage. When the concert had finished and the audience were filing out, Mildred and Russell had both turned to her expectantly. "You're coming backstage with us, my dear," instructed Mildred, sounding like an officious school teacher. "Don't even think about walking away."

Lexi hadn't known what to think. The song had peeled back another layer and she had instantly lost her nerve. George *had* seen her the night of the concert. She hadn't invented it. He must have recognized her on the TV segment and that's how Thesis had ended up as clients. They have both been holding onto the idea of each other for the same amount of time. The thought is overwhelming.

"Mildred. I can't. I won't know what to say."

"If his song is anything to go by, dear girl, you won't have to do much talking."

"Mildred, my darling," said Russell, tugging insistently on the sleeve of her caftan. "I understand you are trying to help, but while George seems a very decent young man, it came to our attention in London that he is somewhat of a philanderer..."

"Nobody's perfect, Russell. Lexi knows that. Do we want her to wait as long as we did, or shall we encourage her to have a crack at true love now?"

"I see your point," said Russell. "Of course."

"The boy is obviously besotted by her. Let's give him the chance to discover that his fantasy is not so far off from the real thing."

But Lexi had remained cemented to her seat, incapable of complying, terrified that both of their fantasies would never compare. What was she to do? Run backstage and fall into his arms? It was never that simple. She knew that now.

Mildred and Russell had stood over her expectantly, until Mildred, accustomed to dealing with production glitches on a daily basis, had kicked into plan B.

"Okay, Lexi, have it your way. Stay here. In fact go and sit right there," she had pointed towards the front of the bowl and her finger landed on the third row. "Russell and I are going backstage!" Before Lexi could protest, Russell and Mildred had joined the last remnants of the crowd jostling their way to the exits. She spotted Mildred talking to one of the security guards and pointing in her direction. She'd stood then, knees like elastic, and headed to the third row.

Lexi hangs her head back and stares up at the starry sky, breathing in the immenseness of the moment. It seems that while she's been busy trying to organize her life, some kind of mystical serendipity has been at work, orchestrating alternate plans. Messier ones. She's remembering her clothes from The Brits discarded in a pile on the floor, crumpled and twisted. She doesn't notice George appear from the side of the stage. She doesn't even see as he swings himself down from the front, dismounting his usual pedestal and landing with two feet on the ground.

When she eventually looks up, he pulls a scrap of paper

from the back pocket of his jeans and pretends to be examining it. Lexi feels a rush of blood to her head seeing him this close again.

"Third row, right? If I'm not mistaken, that's the seat I'm supposed to be in," George gestures to the chair beside her.

"You'd better sit down then. They'll be on soon," says Lexi, feigning indifference and crossing her legs. She can hear her heart buffeting.

George makes his way to the third row and settles in next to her, turning his head to take in an overview of the empty stadium. To think of all the hours he has wasted in the months since he was last in LA allowing his imagination to hijack reality. Looking back, he had barely spoken to Lexi for more than ten minutes combined before he had already mapped out their future. He had mistaken coincidence for destiny. Life was never quite so eloquent. But now that he is sitting next to her again, there is no mistaking the unspoken chemistry between them—the inexplicable charge and curiosity that had first fused inside him the day he ran by her.

"You seen these guys before?" he says nonchalantly. "They any good?"

"Yeah—they're not bad. I've seen them once before. I was dragged by a friend. The lead singer's kinda sexy, in a British sort of way."

George laughs, "You think? I've heard he's a right moody bugger."

"Probably that too—no doubt a full-fledged narcissist. You know how musicians can be?" says Lexi, turning to look at his profile for the first time. He has a slight bump on the bridge of his nose that she hasn't noticed before. A lot has changed since they last saw each other, but not her urge to reach out to him. To touch him.

"Absolutely. Best to steer well clear of them," says George.

"I guess he was really disappointed when he found out that one of his best friends was sleeping with his girlfriend.

You must have read about it?" asks Lexi conspiratorially. "It turns out the baby wasn't even his."

"I did hear something about that," says George, playing along, "but maybe we were reading different articles. I read that she *wasn't* his girlfriend. She never had been. The big disappointment came when he discovered the woman he was falling in love with was actually planning to get married to another man, but had conveniently neglected to tell him. I heard the poor sod didn't eat for weeks."

Lexi swallows hard so she can keep speaking. "Juicy! But you must have missed the second instalment. That woman was never engaged."

"She wasn't?"

"She was asked. But she said no."

George reaches over and takes Lexi's hand. He laces his fingers into hers.

"She said no?" he says with a smile in his voice.

"Yes, she did. She was falling in love with the lead singer as well." Just hearing herself speak the words fills her with nervous anticipation.

"Other people's lives, huh?" says George, finally turning to Lexi. He lifts her hand and presses the back of it to his lips, planting a cluster of delicate kisses all the way to her wrist, sending a ripple of shivers down her spine. Her skin is smooth against his mouth. Without letting go of her hand he leans in and touches his lips to hers and the memory of their first kiss is eclipsed within seconds. This second kiss, under the stars, all the more precious because both of them had imagined it might never happen again, is sweet and warm and urgent. George cups his free hand to Lexi's cheek and when they separate, they immediately are drawn back together again, kissing each other with a slowness and passion that is an entirely new sensation for them both.

One of the roadies on the stage wolf whistles and Lexi and George pull apart laughing. George waves.

"What d'ya reckon?" he says. "These idiots have kept us waiting long enough. Shall we go and get a drink? I think we could do with getting to know each other. Properly." He holds tightly to Lexi's hand. This time around he has no intention of allowing her to slip away.

"I think you might be right," says Lexi, who is more than prepared to live with the mess, and with the sparkling spirals, leaping back to life above her head. "I can catch their show another time."

"Don't bother," says George, pulling her up from the seat and towards him. "I bet they're totally overrated."

"I'll be the judge of that," says Lexi, quietly confident that her verdict is already in.

RORY SAMANTHA GREEN has lived in both London and Los Angeles. She likes to think she has a split personality—British and American. Rory is a published author, trained psychotherapist and creator of Write To Be You, Reflective Writing Workshops.

You can read her weekly blog at

www.writetobeyou.com

and visit her on Facebook at

www.facebook.com/RorySamanthaGreen

27878222R00170

Made in the USA
Lexington, KY
01 December 2013